ROMANTIC TIMES PRAISES REVIEWERS' CHOICE AWARD NOMINEE CONSTANCE O'BANYON!

RIDE THE WIND
"Ms. O'Banyon's story is well written with well-developed characters."

TYKOTA'S WOMAN
"Constance O'Banyon delivers a gripping and emotionally charged tale of love, honor and betrayal."

TEXAS PROUD
"*Texas Proud* is another good read from Ms. O'Banyon. With its excellent characters and strong plot, readers will find enough action and surprises to fill an evening."

LA FLAMME
"Constance O'Banyon tells a tale replete with action-adventure and glorious romance."

SONG OF THE NIGHTINGALE
"Mesmerizing, engrossing, passionate yet tender and richly romantic."

DESERT SONG
"Constance O'Banyon is dynamic. Wonderful characters. [She is] one of the best writers of romantic adventure."

"WHEN WILL THE MARRIAGE TAKE PLACE?"

The situation was so unreal that Lauren felt like an actress in a play, saying words that were not her own. "I suppose you and my father have already decided on a date."

"No. I was not so confident that you'd have me."

"You decided everything else."

"Lauren, this is not the way I wanted it to be between us."

She was ready to do battle, but she had no weapons. "You have won," she shot back. "Enjoy your victory."

"I'm not enjoying myself much at the moment, Lauren." His gaze moved slowly down her body, and he made no secret that he liked what he saw. "Are you ready to listen to me? I want to explain about us."

She swallowed twice before she could answer. "There is no us."

"The hell there isn't." He reached for her and brought her against him. "There has always been us."

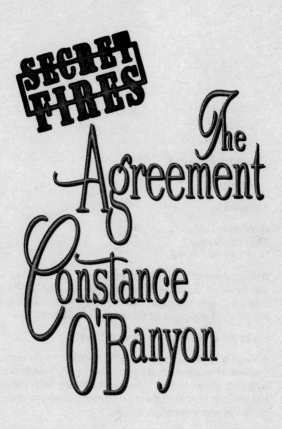

SECRET FIRES

The Agreement

Constance O'Banyon

LEISURE BOOKS NEW YORK CITY

A LEISURE BOOK®

June 2001

Published by

Dorchester Publishing Co., Inc.
276 Fifth Avenue
New York, NY 10001

ISBN 0-8439-4878-7

Printed in the United States of America.

Visit us on the web at www.dorchesterpub.com.

This book is dedicated to my fellow AWOLS, who just happen to be my three best friends. I will never forget the night you three stayed up late to map out a route so that claustrophobic me would not have to ride through that long tunnel the next day.

Bobbi Smith, your insight and ability to laugh at the world have gotten me through many tough times. You never fail to make my days brighter. We are probably AT&T's best customers.

Elaine Barbieri, I was a fan of yours long before I came to know you as a friend. I will always treasure our friendship.

Evelyn Rogers, I admire many things about you: your talent, your wit, but mostly your willingness to go that extra mile for a friend.

And to my agent, Evan Marshall. What would I do without your encouragement? You keep me on a steady course when I get offtrack. You are the best!

Chapter One

Texas, 1882

Would he be there?

Lauren McBride slid her booted foot into the stirrup and settled onto the saddle. She just had to see Garret, even if only from a distance.

The gelding she rode was not fully broken and was certainly unpredictable, but she didn't care. She was a good rider and could handle almost any horse.

Nudging the animal forward, Lauren felt exhilarated as the wind tangled her hair and cooled her cheeks. The gelding ran full-out with a speed that took her by surprise. Her pa had said this horse would be hers when it was broken. But she hadn't been particularly impressed with the gray; it looked more like a plow horse than one she would throw a saddle on. But her pa had an eye for horseflesh, and he had chosen right for her.

Lauren patted the horse's neck and nudged him to a faster pace. "Let's just see what you can do," she said.

To her delight, the horse lunged forward. A fence loomed just ahead, so she kicked the horse's flanks and laughed delightedly when the animal sailed over the obstacle with little effort.

Lauren was so distracted that for a moment she forgot her destination. Riding was her salvation, and it always had been. When her mother died, Lauren had gone directly to the barn to find her horse. She had ridden until sundown and kept going even after dark. Garret Lassiter had found her and had taken her home.

Garret. How she loved him!

Lauren had been riding for over an hour, and her horse was beginning to tire. She slowed her pace, berating herself for running the gelding so hard in the torturous August heat.

She halted for a moment to let her mount rest while staring westward where shards of sunlight cut through a cloud bank—clouds so thin and tattered that there was certainly no rain in them. The land was parched, thirsty, and needed a hard rain to break the sweltering heat.

Lauren glanced at the brittleness of the dry buffalo grass, which should have been green by now. The sun rose higher and seemed to burn right though her clothing. There was not a breath of air stirring, and the spiderlike mesquite trees offered little shade. Many of the ranchers were already suffering, and if it did not rain soon, their herds would start dying off.

Her thoughts returned to Garret Lassiter. She couldn't remember when she had first begun to love him.

Maybe she always had.

Lauren and her brothers had been forbidden to speak to any of the Lassiters because her father hated them, especially the father, Barnard Lassiter.

The Lassiters were what her pa sarcastically referred to as "gentlemen ranchers." He accused Mr. Lassiter of having more airs than brains and more money than the whole state of Texas. It galled Tom McBride that a family who had migrated to Texas had made a success out of the run-down San Reanido Ranch. They didn't run cattle like everyone else in the county, although they kept a few head for their own use. They raised thoroughbred horses that they shipped not only all over the United States, but all over the world as well.

Lauren was not even sure why her pa hated the Lassiters. The feud had happened long before she was old enough to understand. But one thing was certain: when Thomas J. McBride hated, he was good at it. To Lauren's knowledge, her pa never forgave anyone if he felt he'd been wronged in any way, and he seemed to think the Lassiters had wronged him.

She remembered just two years back when Mr. Lassiter had wanted to buy Cedar Creek Ranch. The property was not all that good for running cattle because it was only 150 acres of hills and limestone gullies. But the ranch had something that made it valuable—Cedar Creek. Her pa had not wanted that land for himself but had bought it out of pure spite, paying more than the property was worth to keep the Lassiters from getting it.

Yes, her pa was very good at hating. He was a hard man, who only showed tenderness when he was with Lauren's stepmother, Clare.

Garret's ma and pa were always kind to Lauren, and she had no intention of slighting them as her father had ordered her to. She certainly was not going to ignore their only son. Garret was the kind of man that every young girl dreamed about. At least, Lauren dreamed about him a lot.

Even when she was awake.

Garret's family was so different from hers. They were real quality folks who had moved to Texas after the War Between the States. They had lost everything when the Yankees burned their place in Virginia.

She glanced westward in the direction of the Lassiters' ranch, San Reanido. It was strange in a way, she thought. The Lassiters had been neighbors all her life, and yet she had never been to their home. She had heard that it was mighty fancy, with furniture from Paris and real brocade curtains at the windows. Lauren would like to see where Garret lived so she could imagine him there. But she would never be invited to San Reanido, and even if she was, she wouldn't be allowed to go.

He just had to be there!

Lauren squinted against the bright sunlight. Most of the eligible young women in Sidewinder and on the outlying ranches had an eye on Garret, and probably some of them fancied themselves in love with him—but they could never love him half as much as she did. The talk was that Garret would probably go back to Virginia to find a spouse when he was ready to settle down—that was what his sister had done.

Lauren nudged her horse forward, anxious to get to her destination. She had overheard her brother Stone mention at breakfast that he had seen Garret mending fence between Circle M and San Reanido.

She hope that Garret would be working on that section of fence again today.

All Lauren wanted was one glimpse of him; she would live on that for days. If she actually got to talk to him, it would last her for weeks.

Lately, Lauren had been experiencing strange

yearnings whenever she thought of Garret. She felt feverish, restless, her emotions building like a volcano about to erupt. What would she do if Garret actually touched her?

She imagined how it would feel to run her fingers through his raven-black hair or to stare into his magnificent brown eyes and have him look back at her with love. His mouth was so perfect—what would it feel like if his lips touched hers?

She would love him until the day she died.

The wind suddenly kicked up, and Lauren felt the heat against her face. She reached up and crammed an unruly red curl beneath her battered hat, wishing she had worn something nicer than her leather split-skirt.

Well, she couldn't very well wear her church dress to ride a horse, could she?

Her horse tossed its head and whinnied, so Lauren dismounted, uncapped her canteen, poured water into her hand, and held it out for the animal to drink. After she did this several times, she lifted the canteen to her own lips. She could feel sweat trickling down her back, and her face felt so hot she could imagine the freckles popping out all over it. She should not have come out in this heat—she knew better.

Remounting, Lauren rode along the fence line, noticing the new barbed wire gleaming in the sunlight—its sharp metal points able to deter the most persistent cattle. Garret had probably finished the job by now and gone home. She rode down a gully and up the other side, rounding a butte along a desolate stretch of land that was dotted with delicate bluebonnets and tall sunflowers weaving in the wind.

Her heart stopped.

Garret was there, just ahead!

Garret had not yet noticed her, so she had time to slow her thudding heart.

Taking her courage in hand, Lauren set her hat more firmly on her head and rode forward, hoping Garret would think that she was just out for a leisurely ride.

Suddenly Garret's head swung around, and he looked at her. As she rode closer, he leaned against a fence post and waited for her. Several hundred yards further on, two other men worked another section of fence, but she barely gave them a glance.

Lauren took a deep breath and halted. "Hello, Garret. I see you are mending fence."

"Hello, little redhead. You may not believe this, but I was just thinking about you, and here you appear."

Her heart pounded against her chest, and she caught her breath. He had been thinking about her!

Garret thumbed his hat back and grinned. "Are you a mind reader? Can you guess what I was thinking?"

She stared at him, aware of the way his sweat-damp shirt clung to his lean, muscled torso. He wore faded trousers and scuffed boots. Anyone who came upon him would never guess that he was a Lassiter by the way he was dressed.

"I don't know what you mean," she answered.

His dark eyes met hers. "No, you wouldn't."

She dismounted and stood awkwardly before him, watching a smile tug at his lips. She could feel her face flush. "I can't read minds, Garret. You know that."

He looked at her closely. "You're fifteen now, Lauren."

"I'll be sixteen my next birthday," she answered, trying to make herself sound older.

"You're fifteen," he stated emphatically.

"Ye . . . yes."

He positioned a curled nail over a strand of wire and hammered it into the post. She watched the way his muscles flexed, and her heart felt like the hammer he was wielding.

When Garret had secured the nail, his gaze dropped to her again. "I know when your birthday is, Lauren. You were born on July the third, and that means you turned fifteen just last month. That makes me five years older than you."

"Yes. I know." She was pleased and surprised that he knew the date of her birthday. "Five years isn't so much," she observed hopefully.

His beautiful mouth curved into an almost smile.

"It is right now. But when you are older, it won't seem so much." His dark gaze softened. "I know a lot about you, Lauren. You might be surprised if you were aware just how much."

She was startled by his statement and a little puzzled. Garret would never be interested in a fifteen-year-old girl who was awkward and had freckles scattered across her face. She was all legs, and her breasts had barely begun to develop—she was afraid they never would. Worst of all, she hated her unruly red hair.

Lauren's gaze drifted to the two cowhands, who were busy with the same task Garret was performing. No, he could never be interested in her. She looked at Garret, studying how the heavy curve of his dark brow shadowed his velvet brown eyes. His onyx-colored hair curled slightly at the nape of his neck, and his features were finely honed—his chin strong with the hint of a cleft. He was as tall as her pa, who stood six foot two. She guessed Garret Lassiter was about the best-looking man she had ever seen.

Garret tugged his gloves off and tucked them into his belt, and Lauren's gaze rested on his sun-browned hands—strong hands with long fingers. She went weak all over just thinking about what it would feel like to be touched by him.

"I . . . should go," she said, not wanting to leave but finding no excuse to prolong her stay.

Garret reached through the wire and clasped

her hand, making her heart race and her breathing stop. In that moment, Lauren could not have spoken if her life depended on it.

Garret gave Lauren a steady glance. "Did you ride this way just to see me?"

She felt another blush start at her toes and work its way to her face. "I . . . why'd you think that?" she asked, finding her voice and wishing she could hide her shyness from him.

His thumb moved in a circle over the pulse beating in her wrist. "Because it's true, isn't it?"

She was not about to admit that he was right—no, she could never do that. Instead, she blurted out, "I'm afraid my pa's gonna send me away."

His grip tightened on her wrist, and he frowned. "What are you talking about, Lauren? Send you where?"

"My stepmother . . . Clare . . . wants me to go to Savannah and live with my mother's sister," Lauren stammered. "I don't want to go."

"Your aunt? Why?"

"Aunt Eugenia wrote a letter to pa asking if I could come stay with her." Lauren raised her gaze. "I don't want to. I don't even know her!"

Garret's hand slid up her arm to rest against her shoulder. "You could always say no."

Lauren was having a difficult time concentrating with his hand on her arm. "Clare says I got to go 'cause I need the schooling." She could have added that Clare wanted to get rid of her the same way she had gotten rid of Lauren's brother Tanner—but that was family dealings, and she would not speak of it even to Garret.

"You're lonely, aren't you, Lauren?" Garret asked softly, as if he had read her mind. "Is there some young man that you're interested in? You aren't going to grow up and marry someone else and break my heart, are you?"

She warmed to his teasing. "No, there's no one," she replied with conviction. He was the only man she would ever want to marry.

"You are so young and haven't had a chance to test life. Give yourself time to know your own heart."

She shrugged her shoulders. "I don't attend any of the functions or dances, so I don't know much about boys."

"But someday a man will come along who will . . ." He shook his head. "Enough about that. I believe it would be safer for us to talk about something else."

Lauren felt a rush of sadness that shook her body to the very core. "Do you think anyone will ever love me?"

He slid a hand across her chin and touched her mouth before withdrawing it and cramming it into his pocket as if he did not trust himself. "Oh, yes, little redhead. One day, some fortunate man will love you so much he won't be able to think of anything else but that smile of yours."

"Garret, how does a girl know if love is real?"

Chapter Two

Lauren had just asked Garret the kind of question she should be asking a mother—a question she could never ask her stepmother. Still, he was the last person she should have confided in.

Garret lowered his gaze from her eyes to her lips. "You'll know, Lauren. Sometimes you just know when something's right for you. But," he said shrugging, "you're young yet. You have plenty of time to think about such things."

Lauren looked at him searchingly. She already knew about mating, and her young body told her she was getting ripe for just that. But she wasn't like Clare. She would never let a man have her body just to satisfy his primal instincts—not *any* man!

"I'm old enough to know some things, Garret."

"I'm sure you are." He smiled. Taking a red curl, he tucked it behind her ear. "One day you'll be old enough to know about the feelings that can rip through a man when he looks into those blue eyes of yours."

At the touch of his hand, Lauren felt the blood rush hotly through her own veins. "I already know about those feelings."

"I don't think you do."

"I'm not as innocent as you seem to think I am."

He chuckled. "Aren't you?"

"No . . . Well, maybe." She dipped her head and stared at the ground. "Why does life have to be so hard?"

"I don't know, Lauren." His voice was deep and gentle. "But one day a man will come along who will take care of you and bind all your wounds and hurts, take your burdens on his own shoulders." He shook his head. "Enough of this talk. Just be patient—that's what I intend to be."

Why had she asked him such a question?

What must he think of her?

Lauren stared up at the white-hot sky, trying to think of another subject before she made a complete fool of herself.

"Have you heard any news about my brother Tanner?"

"No, I haven't. Have you?"

"Not since he left." She drew in a deep breath.

"The last words I spoke to him were angry ones. I wish I could take them back."

Garret looked into her confused blue eyes—McBride blue eyes, as everyone in the county referred to them. They were silver-blue, and sometimes, if the light was right, they looked almost transparent. At least, Lauren's did. At that moment, he had the feeling he could see all the way to her soul, and she was hurting. Lauren was still so young and needed tenderness and understanding, things she never got at home. Her father was a real bastard, and her stepmother, Clare, seemed to have no motherly instincts.

Garret had known Lauren all her life, and he almost regretted the way her young body had begun to develop in the last year. He had observed the way men looked at her when she walked down the streets of Sidewinder, and he resented them for it. He had a wild protectiveness toward Lauren, and deep, strong feelings that she was too young to understand.

Regret weighed heavily on Lauren whenever she thought of Tanner. She still missed him. She lowered her head so the brim of her hat hid her face while she voiced her deepest dread. "I'm so afraid that something bad has happened to Tanner. What if he died remembering that I said I hated him?"

"Tanner is too ornery to die, Lauren." Garret smiled. "And he certainly knows that you don't hate him. Don't torture yourself over this."

"Then why hasn't he written to me? He said he would."

"You can bet that if Tanner hasn't kept his word to you, there's a very good reason for it. I know how close the two of you were. His leaving wouldn't change that."

"Not a day goes by that I don't miss Tanner. I'm glad Stone hasn't gone away." She could have added that Clare always found a way to make Stone look bad to their pa, and she wondered just how much longer Stone would take it before he left, too.

Garret slid his hand beneath Lauren's jaw, raising her head so he could see her face. "He'll turn up one day when you least expect him, Lauren."

Her eyes were swimming with tears. It had been over a year since Tanner had ridden out, and she had not spoken to anyone about the pain his leaving had caused her—until now. It had always been easy to confide in Garret. He took the time to listen to her and did not treat her like a child.

"If Pa sends me away, I won't be here if Tanner does come home."

Garret touched her forehead and trailed his finger down her pert little nose. "Don't be melancholy, Lauren."

She angled her head and chewed on her bottom lip. "What does that mean?"

"Melancholy means sad. Don't make yourself sad, Lauren." There was compassion in his tone and a softness in his eyes. "And don't be so impatient. Wait for time to pass." His voice deepened. "Unhappiness passes. I'm learning that."

Lauren thought that if he was sad about something it would break her heart. "You, Garret? You're unhappy?"

He smiled that smile that melted her insides.

"Not exactly unhappy, little redhead. Mine is more a feeling of impatience—of waiting."

"Waiting? For what?"

He looked into those blue eyes and felt his heart thump against his chest. She was half child, half woman, and he wanted her more than he had ever wanted any other woman. "I'll tell you someday."

Sometimes Lauren did not understand Garret's meaning, like now. She had no idea what he was saying. "I tried to get Stone to talk Pa out of sending me away, but he wouldn't do it," she continued. "I thought Stone would be on my side, but he isn't. He agrees with Pa and Clare that I should live with my aunt."

"Perhaps Stone thinks it will be best for you to leave that house. What does your father say about it?"

"Pa wants anything Clare wants." She looked past him at a morning dove that had settled on a fence post, its feathered wings tucked against its body. She could not tell Garret that *he* was the real reason she did not want to leave Texas.

What would she do when she could no longer

see him or talk to him? How would she live when she was so far away from him? "I don't want to leave."

"I wish I could make everything all right for you, little redhead, but I can't. Your father wouldn't even let me set foot on the Circle M, much less advise him on how to raise his only daughter. As for Stone, I believe he'll always want what's best for you."

"Stone just doesn't understand how I feel about anything. Besides, he has his own troubles."

"You may not know it, but Stone is your watch-dog—I've seen that for myself. He's protecting you, Lauren."

Lauren looked puzzled. "Stone? You're wrong about him. He doesn't care about me."

"Unless I'm mistaken," Garret said, nodding to the north, "that'll be your brother riding up now." Garret grinned at her. "Even from here, I can tell he's not happy with me. He'll be thinking he's res-cuing you from me."

She gazed into his eyes wistfully. "I wish Pa didn't hate you and your folks. I don't know why he does."

"I don't care about your pa or any of your fam-ily, Lauren," he said harshly. "As long as you don't hate me." He started to take her hand until he saw how close Stone was and thought better of it. "I don't think I could take it if you hated me."

The love she felt for him wove its way through

her body and around her heart. "I couldn't ever hate you, Garret."

Stone was almost within hearing distance, so Garret spoke quickly. "I'll ask around if anyone has heard anything about Tanner. If I hear something, I'll let you know."

Stone McBride sat high in the saddle as he halted his horse and gazed down at Lauren. "You've been gone a long time." He cast Garret a cold stare, as much as saying it was a good thing that Garret was on the opposite side of the fence from his sister. "It wasn't hard to guess where you'd be."

Garret dabbed sweat from his face with his sleeve, drawing a seething glance from Lauren's older brother.

"Hello, Stone. Sure is hot weather we're having."

Stone muttered, "I've seen worse." His gaze swung to Lauren, and he spoke in a hard voice. "You get on that horse or I'll put you in the saddle myself!"

Lauren considered defying Stone, but she knew he would do just what he threatened. Humiliated, she moved forward, thrust her boot into the stirrup, and swung onto the saddle.

With her head held at a proud tilt, Lauren spoke quickly, too embarrassed to meet Garret's eyes. "Good-bye."

"So long, little redhead."

Lauren warmed under Garret's soothing tone. She liked it when he called her by the pet name he'd pinned on her years ago. As far as she knew, he did not use a special name with any other girl, and that made her feel proud.

Stone rode closer to Garret and spoke harshly. "Stay away from my sister! I don't want to have to warn you again."

The two men glared at each other until Stone whirled his mount and joined Lauren, who had ridden on ahead.

Garret watched Lauren disappear behind a butte, wondering what was going to become of her.

Maybe it would not be such a bad thing if Lauren went to Savannah. She was wild and untamed like a young mare that needed a gentle hand to guide her. Garret did not want Lauren's wonderful spirit to be broken, as it surely would be if she stayed in the same house with her stepmother.

Garret uncapped his canteen and drank deeply, thinking about the soft curve of Lauren's face and those silver-blue eyes that went right to his heart every time she looked at him. Lauren had no notion how pretty she was, or that one day she would be beautiful. When she grew to womanhood, she would break everyone's heart, including his.

But the promise of future beauty was not what drew Garret's interest. It was that indomitable essence of Lauren's that caught and held his heart.

He prayed her family would not destroy her. But they surely would if she remained at the Circle M.

Lauren glared at her brother. "You always treat Garret so bad. Why do you do that, Stone?"

Stone stared straight ahead, his hand tightening on the reins. "You're lucky it was me that came after you instead of Pa. He would have tanned your hide if he'd caught you with Garret Lassiter."

"You're mean, Stone—plumb deep-down mean!"

Stone flinched at her biting words. His lips tightened, but he did not bother defending himself. Tanner and Lauren would never know how many times he had stood between them and their pa's anger, taking blame for something they had done to keep them from being punished. He was a solitary man and kept his feelings to himself.

Lauren kicked her horse in the flanks and shot forward, and Stone had to ride hard to catch up with her.

Angry, hate-filled eyes had watched the exchange between Lauren and Garret.

Estaban Velasquez shoved a new post in the hole he had dug while watching Garret Lassiter. Estaban blamed the whole Lassiter family for ruining his life, but he heaped most of the blame on Garret's shoulders. Why should Garret have everything while Estaban had lost his family, his home, wealth, and the woman who was to have been his wife?

San Reanido had once belonged to the Velasquez family, but now Esteban was only a worker there like the lowest cowhand. San Reanido had come to his great-great-grandfather through a generous Spanish land grant. He stared into the distance, taking stock of the land. He knew every stone, tree, and butte. This land was in his blood—it was his life. Esteban had been born on this land—it should belong to him!

He had watched Garret talking and laughing and touching the pretty señorita, and rage grew and flamed within him.

San Reanido had flourished under his grandfather's guardianship and he had acquired more land. But under his father's guardianship, there had been war, punishing drought, and mounting debts. San Reanido had fallen into ruin. All the cattle had been sold off first, then the furnishings and paintings. Soon thereafter, the *vaqueros* had deserted them. The bank was threatening to foreclose when the Lassiters stepped in and bought a once-proud empire for half its worth.

Esteban's dark eyes centered on the *patrón* who drew the full measure of his hatred. Of course, he also hated the father, Barnard Lassiter, but not as much as Señor Garret. The father no longer ran the ranch, and was no longer a threat. The fault now rested on the shoulders of the son.

The insults to his family had not stopped when the Lassiters moved to San Reanido. Almost immediately, workmen had demolished the Spanish-style house where Estaban had been born, and in its place they had erected a huge place twice the size, which was an affront to Estaban every time he looked at it.

Frank Nelson was becoming irritated. He had pulled the wire tight, and it was taking all his strength to keep it drawn taut. "You gonna stare at the boss or you gonna use that hammer?"

Estaban swung his head in Frank's direction. "One day I will kill the *patrón.*"

Frank had heard all this before, and he knew that Estaban drank too much and was often drunk. The Spaniard had a disreputable look, with hair past his shoulders, a thick mustache, and heavy eyebrows. Frank could not remember ever seeing the Spaniard smile. The other ranch hands refused to work with Estaban, and he never mixed with them. When he was not working, he kept to himself.

Frank did not mind Estaban so much. The Spaniard was a strange one, but he was a hard worker and got the job done. "You shouldn't joke about things like that," Frank told him. "If anyone overheard you, they'd think you meant it."

"I assure you that I was not joking. One day I will kill him."

"Now, why'd you want to do that? As bosses go, Garret Lassiter ain't bad."

"His family has taken everything from me."

"What're you talking about?"

Estaban became secretive, wielding the hammer with such force that he drove the nail into the fence post with one firm swing. "I will say no more."

Frank held another nail in place. "I think the boss is sweet on that little McBride gal."

Estaban grumbled, "I want him to love a woman and marry her. I want him to be happy."

Frank scratched his head, looking confused. "But I thought you said you'd—"

Estaban interrupted as if he had not heard Frank. "I hired on as a hand on a ranch that should be mine. I work like a dog so Garret Lassiter can reap the benefits of my labor."

Frank was troubled by Estaban's irrational ravings, but he thought it might be the whiskey talking. "I've heard it said that your folks once owned San Reanido, but I never believed it."

"It was my home."

"I also heard that your pa gambled and drank, same as you do. Garcia, who runs the cantina in Sidewinder, said your pa shot himself 'cause he couldn't live with losing everything."

Estaban turned his dark gaze on Frank. "Do not make me defend my family honor to a nothing like you."

Frank guffawed, not in the least offended by Estaban's words. "You're one to talk."

"One day I will have my wish because I no longer desire the impossible. I only want the Lassiters to cease to exist."

Frank frowned, wondering if he should tell the boss about Estaban's threats. He shook his head. The Spaniard could not mean what he was saying. And it was not likely that he would ever act on his threats. "Let's get this done so we can get outa the heat."

Estaban still felt the pain he had experienced when his mother had died of sadness, his father had killed himself, and the woman he had loved, his betrothed, had married someone else. It did not matter to him that his father had been weak and a gambler, or that the woman he loved had been faithless and had deserted him for a man who had wealth. He was a desperate man who had lost everything and needed someone to blame for it.

"I want Garret Lassiter to be very happy before I kill him," he said, striking another nail with such force that the stretched wire hummed.

Chapter Three

Late September

It was one of those rare occasions when Lauren accompanied her father and stepmother to town. Dabbing at her forehead with her sleeve, she fixed her gaze on the distant hills, wishing she had stayed at home. First, Clare complained that the horses were going too slow; then when Tom whipped them into a gallop, she complained that the wind was mussing her hair.

In disgust, Lauren watched as her pa tried to mollify his wife by agreeing with everything she said and complying with her slightest wish.

It was revolting!

"Your daughter needs new gowns," Clare said,

staring with irritation at a nail she had just broken. "Nothing fancy, just something serviceable. I suppose she'll need new shoes, too. A pair for church and a pair for everyday."

Lauren was surprised, because her stepmother never showed any interest in anything she wore. That made her suspicious that Clare was up to something.

"I leave the women things to you," Tom answered while concentrating on guiding the team down a steep hill.

"If you should decide to send Lauren to Savannah, what would your first wife's relatives think of us when she arrives in the rags she wears around the ranch?"

Lauren froze. Clare was determined to get rid of her.

"Just look at her," Clare continued. "Her gown's faded and even frayed at the hem. She just doesn't take any pride in her appearance. I can't do anything with her. Maybe her aunt can."

"Dammit, you're her stepmother," Tom reminded her. "Why *can't* you help her?"

Clare cast a disparaging glance at Lauren. "Lord knows I've tried, but she just doesn't listen to me." She looked at Tom with the wounded expression Lauren had come to detest. "I'm afraid your daughter just doesn't respect me."

Tom's broad shoulders tightened, and his eyes were hard when he glanced back at Lauren. "Have you been disrespectful to Clare again? You'd better not be."

Before Lauren could answer, Clare laid her hand on Tom's shoulder. "Don't get yourself upset about this. I have learned to live with hurt. Lauren resents me for taking her mother's place, and she always will. It's best for everyone if she goes to live with her aunt."

"I'm not going," Lauren stated with feeling. "This is my home. Why should I want to leave it?"

"Little girl," Clare answered, reaching behind her and giving Lauren's forearm a painful pinch, "you'll do what you're told. If I say so, you *are* going to Savannah."

The expression in the depth of Clare's gray eyes was chilling, but Lauren would not give in so easily. "Pa, don't make me go to Savannah."

Tom cast a disgruntled glance over his shoulder at Lauren. "Aw, hell! Why must everything be an argument with you, Lauren? If I decide you are going to Savannah, then off to Georgia you'll go." He looked at his wife and added, "And not a moment before."

Lauren felt her hopes shatter. She could not win against her stepmother. Her pa would do anything to keep Clare happy, and at the moment, what seemed to make Clare happy was sending Lauren away.

Clare had a sly smile on her lips, but Tom had not yet agreed that Lauren would leave. "She will need new gowns in the event that you *do* decide that she's to live with her aunt."

"I don't want to go."

"In life you don't always get what you want, little girl," Clare said, her gaze boring into Lauren. "Your pa and I will decide what's best for you."

When Tom McBride halted the buggy in front of the blacksmith shop, Lauren jumped down with every intention of getting away from Clare. But as she stepped into the dusty street and crossed to the other side, she realized with a sinking heart that Clare was just behind her.

She entered Miller's Leather Shop, not thinking about where she was going, and slammed right into Garret's hard chest.

Garret clasped her arms to steady her and smiled. "Whoa, there, little redhead. Where are you going in such a hurry?"

"Ike made me a new saddle," she blurted out, hesitantly raising her gaze to his. A quick glance over her shoulder told her that Clare was not far behind. If Clare saw her talking to Garret, she would tell her father, and Lauren would soon find herself on her way to Savannah.

"You'll look mighty pretty sitting a new saddle, Lauren," Garret said softly, his eyes moving over her in a way that made her blush. He bent toward her and said, "Meet me at the old squatter's cabin tomorrow at noon. I have something important to tell you."

Garret did not see Clare until it was too late. He was not sure if she had overheard him.

Clare was dainty, blond, and beautiful with soft gray eyes and a way of looking at a man that issued an invitation. A man who did not know her might be seduced into accepting that invitation, but Garret had never been tempted by her. He saw her as a conniving bitch who never did anything without a reason. The only person who did not seem to know how duplicitous she could be was her own husband.

"Good afternoon, Mrs. McBride," he said, touching his hat and moving away from Lauren.

"Garret Lassiter." Clare extended her hand, forcing him to pause and shake it. "I haven't seen you in a while."

"We don't seem to haunt the same places, do we, Mrs. McBride?"

Clare hated Garret and his whole family. He always seemed to be talking down to her. And he was one man who did not try to hide his dislike of her. For Lauren's benefit, Clare forced a slow smile. Her hand clamped around his when he tried to pull away. "You are always so formal, Garret. I never know how you really feel about me." Her long lashes swept across her eyes, and she wet her lips. "You're a mystery in many ways." She relinquished his hand. "But then, all men are the same underneath." Her gaze swept down his taut body to rest just below his belt. "Aren't they?"

Garret felt nothing but disgust at Clare's obvious ploy. He was even more annoyed when it worked. Lauren went pale and drew just the conclusion Clare had wanted her to. Garret did not intend to be used by the stepmother to embarrass Lauren, so he said abruptly, "Good day, Lauren." He touched the brim of his hat and stepped around Clare, but not before her hand brushed against his arm and then slid up to rest on his broad shoulder.

"Mrs. McBride," he said, moving her hand away, "I wouldn't want anyone to think you and I are friends. Your husband might not like it." Garret left, closing the door before Clare could reply.

Clare turned to her stepdaughter. "My, my, he was in a hurry, wasn't he?" She lifted a delicate shoulder. "He's so handsome and . . . so male. I could feel his muscles through his shirt. But half the time I don't even understand what he's talking about. It wouldn't be hard for a woman to lose her heart to him, though." Her hardened gaze went to Lauren. "He can have any woman he wants, you know. Don't set your sights in that direction, because he would only break your heart. Take my word for it. If there's one thing I know, it's men."

"He didn't seem to want you, Clare," Lauren observed cuttingly. "He couldn't get away from you fast enough."

There was uncertainty in Clare's eyes as she turned to watch Garret mount his horse. She stared angrily after him as he rode away. But her expression was placid when she turned back to face Lauren. "Oh, he likes me well enough. But he couldn't show it in front of my husband's daughter, now could he?"

"I don't want to hear anything you have to say about Garret."

"Well, just let me tell you this; he'd probably roll you in the hay a few times and then forget you. Men, especially handsome ones, are so fickle."

"I said I don't want to hear it."

"Why shouldn't you learn the truth about men from a woman who knows?" Clare laughed and linked her arm through Lauren's as if they were the best of friends. "If I were to lure Garret Lassiter into the hay, I'd give him something he'd never forget."

Lauren turned away, feeling sick inside. Clare knew just what to say to hurt her. "I don't think Garret would be interested. You're not his kind of woman."

"And you think you are?" Clare asked stingingly. "He probably rushed away because he could envision his lips on mine."

Lauren fought back tears. "Nothing you can say will make me think that Garret would touch another man's wife."

"Well, think about this. I have heard that there is a woman back in Virginia who will soon be his bride—someone of high social standing. How will you like it when Garret marries his Southern lady and brings her back to Texas, little girl?"

Clare felt delighted satisfaction when Lauren flinched and ducked her head. "I thought that would make you think. Ask your Garret the next time you see him if he is in love."

"He's not my Garret. And I know he'll marry someone." Lauren wrenched her arm free of Clare's grasp. "I'm not simpleminded enough to think he'd ever care about me in that way."

"Then bury once and for all any tender feelings you have for Garret Lassiter. He isn't for you. His family is gentry from the old South. The Lassiters always marry their own kind. They marry only *ladies*."

Lauren could hardly breathe because of the pain Clare's words caused her. "I wasn't thinking of marrying him. I'm too young to marry anyone."

Clare tried another tactic. "I hear your mother's sister is considered a lady just like your mother was. Your aunt could probably make a lady out of you, too."

Lauren turned around to face Clare, her red hair swirling about her face and tangling around her shoulders. "I know why you want me gone. You're afraid I'll tell Pa about Tanner and how you always tried to get him into your bed."

Lauren's gaze slid away from Clare's because her stepmother's eyes had suddenly taken on a chilling expression. "I won't tell Pa, but not to protect you. I won't tell him because it would kill him to know what you're really like around other men."

Clare's voice was cold, like ice, when she said, "You don't know anything about me and Tanner."

"I know more than you think I do. It's because of you that Tanner left. If you get rid of me, will you start working on Stone so he'll leave, too?"

"Let's not talk about me," Clare said in a warning tone. "And don't think that your pa would believe anything you said against me."

"Pa believed you when you told him that Tanner was trying to get you in bed. It wasn't true, but he believed you and not my brother. I just bet you're sorry you pushed Pa so far that he made Tanner leave, aren't you? Tanner didn't want you—ever!"

Clare was beyond anger. Her eyes took on a predatory expression, and Lauren had to turn away from the hatred she saw reflected there. "Let's talk about you and Garret, hmm? Even though you deny it, I know you fancy yourself in love with him. His family won't let him marry the likes of you." Clare took a moment to choose her next words. "Maybe with a little polish from your aunt in Savannah"—she gripped Lauren's arm and steered her toward the blacksmith shop where Tom was waiting for them—"who knows, you might come back as Garret's equal."

"You're just trying to get rid of me."

Clare drew in a deep breath as if she were attempting to be patient. "Oh, I think you'll go.

There's nothing for you here. You're such a homely, freckle-faced little redhead. You'll have a hard time getting any man to look past your flaws, you know."

Tears gathered in Lauren's eyes, and she angrily brushed them away. "Why should I care what any man thinks about me? I don't need anyone!"

Clare grabbed her and turned her around, not caring that she drew curious glances from several people who passed by. "That's good, because you'll never get a man who amounts to anything. Some broken-down old cowboy may take pity on you someday, but that's about the best you can expect."

Lauren was daily exposed to her stepmother's cruelty, but it hurt most when Clare pointed out her flaws. "Don't pretend you care what happens to me, Clare. We both know you don't."

"You're right, I don't care what happens to you at all. But I don't want you hanging around the house the rest of your life, little girl. I always get what I want from your pa, and I want you gone. Do you understand me?"

"I suppose you can't wait to tell Pa that I spoke to Garret."

Clare looked thoughtful. "You should know there are no secrets between a husband and wife."

"No secrets, Clare? I can only imagine the passel of secrets you keep from Pa. If you ever told him the truth about yourself, you'd be the one leaving the Circle M." She raised her head. "And I don't care if you do tell him about Garret. You were the one with your hands all over him. I'm sure Pa would be interested to hear about that."

Clare walked beside Lauren, quiet at first, as if she were carefully choosing her next words. "I won't tell your pa about Garret."

Lauren lowered her head in total defeat. Her fists balled at her sides as she fought for control. "Why can't Pa see you for what you are? Everyone else does."

Clare laughed snidely. "Your pa sees just what I want him to see and nothing more. You might want to remember that if you try to speak against me." She stepped in front of Lauren and lowered her voice. "You can either tell your pa you're willing to go to Savannah, or wait until I make it hard on you. It's your choice."

Lauren stepped into the heat of the blacksmith shop, her eyes searching the shadows for her father. "Leave me alone."

Clare stamped her foot and swallowed her anger. It was going to be difficult to bend Lauren to her will. But she would do it, one way or another. Garret was Lauren's weakness, and that was the tool Clare would use to get her out of the house once and for all. She had no intention of sharing the Circle M or any of Tom's money with his sons and daughter. Well, she might share it with Tanner, but not the others.

"Tom," she called out, moving into the blacksmith shop. "Your daughter is being stubborn again. Make her come with me to the general store."

Tom glared at his daughter. "What's the matter with you, gal? I thought you females liked buying new doodads. Go with your stepma and don't be sassing her." He saw the forlorn look on Lauren's face. "Did you get your saddle?"

She shook her head. "No. I forgot."

"Hell, gal. Can't you do anything right?"

She lowered her head. "I guess not."

He made a helpless gesture. "You and Tanner always were trouble. Why can't I have respectful kids like—"

"Like the Lassiters?" Clare offered, her gaze boring into Lauren, clearly reminding her that one word from her about Garret would send Tom McBride into a rage. "Like Garret Lassiter?"

"I'll go with you, Clare," Lauren answered, hurriedly moving toward the street, defeat weighing down her footsteps.

Clare caught up with her and smiled that self-satisfied smile she always used when she got her way. "I told you—I always get what I want, little girl. Try to remember that. It'll save us both some trouble later on."

Chapter Four

Clare glanced behind her to make sure no one was watching before she approached the barn and slipped silently inside. The interior was dark, but some light filtered through the open door in the loft. When she reached the first stall, she nodded with satisfaction.

It was empty.

Manuelo had done exactly what she'd told him to. All the horses had been herded to the east pasture—all but one: Raja.

She approached Raja's stall with trepidation because she was afraid of that horse, and with good reason. The stallion reared and snorted; his ears went back threateningly.

He was a killer!

Raja had trampled one of the cowhands last spring—stomped him into the ground before anyone could stop him. The horse should have been shot at that time, but Tom refused to let anyone harm his prized stallion. There wasn't a horse living that Thomas McBride could not ride, and he took particular delight in proving his mastery over that black devil.

Clare smiled with satisfaction, congratulating herself for being brilliant. No one would ever blame her if Lauren chose to ride Raja. Who would have thought that Raja would be the tool that would relieve her of her tiresome stepdaughter? Even if the horse did not kill Lauren, her pa would be so angry at her for riding the beast that he would send her packing.

Clare had overheard Garret's conversation with her stepdaughter in the saddle shop the day before. There was not a doubt in her mind that Lauren intended to meet him at the old squatter's cabin—even if she had to ride Raja to get there.

Lauren was headstrong and would not care that she had been strictly forbidden to go near the stallion. Lauren usually acted impulsively, and Clare was depending on that.

Manuelo was loyal to her alone, and she could trust him not to say anything about pasturing the other horses. As soon as Lauren left, she would have him bring the horses back before Tom got home. Manuelo lived to serve Clare, and she

would use that to her advantage, as she had in the
past.

Lauren grabbed up her hat, crammed it on her
head, and rushed out of the house. When she entered the barn, she was shocked to find that all the
stalls were empty. Why had her pa sent all the
horses to pasture when they were needed there at
the ranch? It didn't make sense.

A sudden noise at the back of the barn caught
her attention, and she walked toward Raja's stall.
The black stallion pawed the floor and backed
against the far wall with a wild look in his eyes.
The animal was a thing of beauty, a wild spirit that
would never be entirely tamed. But he was a rogue,
a killer, and that disgusted Lauren. Why did her
pa keep such an animal?

Disappointment settled heavily on her shoulders as she went to the paddock and found it
empty, too.

She would not be able to meet Garret today.

Going back inside the barn, she moved slowly
toward Raja. The stallion reared and pawed the
air. "Raja," she said in a calm voice, "Thomas J.
McBride's pride is about to be ridden by Thomas
J. McBride's daughter."

Lauren hurried to the tack room and hoisted her
saddle over her shoulder. If her pa could ride Raja,
then so could she. She remembered her pa once
commenting that he always gave Raja his head and

allowed him to run until he was tired, making him easier to handle.

It was surprisingly easy to saddle the horse, but Raja pulled back and reared when she led him out of the stall. Calming him with quiet words, she carefully slid her boot into the stirrup and hoisted herself onto the saddle.

As she nudged Raja forward, he shot out of the barn at a full run, and Lauren made no attempt to hold him back.

Clare pulled aside the lace curtains and smiled as she watched Lauren ride away from the house. "There's more than one way to skin a cat," she whispered. "I've done my part. Now Raja can do the rest."

Manuelo stroked his thin gray mustache, looking worried. "That horse will probably kill Señorita Lauren. Is that what you want?"

"I do, if that's the only way I can be rid of her."

Manuel nodded. "If that is your wish, then that is the way it will be, señora."

Lauren had never ridden a more superb animal. Her father was right—Raja was exceptional. It took all her strength to hold him back, but she was laughing as she bent low over his neck, feeling as if she were flying. His movements were fluid, and he was the most powerful horse she had ever mastered.

The Agreement

After a while, Lauren slowed Raja to a canter, delighted with his smooth gait. He was a bit skittish and shied when a jackrabbit jumped across their path, but she was able to control him by pulling back on the reins and hugging his belly with her knees. There was an unexplainable excitement about riding a horse that had such spirit.

When Lauren reached the squatter's cabin, her heart was thundering with anticipation. She dismounted and tied the reins to a branch of a mesquite tree and patted Raja's twitching flank. Glancing around, she discovered that Garret had not yet arrived. Lauren looked in the direction he would come from, but he was nowhere in sight.

When she walked toward the cabin, her boots crunched on broken pottery. There was not much left standing of the old house. The logs had rotted and fallen away, and the door hung on one rusty hinge. In a way, it made her sad to think that a family had built this cabin and had once made it their home. She wondered what had caused them to abandon it—hard times, or maybe Indians. Maybe even her pa, who took offense at anyone squatting on his land. And when Thomas J. Mc-Bride took offense, people trembled.

She glanced inside the ruins, but decided not to enter. The place was probably infested with rattlesnakes. In the distance she heard a rider approaching, and she held her breath as Garret rode over the hill toward her. He looked magnificent riding a spirited white Arabian.

He dismounted and walked toward her with long strides. The closer he got, the faster her heart beat. If he knew how much she loved him, would he be amused?

Probably.

"I wasn't sure you would come," she said, glancing up at him. With the sun behind him, Garret appeared to be surrounded by a halo of light. "But you did."

He smiled. "There was never any question about that. However, I wasn't sure you could get away."

"I almost didn't. I had to ride Raja."

Garret frowned and swung around to look at the black stallion, then gazed back at Lauren. "What do you mean by riding that horse? He killed a man!"

She shrugged. "I can handle him just fine."

Garret stared at Lauren as if she had lost her mind. "I can't believe your father would approve of your riding that horse. I sure as hell don't. What were you thinking?"

His tone was harsh. He had never spoken to her in anger before, and it put her immediately on the defensive. "I can handle him. I rode him here, didn't I?"

"Well, you aren't going to ride him back. I'm taking you home even if your father shoots me."

"No, you won't!" She had never been angry with

Garret, but she was close to it now. "I won't let you."

Garret drew in a deep, intolerant breath. "You just see if I don't. I'm not going to allow you to ride home on that devil."

There was a part of her that was pleased he cared about her safety, and a part of her that balked at any man telling her what she was going to do. She did not want anyone to order her about.

"We'll talk about the horse later," he said, watching the angry flush on her cheeks. Lauren was just too damned impulsive for her own safety.

Lauren shielded her eyes from the sun. "I couldn't sleep all night for wondering what you wanted to see me about."

He drew her into the narrow shade that was cast by the cabin. "I have some news for you, and I didn't know how else to tell you. I realize now that I may have caused you trouble with Clare. I'm sorry if I did."

"I . . . don't think she knew I was going to meet you." She looked puzzled. "What kind of news?"

"It's about Tanner. I know how worried you've been about him. Remember I told you I'd ask around?"

Hope sprang to life within her. "You know where my brother is?"

"I know where he was two months ago. One of our hands saw him down Pecos way. Tanner had hired on with a drover who worked for a large spread near El Paso."

She studied the toe of her scuffed boot. "El Paso. That's a long way from here."

Garret's tone was gentle. "Tanner will come home one day, Lauren. You know he will."

Lauren glanced up at Garret, wishing she could tell him how she felt about him, but she could never do that. The friendship she had with him would end if he found out that she loved him. "It was kind of you to ask around for me. It eases my mind a bit to know that Tanner was alive two months ago."

Garret uncapped his canteen and handed it to her. "I told you, Tanner is tough. Don't worry about him. He wouldn't want you to."

She took a drink, thinking all the while that her mouth was touching where Garret's had touched. She felt weak all over and jerked the canteen away. She handed it back to him, wishing she would not have such thoughts.

"Thank you," she said abruptly.

Garret watched Lauren carefully, thinking she looked a little pale. Perhaps she'd been out in the heat too long. "Are you all right, Lauren?"

Her forehead furrowed. "Yes. Why wouldn't I be?"

"I just wondered. I worry about you sometimes."

She met his gaze, touched deeply by his kindness. "You worry about me?"

He reached for a red curl and held it between his fingers. "Someone has to, little redhead." A curl wound around his finger, and he smiled. "Will you give me a lock of your hair, just in case you are sent away where I can no longer see you?"

She had thought men only asked for locks of hair from the women they loved. He must be teasing her. "If . . . you want it."

He wore a knife on his belt, and he unsheathed it. "This is sharp, so it won't hurt you."

Before Lauren knew what was happening, the blade sliced off a curl. Garret tucked it in his pocket, then slid the knife back into its sheath. "Now," he said smiling, "if I want to remember the color of your hair, I'll always have a reminder."

She blushed and lowered her head. "Do you do this often? Do you collect locks of hair like trophies?"

He laughed, his eyes sweeping her face adoringly. Then he gently touched her cheek. "No, sweetheart. I have only yours. Why would I want anyone else's?"

He had called her sweetheart! And he wanted a lock of her hair. He had never acted this way before. She watched him step away from her as if he did not want to touch her, and she was more puzzled than ever.

Garret needed to put a little distance between

him and Lauren. He glanced upward for a long moment and then back at her. "Are you ready for me to take you home?"

She was disappointed that he wanted to leave so soon. "Garret," she said, trying to prolong their meeting and knowing she was not going to let him take her home. Her pa would shoot him on sight. "Do you know who you're going to marry?" she blurted out, and then wished she could call back her words.

Garret was quiet for a long time as he watched the wind play through Lauren's tangled hair. He resisted the urge to touch a tantalizing curl that had fallen across her cheek. "Yes, I do. Do you know how if feels to recognize when someone is right for you, to know that no matter how long and hard you look, you will never find a more perfect match for yourself?"

Pain stabbed at her heart and tears gathered behind her eyes. Yes, she knew, because she felt that way about him. "You're talking about love."

His deep voice shook with emotion. "Yes, love," he mused gently. His voice softened, and his eyes took on a tormented expression that she did not understand. "The kind of love that lasts a lifetime, Lauren."

"I wouldn't know about that, Garret." She felt her heart shatter into a million pieces. "Do I know her?" she asked.

He smiled. "At this time in her life, I don't believe she knows herself. But I am willing to wait until she is ready to hear what I have to say." He felt compelled to add, "Of course, I don't know if the lady of my choosing will have me."

She could not imagine any woman not wanting to be Garret's wife. Disappointment burned through her young heart, and she dared to raise her gaze to his. "I don't ever want to get married," she said, trying to envision the porcelain-perfect lady that would entice him to give up single life.

"You say that now because you are so young. The day will come when you'll feel different."

She had to know more about the woman he loved. "Tell me about her. Would I like her?"

He arched a dark brow. "I like her more than anyone I know. She's just on the edge of discovering life."

His eyes were on her as if he were undecided about something. Or perhaps, Lauren thought, he did not want to talk about the woman he loved with anyone. She moved closer to Garret as if compelled by some unseen force. "I . . . was just . . . wondering what she would be like."

"I only hope that when I ask her to marry me she'll feel the same way I do."

Lauren tried to turn her head away, but he caught and held her chin so she was forced to look at him. "I only hope my love cares about me even half as much as I love her."

Lauren pulled away from him, feeling so distraught she could hardly hold back the tears. The truth whispered through her mind. Garret would never belong to her. All along she had secretly hoped he might love her. But now that hope was shattered.

"She'll love you," Lauren said, trying not to show how devastated she felt.

"Do you think so?"

Lauren watched his eyes glisten and darken. "Yes, I do." She was aware that his fingers trembled against her cheek, and she wondered why.

"I should take you home now, Lauren."

In a wild moment, she wanted to know what it would feel like to have that wonderful mouth against hers. Let him marry his lady love—all she wanted was one kiss. Without considering the consequences, she drew even closer to him, her arms boldly sliding around his broad shoulders. She quickly pressed her lips to his before he could react.

At first, Garret was startled by Lauren's action, but then his lips softened, and his arms tightened about her, and he deepened the kiss.

Torrid heat engulfed her as she was hit by a new awareness of life, of love, of feelings. Desire burst through her, rampaging within her young body. She had not known that a kiss could open the door to so many emotions—powerful emotions that she did not really understand.

Garret was holding her and kissing her and, for that moment, he belonged only to her.

This is the man I was born to love! This is the man I will love until the day I die!

Chapter Five

Dazed, Garret held Lauren tighter to him, his heart beating like a drum. He had wanted this, dreamed of it, but not yet—not yet. She was not worldly enough to know about the love that burned inside him. She was so sweet and trusting, not realizing that she had stirred fires within him that he could not control. Without breaking off the kiss, he shifted her weight until she nestled against him. His tongue slid into her mouth and caressed hers, drawing a passionate moan from her.

Garret groaned. Gripping her shoulders, he tore his mouth from hers. He took a quick step away from her, holding her at arm's length. One day he would have her, but not now. "I should never have let it go that far, Lauren. Say you forgive me."

They both knew it was she who had instigated the kiss, but he was a gentleman and was taking the blame on himself. His chivalry only added to the shame she felt. How could she have done such a wicked thing?

Lauren's pride rose up to save her as it always had. "I'm leaving now," she said, turning toward Raja, her footsteps hurried. She did not want Garret to witness her complete collapse. He must have been shocked by her boldness; maybe he thought she did this with every man she met. He could not know that this had been her first kiss. If only the ground would open up and swallow her—it was what she deserved.

"Lauren, don't leave like this. I need to tell you—"

She only ran faster. "Please forget about it. I don't know why it happened."

He caught up with her and turned her toward him. "You did nothing wrong, Lauren. Please don't torture yourself."

His kindness only made her feel worse. "Just leave me alone."

"No, I won't. I'm not going to let you ride that horse, Lauren. I told you I'd take you home."

She wished he would just go away. "I came on Raja, and that's the way I'm going home."

She twisted out of Garret's grip and lunged at Raja. Her sudden movement spooked the stallion, and he reared, his powerful hooves pawing the air.

His ears went back, and his eyes bulged wildly. With a snap, Raja broke free of the branch and turned on Lauren.

The horse was out of control, and Lauren knew it. She moved quickly to the side, trying to dodge his deadly hooves, and in her haste tripped and fell backwards, hitting her head against the hard ground. The hooves seemed to hover above Lauren, and she knew she was going to be trampled. Fear kept her rooted to the spot, unable to move.

A shot rang out. The magnificent animal, her father's prize stallion, lowered his hooves and tossed his mane as if in final defiance. Then, slowly, he slumped to his forelegs and fell over on his side, mere inches away from where Lauren lay, a bullet dead center in his forehead.

Lauren watched in horror as the animal twitched and then subsided in death.

Garret threw down his rifle and rushed toward her. Going down on his knees, he ran his hands over her arms and legs, fearful that the horse had struck her.

Lauren felt something hot and sticky on her face, and she realized that she had been splattered by the stallion's blood. She tried to rise, but she could not stop shaking enough to stand, and Garret's grip only tightened.

"You killed him!" Lauren whispered, looking into Garret's eyes. "You killed Pa's horse!"

Garret gathered her so close that he could feel

her trembling. She was not half as frightened as he had been.

He had almost lost her.

What if he had misfired and the horse had trampled her to death right before his eyes? "You're all right, sweetheart! That's all that matters. It's all over."

She was sobbing now. "Why . . . why?"

"That horse would have killed you, Lauren. And I could never have allowed that to happen."

Before Lauren could say anything more, she heard riders approaching. She drew away from Garret, standing on shaky legs.

"That's probably Stone. I'll ride back with him. You'd better go, Garret. I don't know what Stone'll do to you."

"Lauren—"

"I know you had to do it, Garret." She also knew that her father would never forgive her or Garret for the death of Raja. A strange calm settled over her as she accepted the fact that Clare had won. She would be going to Savannah, after all. It did not matter now, though. She did not want to be anywhere near when Garret brought his new bride home.

Garret stared into her cold blue eyes. "Lauren, we'll talk about this later. Don't leave mad at me."

"I'm not mad, Garret. I understand why you shot Raja. I won't be seeing you again, though. Pa will make me go to Savannah now."

He closed his eyes, feeling as if she had physically hit him. "This isn't about the horse, is it?"

"Just ride away before Stone gets here."

"Lauren, let's talk about this. I want to tell you how I—"

She raised her head and watched her brother ride closer. "You had better leave before my brother gets here," she repeated.

"Lauren, we can't leave it like this."

She knelt down and placed her hand on the sleek neck of the black stallion while bile rushed into her throat. "I'm obliged to you for saving me. But Pa's going to be plenty mad at me and you."

By now, Stone had dismounted and was walking toward Lauren, accompanied by the foreman of the Circle M. Stone grabbed Lauren's hand and tugged her up next to him while Jeb examined Raja.

"I warned you to stay away from my sister, Garret. Apparently, you didn't listen too well."

Lauren grasped her brother's arm. "Just take me away from here."

Stone gathered her even closer to him, his piercing gaze on Garret. "I saw what happened from a distance. You had no choice but to shoot Raja. Still, if I were you, I'd make myself scarce. Pa won't take kindly to what you did."

Garret's lip curled in anger. "I'm not afraid of your father, Stone."

"Well, you sure as hell ought to be. He may well

kill you for luring my sister out here."

"Your sister was never in any danger from me, Stone."

Stone didn't raise his voice, but there was a threat there all the same. "I'm telling you for the last time, stay away from Lauren. I don't know what you have in mind for her, but it ain't gonna happen."

Garret saw how pale Lauren was, and knew she was still dazed by what had happened. "Take her home, Stone."

Garret turned his back and walked over to Jeb, who had cut the cinch of Lauren's saddle and was attempting to pull it free of the dead animal. Between Garret and Jeb, they managed to yank it free.

"Stone's right about the boss," Jeb told Garret. "He'll shoot first and ask questions later."

"What would you have done in my place, Jeb?"

"I'd have shot that damned rogue dead, same as you," the tall, angular foreman admitted. "But I'm not sure the boss wouldn't shoot me if I'd done it."

Stone dampened his handkerchief with water from his canteen and wiped some of the blood from Lauren's face.

Lauren was in tears by the time he lifted her onto his horse. She did not look back as they rode away from the squatter's cabin. Her heart was broken, and it would never mend. She felt as if she were suffocating. Garret thought she blamed him for shooting the horse, but she did not. "I want to leave Texas, Stone."

He shifted in the saddle and looked at her. "Did anything happen between you and Garret?"

"No. Not the way you mean. Garret would never do anything to me. Pa's going to be mad at me."

"Yeah, he will."

Lauren's throat burned, and suddenly dry sobs heaved through her, becoming choking sounds that tore at her heart. She leaned her head against Stone's back and cried.

"It's all right, Lauren," Stone assured her in a gruff voice, misunderstanding the source of her misery. "That horse should have been shot a long time ago. If Pa had cared about anyone but himself, he would have done it when Raja stomped Chad." He lifted her chin and stared at her. "You weren't hurt, were you?"

Not hurt? She was wounded to her very soul with a hurt that would never heal. The only man in the world she could ever love loved someone else. And to make matters worse, she had humiliated herself by kissing him.

She would never forget the shame of this day.

Estaban Velasquez had watched the exchange between Señorita McBride and the *patrón*. It was fortunate for the girl that her brother had come along when he had. Otherwise, the innocent se-

ñorita might have found herself less pure. He hol-
stered his six-gun. He would not have interfered
to save the woman. But he would have if Stone
McBride had attempted to shoot Señor Garret—
that was a privilege that belonged to Estaban
alone.

Estaban mounted his horse and rode down a
gully back toward the ranch. He could wait for his
revenge. He was good at waiting. But perhaps it
was time for Garret to lose his mother. She had
never spoken three words to him, and yet he was
the one who would introduce her to death.

Estaban frowned. He did not like Señora Lassiter. She was pale and sickly, always complaining
about what she had lost when the Yankees burned
her home, never appreciating the land under her
feet—and that should belong to him to be passed
down to his children and, through them, to their
children.

With a satisfied smile, Clare listened to her husband curse and rant, berating his daughter for over
an hour. She almost laughed aloud when Tom
yanked a pale Lauren to her feet. "You are going
to your Aunt Eugenia's as soon as I can get you
there! I've had enough of your nonsense, gal.
Damn Barnard Lassiter for siring such a son, and
damn Garret Lassiter for shooting my horse! They
haven't heard the last of this."

Stone leaned against the mantel in a seemingly

unconcerned manner. But his eyes were on his father. He would let his pa carry on as long as he did not lay a hand on Lauren. He would never allow his pa to hurt her.

"I don't want to live here anymore," Lauren said, angrily brushing tears from her cheeks. "I want to leave, and I don't care where I go." She raised her head and looked at her stepmother. "I'll be glad when I'm gone."

Clare's eyes gleamed like those of a cat about to pounce on some poor unsuspecting creature.

"This is the best thing for you, Lauren," Clare said. "Best for everyone."

Tom's anger seemed to lessen suddenly as he looked into his daughter's eyes. "You actually rode Raja," he remarked with an expression of pride shining in his blue eyes. "If only you'd been born a boy . . . what a son you'd have made me." He shrugged. "Go to your room and get yourself packed, gal."

He abruptly left the room, and Lauren soon heard the slamming of the back screen door.

Clare moved closer to her stepdaughter. "I told you you'd be leaving, Lauren. You should have believed me."

"It doesn't matter anymore," Lauren stated in total defeat.

As she left the room, Clare's lips were curved in a smile of sheer joy. She would not have shed one tear if that horse had trampled Lauren to death, but as it was, everything had turned out to her satisfaction.

"Lauren, it'll be all right. You'll see," Stone told her gently.

"You can say that. You aren't the one being sent away."

"Take heart." He went to her and stared down into her small face, wishing he had words to comfort her. "I met Aunt Eugenia once, and you'll like her. She's like Ma."

Lauren's footsteps were heavy, as if her troubles were weighing her down. "Good night, Stone."

"I'll go with you to Savannah if you want me to."

"No. I want Jeb to go with me. Pa needs you here."

Stone had wanted to see that Lauren was safely deposited on their aunt's doorstep. He always seemed to have trouble explaining himself to his little sister. He was not open with his feelings like Tanner. "Well, then, I'll see you in the morning. I'll just go and tell Jeb that he'll be taking you to Savannah."

That night Lauren cried herself to sleep.

She would go to Georgia and never come back to Texas!

Jeb assisted Lauren into the stage and climbed in beside her, his leathery face etched with worry. "It'll be the best thing for you, Lauren. If your aunt's anythin' like your ma, you'll be treated kindly."

She leaned back and sighed. "Everyone keeps telling me that. I suppose anyplace is better than here."

When the stage pulled away from Sidewinder, Lauren closed her eyes. There was nothing for her in this town—not anymore. She opened her eyes and found Jeb watching her. "Thank you for coming with me, Jeb."

"Lauren, you should've said good-bye to Stone. It wasn't right, you leavin' him like that."

"I know, and I'm sorry. You'll tell him, won't you?"

"Stone thinks you still hold it against him 'cause of the way Tanner left. It wasn't Stone's fault. Ask yourself why he's stayed on so long with Clare makin' it hard for him. He'd have left long ago, but he stayed for you."

Jeb's words made her feel ashamed of the way she had treated Stone. "I'll write him a letter as soon as I get to Savannah."

"You do that."

She sighed. "I wonder what it'll be like, living with my aunt and her family."

Jeb saw so much of her mother in Lauren that it was almost painful for him to look at her. He had secretly loved Emily McBride before her death—he still loved her. He would certainly have left the Circle M years ago if it had not been for

Emily's children. He felt obligated to look after them for her. His gaze went back to Lauren, who had her mother's red-gold hair and delicate features. But she had her pa's eye color, and his hair-trigger temper. Emily, sweet Emily, he thought. She had been a fine lady, too good for Tom McBride.

"The way things are, Lauren, I believe your ma would have wanted you to live with her sister."

"Ma's dead."

"Lauren, don't let this get you down. You'll be back one day. You're Texas-born, and you'll always come back home."

"There's nothing for me here, Jeb." She felt the sway of the coach and leaned her head back against the worn leather seat. Her past was gone, and the future was unknown and frightening.

"I have a letter for you," Jeb said, reaching into his breast pocket. "I was gonna wait and give it to you when we reached Savannah, but I think now would be a good time."

Lauren stared at the envelope he extended to her. "Who's it from?"

"Garret Lassiter. He brought it to the ranch early this mornin' and asked if I'd give it to you. I said I would."

Her hand trembled, and she reached for the letter, but then she reconsidered, shoving it back at Jeb. "I don't want Garret's letter."

"He went to a lot of trouble to get it to you."

"I don't care. I'll never read it. Give it back to him."

Jeb replaced the letter in his pocket. "Maybe you'll change your mind one day. I'll just keep it until you ask to read it."

"Jeb, I don't want Garret to write to me, and I don't want to know anything about him."

"What'd he do to make you feel like this? Only last week you were half in love with him."

Lauren shook her head. "I don't want to talk about him anymore."

Jeb wished he knew how Emily would have advised Lauren in this instance. Hell, he knew the girl thought she loved Garret, and he was not so sure Lassiter did not love her, too. "Don't forget, I'll have this letter for you, if you ever want it."

Lauren's brow wrinkled in a frown. "I won't ever want it." She knew the letter would only contain an apology. Why should he apologize when she had been the one who kissed him? It was all so awful.

Lauren stared restlessly at the bleak landscape. How many years would pass before she forgot how Garret's eyes shone when he smiled, before she forgot the feel of his mouth on hers?

She straightened her spine. Garret was her past, and Savannah was her future. She had to let him go, put him out of her mind. The love she felt for Garret was not that of a young girl captivated by the charms of an older man. It was real, and it hurt so very much.

She closed her eyes, lulled by the rocking of the stagecoach. She would bury her love for Garret so deep in her heart that she would never think of him again.

Chapter Six

Savannah, Georgia—four years later

It was just after the dinner hour, and Lauren was in the parlor with her aunt and uncle. A chessboard was positioned between her and her uncle, and Lauren's face was drawn in concentration as she contemplated her next move.

Suddenly her face brightened.

Lauren's knight was directly in line with her uncle's king, and she moved her bishop into place. "I have you!" she cried gleefully. "You fell into my trap this time."

Uncle Morgan leaned back and smiled graciously in defeat. "The vanquished salutes the victor, my dear. The student conquers the teacher."

Lauren glanced up at Aunt Eugenia. "I finally beat him."

Her aunt's hands were busy at her sewing, and she paused, looking over her glasses. "About time someone took you down a peg, Morgan. You were getting far too confident about your mastery of chess."

Before Morgan Colfax could reply, there was a tap on the door, and the maid, Molly, entered, carrying a letter on a silver tray. "Excuse me, Miss Lauren, but this post came for you," she said, extending the tray to her.

Lauren looked puzzled. "Please excuse me, Uncle, while I read this." She never gave up hope that Tanner would write her. But the handwriting was unfamiliar. It was from Sidewinder, all right, but it was not from her brother. It was from her father's solicitor, William Hanes.

With worry tugging at her mind, Lauren opened the envelope and read the letter, her heart growing heavier as she absorbed its contents. At last, she glanced at her aunt in fear and confusion.

"The letter says my father is ill and dying. How can that be?" Her bewildered glance went to her uncle. "I cannot believe it. It must be one of my stepmother's ploys to get me back to Texas."

"You must consider, my dear," her aunt said wisely. "Do you think your stepmother would want you to return? After all you have told us

75

about her, I would think she desires your absence."

"My father was always so big and strong, how could anything strike down Thomas J. McBride?"

Eugenia Colfax rose and went to her niece, sliding a comforting arm around her waist. "What exactly does the letter say, dear?"

Lauren glanced back at the letter and read aloud:

"Dear Lauren Emily McBride, In accordance with instructions contained in the last will and testament of Thomas J. McBride, dictated to me and dutifully signed and witnessed on this date, the fifth of March, in the year of our Lord 1886, I am forwarding this letter to all potential heirs to his estate that they be informed of the conditions of inheritance prescribed in the above legal document. It is the intention of your father, Thomas J. McBride, to bequeath equal shares of the Circle M Ranch and all his remaining assets to each of his progeny, and to his wife, Clare Brown McBride. Mr. McBride has stipulated, however, that in order to be eligible for this bequest, his progeny must present themselves at the Circle M Ranch no later than nine months from the date of this letter; to remain there pending the arrival of the other heirs, at which time the details of the inheritance will be specified. Those of his progeny who do not appear within that period will forfeit their shares of the estate. The forfeited shares will then be added to the award of Clare Brown McBride. Thomas McBride has made it clear that no exceptions will be made to the conditions he has outlined. The official business of this letter concluded, I feel it is my duty as solicitor to the estate and longstanding friend of the McBride family to include the information that Thomas McBride is gravely ill, that his condition has been pronounced terminal, and that he is not expected to live out the year. Hoping to see this matter drawn to a conclusion that is satisfactory to all, I remain, yours most sincerely, William Benton Hanes, Esq."

Lauren's voice trembled as she read the letter. Disbelief and sadness battled for control of her mind. "Can it be true? If it is, I must go home at once."

Morgan laid a comforting hand on Lauren's arm. "Before you do that, I advise you to write to William Hanes, my dear. Inform the solicitor that you want more information on your father's health. I'll help you draft the letter if you would like."

Lauren took comfort from the two people who had become so important to her during the past four years. Her aunt, though in her early fifties, still looked youthful and lovely, her skin flawless, her red-gold hair laced with just a touch of white. Uncle Morgan was not a tall man, and rather thin, but it was his eyes that drew attention—they were light gray and always seemed to be softened by laughter. He had shown Lauren what it was like to have a loving father. She loved them both so much; nothing would induce her to leave them.

"Uncle, I don't think there can be any mistake. I know Mr. Hanes, and he is likely to err on the side of caution rather than alarm. My father must be very ill for him to have written such a letter."

"Come into my study," her uncle said. "We shall draft a letter and send it in the morning post."

Lauren nodded. Since her uncle was a solicitor of some renown, he would know just how to put her concerns in a letter. She paused in the doorway and glanced back at her aunt, watching her dab at her eyes with a handkerchief. "I don't want to leave you, but I fear I must. It is surprising how a letter can change one's whole life."

"I love you, Lauren, as if you were my own daughter." Eugenia folded her handkerchief and neatly pressed it into her pocket. "I cannot imagine this house without you in it."

Lauren ran into her aunt's arms. "You have been a mother to me, and Barbara and Carolyn have been like my own sisters. I have known only happiness here with you and Uncle Morgan. I don't want to leave you."

Eugenia straightened her spine and gathered her courage, knowing that if Tom McBride was dying, Lauren had to go back to Texas. "I somehow knew that the day would come when you would have to leave. But I am not quite prepared to—"

"Eugenia," her husband cautioned softly, "we must not make this more difficult for Lauren than it already is."

"If you must go, I shall go with you," Eugenia stated with feeling. "I won't let you go alone."

"As much as I would love to have you with me, Aunt Eugenia, Barbara will need you when her baby comes." She lowered her head, thinking about the trouble and heartache that awaited her in Texas. "I thought I would be with Barbara, too, when her time came. I was so looking forward to the birth of her baby."

"There, there," her uncle said, patting Lauren's shoulder. "Let's get this letter written."

Lauren spent an hour with her uncle while he helped her compose the letter to her father's solicitor. When it was finished, she read it to herself.

To William Benton Hanes, Esq.
Sidewinder, Texas
Dear Sir:

I am in receipt of your letter in which you stipulated the terms and conditions of the last will and testament of my father. Thomas J. McBride, as dictated to you on the fifth of March, this year of our Lord, 1886. Since I have not seen or heard from my father in the four years since I came to Savannah, and since I have, during that time, established a full and busy life apart from the Circle M. I hope you will understand that I have a few questions and comments regarding your communication.

First and foremost is my question about my father's state of health. You mention that he is gravely ill and not expected to live out the year. I hope you will excuse my surprise at that statement. My father was always a physically sound and robust person. The fact that he married a woman twenty-three years his junior, who was not the first of his many paramours, would seem to bear proof of the statement that he had the health and vigor of a man far younger than his forty-nine years. Therefore, before undertaking a journey of such a considerable distance, I would appreciate a clearer definition of his illness.

Secondly, it is my understanding that my brother Stone left the ranch after I did, leaving the Circle M to my father and his bride as my father apparently wished. Remembering Stone's unforgiving nature, and recalling the bitterness with which my brother Tanner departed the Circle M, I find myself sincerely doubting that either of them will respond to your letter. I know I need not tell you that my own departure from the Circle M was under equally unpleasant circumstances. I have not heard from either of my brothers in several years, yet the familial connection remains on *my part. For that reason, I beg your indulgence when I ask if you would be kind enough to convey whatever information you might have as to their present situations.*

I wish to make clear that you need not include any reference to my father's wife, Clare Brown McBride, in whatever response you choose to make to this letter. The reason is rudimentary. Due to the complicated history of ill feeling between Clare Brown McBride and myself, I made the decision four years ago that I would no longer allow her to affect my future in any way. For that reason, any information you might relay would be superfluous, as it would have no bearing on whether I will eventually choose to return to the Circle M, or how briefly I will stay.

I hope you will not consider it a conflict of interest as my father's lawyer if I ask you to keep your receipt of this letter from him. I would prefer that my father remain ignorant of this communication until I have made my decision.

Thank you for your forbearance in the reading of this letter. I hope to receive your prompt reply so I can make the appropriate determination with regard to the stipulation my father has outlined.

Lauren nodded in satisfaction. Her uncle

had polished the legal prose for her. She picked up the pen and signed:

> *Yours most sincerely, I remain,*
> *Lauren Emily McBride.*

Grief surged through Lauren as she wearily climbed the stairs to the bedroom that had been hers for four wonderful years. From the moment she had arrived in Savannah, she had been welcomed into this house with love and kindness. Her cousin Barbara was three years older than she, and Carolyn was her same age. They had embraced her as family and had wiped her tears when she cried of homesickness. It would be so difficult to leave them—they were her best friends.

Lauren sat on the edge of her bed, running her hand over the lovely lace coverlet her aunt had made for her—just one of the many kindnesses she had been showered with. Her aunt and uncle lived in a beautiful home, and they had introduced her to a gracious way of living. She wore fashionable and expensive gowns and had attended one of the South's best schools for young ladies.

Lauren allowed her thoughts to drift back to the time when she'd first arrived in Savannah. She had not been there a month when her aunt had enrolled her in Mrs. Dickerson's School for Young Ladies, the same school Carolyn attended. Lauren and Carolyn had taken only day courses because her aunt wanted them to live at home and not at the school as many of the young ladies did. Aunt Eugenia had engaged a diction teacher, a music teacher, and a voice teacher to come to the house to teach Lauren.

At first Lauren had been lonely, but the love of this family embraced her and drew her in so quickly, it seemed that she had always lived there. Although there had been times when she wished for her old life, the loneliness became less and less.

Now, if her father was indeed dying, she must leave the people who had become so dear to her.

She did not want to go back to Texas, where she had been so unhappy.

But she must.

How would she bear the separation?

It was with a heavy heart that Lauren read the answer to her letter. William Hanes's letter was put in simple terms and was less formal than the first one.

Dear Lauren,

If my first letter to you was unclear, let me put this bluntly and assure you that your father is indeed gravely ill. As you requested of me, I will say nothing to your father or stepmother, Clare McBride, about your previous correspondence. I have had no word from Stone and cannot even be sure that my letter ever reached him. But Tanner has come home and is residing at the Circle M, as the will stipulates he must. If you are asking my advice about returning home, I must inform you that the doctor fears your father will not live for very long. I believe you should come home with all dispatch.

Sincerely,
William Hanes, Esq.

Tanner had returned to Sidewinder! He was living at the Circle M.

More than anything else the attorney had written, the part about Tanner's return convinced Lauren that their father was indeed gravely ill. Otherwise, her brother would never have returned to Sidewinder.

Lauren found her aunt in the pantry, overseeing the butler while he polished the silver.

When Eugenia saw Lauren's face, she took her arm and led her into her husband's study. "Sit down, dear. From your expression, I take it you have received an answer to your letter."

"Yes. I must leave for Texas."

Eugenia drew Lauren into her arms. "Then leave quickly so you can return to us all the sooner."

On the day Lauren left, she tried not to cry, but tears seeped from her eyes and ran down her cheeks. She hugged her aunt tightly, as if she could take the essence of her back to Texas with her. Barbara and Carolyn clung to her, wiping tears from their eyes. She was sure she had seen tears in her Uncle Morgan's eyes as well when he hugged her to him.

Once more, Lauren's life was spinning out of control. She did not know what she would face when she returned to the Circle M, but the thought that she would see Tanner gave her strength.

Her aunt's maid, Molly, and her uncle's man-servant, Albert, were accompanying her to Sidewinder, though they would not remain with her.

When the train pulled away from the station, Lauren waved from the window until she could no longer see Aunt Eugenia. She collapsed in a seat, wishing the train would stop so she could run back to the safety of her aunt's arms. She had cried herself to sleep the night before, and she was not sure which was more painful—the fact that her father was dying, or the fact that she must leave her aunt.

The tedious journey dragged on for almost three weeks. Lauren was so weary when she finally reached Texas that she was ready to collapse. They were in Dallas now, and it was not much farther to Sidewinder.

Today, Lauren would began the last leg of her journey by public coach. As she left the hotel, she watched Albert direct the men who were loading her baggage onto the stage.

"You there, have a care. If you dent that trunk, you'll pay for it," Albert stated with authority.

Molly walked beside Lauren, and it soon became apparent to them both that they were objects of curiosity. People, men mostly, were stopping to stare at Lauren. Two drunken cowboys, weaving their way down the boardwalk, stopped to openly admire her, and it made her most uncomfortable. This had never happened to her in Savannah.

One of them doffed his hat, bowed, almost tipping over, and said admiringly, "Ma'am, you're 'bout the prettiest gal I ever did see." He turned to his companion. "Ain't that so, Billy?"

Molly grabbed up Lauren's sunshade and wielded it at the two cowhands like a weapon. "Get on with you! Don't you know a real lady when you see one? Get out of the way, and let us pass."

"Yes, ma'am, I surely do know a lady when I see one—and I'm a-seeing one right now," the cowboy named Billy stated admiringly. He smiled at Lauren, and she had a difficult time not smiling back. " 'Scuse my condition, ma'am. I'm just off the trail and had me my first drink in weeks. Would have stayed sober if'n I'd a-knowed I'd see such a pretty lady."

Lauren whisked past them with a slight smile. There was no harm in them. She knew how isolated cowboys were when they drove a herd to market, and how they looked for amusement when they finally reached a town.

"Good day to you, pretty lady."

Lauren stepped into the street, and Albert helped her into the coach. She would be home in two days.

Home.

How strange that sounded.

The scenery outside the coach window now looked familiar to Lauren. She did not invite the memories into her mind, but they came anyway, unasked and unwanted. Her father was ill and dying. She loved him, even though he had been a hard man to love at times. She wanted nothing to do with any inheritance he might leave her. She only wanted to be with him and give him what comfort she could. Then she would return to Savannah.

Tanner was at the Circle M. And Stone—had he returned, too?

She closed her eyes. Clare. She did not look forward to bring reunited with her stepmother. The woman would hover over everyone, sneaking around corners and offering snide remarks. Lauren studied her manicured hands. How different she was from the wild, unkempt young girl who had left Sidewinder four years earlier. Now she would never allow Clare to intimidate her as she once had.

Lauren glanced down at her exquisite green

traveling gown, which was cut in the latest fashion. A matching hat with a red cockade sat atop her elegantly arranged hair. Her aunt and uncle had insisted on showering Lauren with beautiful clothing. No, she was not the same unkempt girl who had left Texas with a broken heart and spirit.

Even her diction had changed. She now spoke with a softer Southern accent, which had been drilled into her by an insistent speech teacher. Outwardly she had changed, but inwardly she still felt a prickle of uncertainty about what lay ahead.

Her mind went where she did not want it to go—to Garret Lassiter.

Garret was probably married by now. Lauren's only contact with Sidewinder had been the short letters she always received from Jeb at Christmas time, and Jeb never wrote more than a few lines. She had no idea what had been going on during her absence.

Now was not the time to think about Garret, so she pushed all thoughts of him to the back of her mind.

"Will someone be meeting us, Miss Lauren?" Albert inquired.

She turned to him and looked thoughtful. "Uncle Morgan sent a letter to my father's solicitor advising him of our arrival. And if I know my uncle, he's probably sent wires as well."

"Will we be going to the ranch with you?" Molly wanted to know.

Lauren knew that Molly wanted to be back in Savannah by the time Barbara's baby was born. "Do you want to go with me?"

"Miss Lauren, if it's all the same to you," Molly said hesitantly, "I'd like to get back home. Mrs. Colfax is sure to need my help when Barbara has her baby."

"I understand how you feel." Lauren opened her reticule and handed a packet to Albert. "This is the money Uncle Morgan instructed me to give you. You have the return tickets you'll need, don't you?"

Albert patted his pocket. "Yes, Miss Lauren."

Lauren nodded in satisfaction. "I'll arrange rooms for you at the hotel in Sidewinder. When you feel rested enough, you can make the return trip."

"There sure is a lot of space out here, Miss Lauren," Albert observed. "Most of it seems uninhabitable to me."

Lauren's gaze followed Albert's. "It's not, though. You would be surprised at how many people live out there. This is some of the best ranching country in the United States," she said, nodding out the window. "You can see for miles in any direction. I guess I have missed that without really knowing it."

At that moment, the coach made a wide turn, and Lauren knew that Sidewinder was just ahead. She could hear the driver urging the horses into a slower pace. By the time they entered the town itself, the horses had slowed to a walk.

Lauren glanced at the town she had not seen since she was fifteen years old. She sat forward and frowned. She hardly recognized it. "What has happened here? This is not the Sidewinder I remember."

Albert looked amazed. "I count three saloons, Miss Lauren. No, four."

"How could this happen?" Lauren questioned. "There is a saloon where Darby's Feed and Equipment once stood." She saw a gaudy red gown displayed in one of the storefront windows. The streets were crowded with people, but she did not see one familiar face.

Lauren saw the worried frown on Molly's face and attempted to calm her. "It's probably not as bad as it seems." She glanced at Albert. "I'll expect you to stay close to Molly at all times while you're here. I think perhaps the two of you should leave as soon as possible. I don't like the looks of the town." She shook her head. "I don't understand it."

"You're not to worry about us, Miss Lauren," Molly said with assurance. "You just get yourself home to your papa and do what has to be done there."

They passed the sheriff's office, which gleamed with a new coat of paint. A man stood near the street, his tin badge shining as the sun hit it. He was tall and broad-shouldered with dark hair and skin.

For the merest moment, their eyes met, and Lauren saw something questioning in his gaze— or had she only imagined it? His light-blue eyes were familiar somehow, and yet she knew they had never met.

She broke eye contact with him and smiled at Molly. "It seems that I am home."

The coach came to a swinging halt, and Lauren almost wished they had kept on going right through Sidewinder. She hoped the change in the town was no indication of what was to come, but she feared it might be.

Chapter Seven

Tanner McBride watched as the Overland Stage approached. It had been a long time since he'd seen his sister. He had tried to picture what she would look like many times during the last years. But his image of her was always of a spirited young girl with red curls flying and a mischievous smile that had melted his heart. Lauren was a young lady of marriageable age. What would she be like now?

As the coach slowed, Tanner suddenly felt nervous. He had always felt guilty for leaving her under Clare's domination. He had left Lauren in tears, and she had said some cruel things to him at the time. He hoped she had forgiven him by now.

*   *   *

Other eyes watched the stage arrive. Garret Lassiter had waited for this day for four long years.

Lauren . . . had she changed? Of course she had. She was nineteen. He still carried the lock of her hair with him in his saddlebag, although he rarely looked at it anymore. The thought of her, the memory of her freshness was always with him.

And now she was home.

Still other eyes watched Lauren's arrival. The young sheriff had a particular interest in the woman he had seen briefly through the stage window. Faith, his wife, came up beside him and followed his gaze.

"Is that her?"

"Yes. That's her."

"Are you going to meet the stage?"

Chase McBride glanced down at his wife. Her golden hair was worn in a braid like a halo around her head, and her eyes shone with sweetness. But he knew that if anyone crossed Faith McBride, she could fight with the best of them. "No," Chase said at last. "I will not be meeting that stage."

"I would like to meet Lauren."

"I want you to understand that you might never meet her. She probably has very definite ideas about me—or will when she finds out about me. Tanner said that no one has told her she has a bastard brother. I don't think she'll welcome me."

"Don't feel that way. I'm sure when Lauren learns of your existence, she will want to see you."

He smiled at her. "Even after everything you've been through, you still look for the good in people."

Faith knew Chase as well as anyone could know him. There was a churning unrest inside her husband. She knew he loved her, and that their marriage had made him happy, but would he ever find rest for his troubled spirit? "Although you may not admit it, I believe you want your sister's acceptance."

Chase did not bother to deny his wife's words. "I'll probably only meet her in passing," he said. "I want you to realize that's the way it's going to be, so you won't be hurt. You can be sure we'll never be part of her life."

"I won't be hurt for myself. But I will be for you."

"Don't be." He took her small hand in his. "It doesn't matter to me. Don't let it matter to you."

She stood on tiptoe and kissed his cheek, knowing he was hiding his true feelings from her. He would never admit it to her, and probably not even to himself, but what Lauren thought of him would matter a great deal. "I'm on my way to visit with Annabelle Chapin. I'll see you at supper."

He nodded, his eyes still on the stage. "I'll see you then."

When the stage halted, Garret and Chase both watched Tanner step forward. This was Tanner's time with his sister—they would both wait their turn. Garret wanted his meeting with Lauren to be away from curious stares and prying eyes. Chase did not know if Lauren would ever want to meet him.

Garret watched a woman dressed in a gray gown and bonnet step down from the stage. The matronly woman looked startled by what she saw of Sidewinder. Then he saw a delicate ankle appear at the door and slide to the ground. The stage driver offered his hand to the lady who emerged, for lady she was from head to toe.

Garret had been with other women over the years to satisfy his urges, but always in the back of his mind lurked an adorable young redhead with freckles scattered across her nose, and the brightest, bluest eyes he had ever seen. Gone were the freckles and the long, gangly legs, and in their place was a beautiful woman with pale smooth skin and a woman's body. She was taller and more assured, but it was still his Lauren. Everyone was staring at her, and no wonder. Sidewinder had not seen her like before. She was poised and self-possessed. Her green traveling gown bespoke good taste and money. She was every inch a lady.

Lauren anxiously stepped down, her gaze going immediately to the tall man with McBride blue eyes.

"Tanner!"

Without hesitation, she flew across the distance that separated her from her brother and right into his open arms. She nestled her face against his rough shirt and closed her eyes. His arms were strong and protective, and happy tears blurred her vision.

This was what coming home meant. To be reunited with Tanner.

His arms tightened about her, and he just held her for a long moment without saying anything.

After a bit, Tanner chuckled and held her away from him. "Can this be my Lauren—the pesky little girl who followed me around, badgering me with questions and dogging my every step?"

She turned around in a circle and smiled at him. "As you see, I'm all grown up now." She raised an eyebrow. "But I'm still pesky, and I'll probably still dog your steps."

He hooked an arm around her shoulder. "I see I will have to keep the shotgun handy or some man will try to steal you away. Or has some man in Georgia already done that?"

"My heart belongs only to you," she teased lightly and went back into his arms again. "I have missed you."

He hugged her to him. "I know." His voice shook with emotion. "Me, too."

Lauren pulled away from him, her eyes suddenly clouding. "How is Papa?"

Tanner shook his head. "He's not good at all,

Lauren." He took a deep breath. "He won't allow me to see him very often, and he may not let you, either. He's as stubborn as he ever was."

"I had hoped he would be better by now. I guess I just don't want to accept the fact that our father is . . . so ill."

"You need to be prepared when you see him, Lauren. Our pa's getting weaker, not stronger." Tanner noticed a drunk weaving his way down the street. "Let's get you away from here. I'll tell you all about Pa on the way home."

Lauren turned her attention to her aunt's servants. "Tanner, this is Molly and Albert. They will need a place to stay here in town until their stage leaves for Savannah." She looked doubtful. "A nice place if there is one."

"I think we'd better put them up at Annabelle Chapin's boardinghouse. I'll ask Annabelle to look after them."

Molly and Albert looked to Lauren for direction. "Go with my brother, and he will see you both settled." She hugged Molly and gave Albert's hand a quick squeeze. "Thank you both for accompanying me on this journey," she said, already feeling the loss of their company. When they left, it would sever her ties with her aunt and uncle. "Assure Aunt Eugenia that I shall keep her informed about what is happening with my father. And have a safe trip home."

Tanner nodded toward the stage office. "Wait

there 'til I return, Lauren. I won't be long."

Lauren watched Tanner steer the two servants in the direction of the boardinghouse. Instead of going inside the Overland office, she settled on the wooden bench just outside the door. The afternoon heat was stifling. She had forgotten how hot it could get in Texas.

She glanced about her, somewhat alarmed by the transformation that had come over Sidewinder since she had been away. She watched as women dressed in outlandishly gaudy, low-cut gowns paraded around, enticing men into the saloons. The town bustled with shuffling feet and people bumping shoulders. What was wrong here?

Lauren looked across the street, and her throat tightened when her gaze collided with Garret Lassiter's. Even after all this time, the sight of him made her heart leap. She was painfully reminded that he was not the kind of man a woman could ever forget. He stood with his shoulder casually propped against the building, his intense gaze on her. She had not forgotten those eyes that had visited her so often in her dreams and haunted her in her waking hours during the four years since she had last seen him. His mere presence had recaptured her heart, and it thudded inside her like a wild thing. In the depths of her very soul, she had ached for him. She realized a painful truth: her love for him had not diminished—it had simply become torture.

Panic touched Lauren's mind as she watched Garret push himself away from the wall, untie his horse from the hitching post, and lead it across the street in her direction. His stride was slow, almost as if he were stalking her; his eyes were compelling. He exuded power, and she was afraid that power would reach out and snare her again as it once had.

Garret dropped the reins of his horse, and the animal stood as if at attention while Garret climbed the steps and stopped in front of Lauren. His eyes were silently asking for something from her—but she did not know what it was. It was as if he were expecting some reaction. She raised her chin a little higher and waited for him to speak.

The glacier blue gaze Lauren gave Garret was as impersonal as one she would bestow on a stranger. Her coldness was like a physical fist driven into his gut.

"Hello, Lauren."

Her instinct was to tell Garret how glad she was to see him, but she faltered, and then decided against it. "Hello."

She looked into the velvet brown eyes that had made her reject every suitor who had courted her in Savannah. He was the man she had unconsciously used to take the measure of every other, and the others had certainly paled in comparison to him. He was even more magnetic than before, and much more dangerous and exciting.

Lauren realized that she had been staring at

Garret, so she turned away. Somehow he willed her to turn back to him. He was the last person she had wanted to see, and yet . . .

His lids slid down to hood his eyes, but the glimmer in the brown depths was compelling.

His voice was deep and resonant. "It's wonderful to see you again, Lauren."

Stiffly she said, "I didn't expect to see you today." Her insides churned with emotion.

Oh, why did Garret have to be there?

"Didn't you?"

"I should have thought of the possibility, since Sidewinder is such a small town."

"It's no accident I'm here, Lauren. I knew you would be coming in on the afternoon stage."

What did he mean by that? she wondered. How little he had changed. Only his attitude was different. He was not smiling as he once had whenever they met.

Lauren's voice quivered as she asked politely, "How have you been, Garret?"

His mouth shaped the words, but he seemed to have difficulty speaking. At last he admitted, "I have been dead inside."

"I don't understan—"

His rich laughter cut her off in midsentence, and the sound of it sent a thrill through her. "I'm fine now, Lauren—alive again. I'm just fine."

Memories tumbled through her mind, memories she had thought she'd put behind her. She recalled the unpleasantness of their last meeting and jerked her mind back to the present.

Garret had not missed Lauren's exquisitely polished manner, or her smooth diction. "You seem to be well."

"I . . . yes. As you see. I came home because my father is ill. You must know that."

"I do know. I'm sorry." He reached out and laid his hand on her shoulder as if he could not resist touching her. His gaze moved slowly over her, taking in every detail.

"How was your journey?" he asked as casually as if they had seen each other the day before.

She had envisioned their meeting many times, but she was not prepared to face him so unexpectedly. "Uneventful and long," she said, giving him a tight smile. To have something to do with her trembling hands, she snapped her parasol open, and at the same time rose from the wooden bench, twisting away from his touch.

Garret looked amused, as if he knew the effect he was having on her. "You are very beautiful, Lauren. More so than ever, if that's possible." His soft gaze moved slowly across her face. "I do miss the freckles, though. I don't see a one."

She raised her chin the merest bit and turned back to him, wishing he would just go away. "I grew out of my freckles, Garret, just as I grew out of many childhood traits."

Garret looked as if he wanted to say something

more, but he touched his hat and moved away from her. "So you have." He shoved his boot into the stirrup and mounted, his gaze settling on her. "I'll be seeing you, Lauren."

She stared after him as he rode away with his back straight and his eyes ahead. After four years she still loved him—today she was reminded just how much.

Had he married the woman he had told her about the day he shot Raja? She had not gathered the courage to ask him.

Probably, he had.

If only she did not care. If only . . .

The young sheriff had watched the interchange between Lauren and Garret Lassiter. There was something unsettled between those two, but he did not care to speculate about their past relationship. He was not interested in Lassiter. His eyes went to Lauren. Would she reject him without giving him a chance? He was more uneasy about meeting her than he'd been about Tanner or even the still absent Stone. For some reason, he wanted her approval more than that of her brothers.

At that moment, Lauren turned toward Chase, and their gazes locked. He gave her a half smile, but she lifted her chin and turned her back to him.

Just the reaction he would have expected from a white woman of her class. He decided in that moment that he would never seek her out. If she came to him, that would be another matter, but he doubted that she ever would.

Estaban Velasquez loaded supplies into the wagon and watched the scene being played out on the streets of Sidewinder. No one knew better than he what all the players were thinking and feeling, since he made it his business to find out about anyone who interested the *patrón*, and Señorita McBride definitely interested Garret Lassiter.

Hoisting a heavy sack of flour, Estaban placed it in the wagon with such force that the weathered boards creaked. Each time he had to take orders from a Lassiter, his hatred of them deepened. He had been told to come for supplies today, because no one else on the ranch liked that chore. Well, he had wanted to be here today—he wanted to see Garret's reaction to Señorita McBride's arrival. Now he knew that there was still much emotion between them.

He gave a careless wave to the storekeeper, hopped into the wagon, and drove out of town. It appeared to Estaban that Señorita McBride had been cold in her greeting to the *patrón*. He had studied Garret Lassiter for years, and he knew him. There had been no woman in Garret's life since Señorita McBride had left Texas, at least none that counted.

Garret Lassiter was tortured by love for the beautiful señorita.

Estaban remembered when he had loved a woman with such intensity. Bitter memories overwhelmed him. His beautiful Carmelita had not wanted a man with no land and no money. She had married another man who had both. Carmelita had been faithless, *pérfido*!

But she belonged to the past. He hardly allowed himself to think about her anymore.

Estaban smiled and then laughed aloud. Let the *patrón* pursue his woman and catch her. He was still willing to wait and strike when Garret Lassiter had much more to lose.

"You want her, Señor Lassiter," the Spaniard said in a harsh voice. "Love her, ache for her. And when the beautiful señorita agrees to marry you, and you are happy, I will kill your father, as I did your mother. Then it will be your turn." It gave him a feeling of power to know that he could punish the *patrón* at will.

Chapter Eight

Lauren sat beside Tanner, her arm linked through his as he maneuvered the buggy through the congested traffic of Sidewinder. For Lauren, there had been sadness in coming home but happiness as well. The happiness came from seeing Tanner and knowing he was all right. She had worried about him for so long that her heart now surged with joy.

"It's so good to see you again," she said, glancing into his handsome face. "I've missed you so much."

He looked down at her, his eyes soft, his lips curved with a smile that had always been reserved for her alone. "Just look at you, all grown up." His smile deepened. "And you turned out right pretty for a redhead." His voice softened. "You remind me a lot of Ma."

Tanner had always teased her about her red hair, but she had never resented it coming from him, just as she had not minded Garret calling her "little redhead." "The sad part for me," Lauren said, "is that I can hardly remember our mother. As time passes, my vision of her becomes less clear."

"If you want to remember what she looked like, just look in the mirror."

"Really?"

"You're taller than she was and have some of Pa's features, too, but you have the look of Ma about you."

"Why didn't our father love our mother?"

He lifted an eyebrow. " 'Father and mother,' not 'Ma and Pa'?" A teasing light came into his eyes and he said, "Lauren, you have come home a refined young lady. What did they do to you in Savannah?"

She pressed her cheek against his arm. "They trimmed away the rough edges." She laughed as she remembered when she had first arrived in Savannah. "You should have seen the diction teacher Aunt Eugenia engaged for me. Miss Primpton was horrified by what she called 'my wild Texas accent.' " Lauren's voice rose as she imitated her teacher. " 'My dear, you will never be a proper young lady if you cannot speak correctly.' "

"It couldn't have been easy for you."

"At first I was lonely. But Aunt Eugenia and Uncle Morgan were good to me and made me feel like I was part of their family. I had a good life with them, Tanner. I wish you could meet them."

"And now you've come back"—he thrust his hand out—"to this."

"I almost didn't come. After receiving the letter from Mr. Hanes, I thought about not coming home. At Uncle Morgan's suggestion, I wrote Mr. Hanes a second letter, and he assured me that our father was gravely ill. After that I had to return."

Tanner stared into the distance. "There's three of us home now."

"Then Stone's already arrived." She felt another surge of pleasure at the thought of seeing her older brother. She had never told Stone how much she loved him. And now, looking back, she realized that her older brother had been in the background of her life, taking care of her all along. "It will be good to see Stone. Has he changed much? I hope the two of you have settled your differences. Now that I am older, I realize how important family is."

Tanner stared at her so he could judge her reaction to what he was about to tell her. She had to be told, and it would be better if the news came from him. "It's not Stone. He's not here, yet."

She looked puzzled. "Not Stone? Then who is the third one?"

"Lauren." Tanner shifted uncomfortably. "I

have to say something, and I don't know quite how."

She slid her hand into his. "The best way is to just say it right out. Isn't that what Papa always says?"

"Yeah, I guess," he agreed. "Lauren . . . we have another brother."

She smiled. "Yes, I know . . . Stone."

He shook his head. "I wasn't referring to Stone, although Chase McBride is Stone's age."

She frowned, knowing she was not going to like what Tanner was telling her. "I don't understand. What are you saying?"

"Pa . . . was . . . with another woman while Ma was carrying Stone. The result was . . . is that we have a brother. His name's Chase, and he's in Sidewinder. Pa called him home the same as the rest of us."

Lauren frowned, fighting back the sick feeling inside her. "How can that be?"

"Lauren, you probably don't know it, but Pa was with many women while he was married to Ma. Chase is the result of one of his indiscretions. And there's more. Chase's Ma was a Comanche."

"Why are you telling me this now?"

"Because Chase is a McBride, and you are going to have to see him from time to time."

"A McBride."

"He's our brother. We may not like what Pa did, but it wasn't Chase's fault. I don't know how you

and Stone will feel about him, but I've already acknowledged him as my brother."

She took a deep swallow, trying to ingest all
Tanner had told her. "You are asking me to accept
this . . . person who is the result of Pa's indiscre-
tion?"

"No. That's a decision you'll have to make on
your own." He stared down at her. "But you might
want to think about this—Chase probably suffered more than any of us. I hope you will think
about the hardships he faced by not having a pa."

Suddenly Lauren remembered the man she had
seen through the stage window. He had looked
familiar because he was a McBride. "Is he the sheriff?"

Tanner looked amazed. "Yes. How did you
know that?"

"I saw him as the stage was pulling into town."

"He was a Texas Ranger before he became sheriff. He's trying to clean up Sidewinder, and I believe he will. The town's gotten rougher in the last
few years."

"I noticed."

"It would be good if you'd pay Chase a visit,
Lauren. He's proud, and he'll never come to you."

She thought of her mother and wondered if she
had known about the other son her husband had
sired. "I'm not sure I can do that. It seems disloyal
to Mama."

"This has nothing to do with Ma. I think Chase

expects you to reject him outright. But I don't think you will when you've had time to reflect on his situation."

Lauren was quiet for a moment. Then she asked softly, "He uses the McBride name?"

"Yes. Chase gives the impression that he doesn't give a damn about anything—but why do you suppose he took our name if he didn't care?"

"I don't know." She stared into the distance. "I don't know how I feel about him. It's all so unexpected. Give me some time."

"Take all the time you need."

They were quiet for a long moment, and Lauren knew that Tanner was giving her time to compose her feelings.

Then he asked, "Have you heard from Stone?"

Lauren shook her head. "Not in a long time and only one letter. He wrote to let me know that he had left the Circle M the day after I left for Savannah. I didn't have an address, so I couldn't answer him." She looked at Tanner, wondering why he had not written her when he had promised that he would. "I would have written you, but I didn't know where you were, either."

"When you didn't answer any of my letters, I thought you might still be mad at me." He gave her a searching look. "You were furious with me when I left."

Lauren frowned. "Tanner, what are you talking about? I never received a letter from you."

"What!" He flicked the reins and settled the horses into an easy gait now that they had left the town behind. "I can believe that one letter might go astray, or even two, but I wrote you every two weeks for over six months. All those letters couldn't have gotten lost."

They both came to the same conclusion at the same time, and said the name in unison: "Clare!"

"Damn that woman," Tanner said angrily. "She's nothing but trouble. Why would she do that?"

"You know why. She was infatuated with you and probably read your letters over and over. Let's not allow her to spoil our reunion. It would give her too much pleasure if she knew she had that kind of power over us. We'll deal with Clare in our own time. Tell me more about Papa."

"As I said, he's dying. It's his heart mostly, but other things too, I suspect."

"I won't know what to say to him when I see him. Especially now that I know about . . . Chase."

"That might not be a problem. Pa may not let you into his room until he's good and ready. And Clare will probably try to keep you away from him altogether."

"Just let her try." Lauren's eyes glinted with defiance. "I just hope she does try. I will never forgive her for keeping your letters from me."

He chuckled. "You're a regular little pistol, aren't you?"

"I'm not the frightened little girl I once was." She fanned herself with her handkerchief. "What kind of care is Papa getting?"

"Aside from the frequent visits from Doc, there's a man, Tiny, who looks after him. Clare doesn't like Tiny at all, which makes him all right with me. He seems to take good care of Pa."

"Tiny who? And where did he come from?"

"I don't know where he came from. Jeb said Pa once did him a kindness, and he's devoted to him now. If he has a last name, I haven't heard it. He's a mute, Lauren. You'll never know what's going on in his mind. I've managed to communicate with him through Indian sign language, though, if you can believe that."

"I will be happy to see Jeb. How is he?"

"Jeb's always the same—steady and strong. Clare's tried to get rid of him over the years, but she can't." He smiled. "It must be hard for her to have a man around who despises her." He snapped the reins, and the horses broke into a faster gait. "I think I should warn you that Manuelo is still Clare's eyes and ears. That man would do anything she asked him to do."

Lauren gazed out at the familiar prairie. She had come home, but it no longer felt like home to her. "I don't want the inheritance, Tanner—none of it."

"I feel the same way, and so does Chase. You can be sure that Clare will do her best to see that we continue to feel that way."

Lauren shuddered. "I hoped I'd never have to see her again."

Tanner smiled. "I think our stepma is in for a surprise when she sees you. She never did know how to act around a real lady."

Lauren stiffened. "I'm ready for her." Then she said with less assurance, "At least, I think I am."

"I'll watch out for you as much as I can, but be careful, Lauren," he warned. "Right now she's desperate with all of us coming home, and she's capable of anything."

"You and I both know why you left, Tanner. I wasn't sure you would come home."

"You don't believe the lies Clare told about me, do you, Lauren?" He looked deep into her eyes. "I mean, about me . . . and her."

"Of course not! How can you even ask?"

"I never touched that woman, but she sure as hell tried to get me to. She lied to Pa and is still lying to him. I don't know if he believes her. I don't see how he can."

"She would say and do anything if it was to her benefit. We both know that."

"Yeah."

"Tanner, did you see Garret in town today?"

He studied her more closely. "I did see him. Why?"

113

"I was just . . . wondering."

A teasing light came into his eyes. "If I remember, you were kinda sweet on Garret at one time."

"That was four years ago. It all seems a lifetime ago. I was a different person then."

"I saw you talking to Garret while I was getting Molly and Albert settled. He was hanging around town all morning like he was waiting for something. Now that I think about it, he was probably waiting to see you."

"I can't think why. He never gave me a serious thought." She felt a tightening in her chest. "He's married now, I suppose."

"Nope."

A sudden giddiness took possession of Lauren, and she felt lighthearted. "Not married? I thought he would be."

The sun was going down, and the western sky was a deep crimson red when they pulled through the gates of the Circle M. They were still too far away for Lauren to see the house, but she knew every nook and cranny of it. And it was the last place on earth she wanted to be.

She glanced up at the weathered Circle M sign as the buggy passed beneath it, and moments later Tanner pulled back on the reins and halted the horses. It took Lauren a moment to realize where they were. Her gaze swept the familiar arroyo, the craggy cliffs, and the dry riverbed below where their mother had lost her life in a wagon accident.

The Agreement

Lauren turned to Tanner, seeing the pain in his eyes. "Are you still torturing yourself over Mama's death?"

"Pa and Stone never believed me, but I fixed the wagon wheel that day, Lauren. I don't know how it came off, because I tightened all the bolts."

"You have nothing to feel guilty about. Let the past die, Tanner. We both know you're innocent."

"That's not the end of it," he said flatly. "I need to know what caused the accident that day. I put a new wheel on, and there isn't any way in hell it would have come off unless someone tampered with it."

Her eyes widened in horror. "You think that someone deliberately loosened the wheel? Who would do that to our mother?"

Darkness was encroaching, casting the craggy land in partial shadow. "I don't know what happened. But I sure as hell intend to find out."

"Perhaps we'll never know the full truth. But you must stop torturing yourself."

He took her gloved hand and laced his fingers through hers. "It helps that you believe me."

She smiled and kissed his cheek. "I would believe you if you told me yesterday was today."

He returned her smile and pulled her head against his shoulder. "I never knew how much I needed my little sister until now."

She drew away from him and gave a mock look of horror. "What? The great Tanner McBride needing his sister? Or any woman, for that matter?"

"There is a woman." He allowed his gaze to roam over the broken hills before he glanced back at Lauren. "I've been trying to think of a way to tell you about Callie."

"Who is Callie?"

"She's my wife, Lauren."

Lauren's mouth settled into a smile, and her eyes sparkled.

"Wife! So some woman finally tamed you, Tanner McBride." She threw her head back and laughed with joy. "That must disappoint a lot of women who had hopes you might look their way. Tell me *all* about this new sister-in-law of mine."

"I can't explain what happened to me when I first met her, but I knew in an instant that she was the one woman in the world for me." He paused as if remembering. "There were times I was afraid we would never get together."

"But you did."

"You have no idea what I went through to win Callie." He smiled slightly. "But I got the girl."

"I bet your marriage has put Clare's nose out of joint."

Tanner wrapped the reins around his hand. "Don't worry. My Callie can handle Clare just fine."

Lauren studied him closely. "Then I'm already inclined to like her."

"I've told her all about you, and she's eager to get to know you."

She eyed her brother carefully. There was still a tenseness about him, and she knew that he was worried about their father, but there was no sign of the restlessness that had once plagued him. She imagined that was because he had found happiness in his marriage. "How does Callie like living in the same house with Clare?"

He glanced down at her. "You know better than that. I'd never expose my wife to that viper. We fixed up the old line cabin real nice. Callie has a way of making that old shack look like a real home. But today she's waiting at the ranch house to see you."

"Then let's go! I want to meet my new sister-in-law."

Callie had been watching for the buggy for over an hour. Surely they should have arrived by now. She walked out onto the porch and felt a cool breeze touch her cheek. She was a bit apprehensive about meeting Lauren. What if Lauren did not like her?

She saw dust just over the rise and gripped the porch railing. She would soon find out. As Tanner halted the horses, it was too dark to see Lauren very clearly.

Without waiting for introductions, or for Tanner to help her out of the buggy, Lauren slid to the ground and approached the woman on the porch. She stopped a few paces from Callie and looked her over carefully. Callie McBride had eyes the color of honey that were wide with uncertainty at the moment. Her hair was brown with streaks of gold that caught the dying sunlight.

"So you're the woman who convinced my brother to give up the single life. I'm happy to welcome you to the family."

"I . . . thank you."

Lauren saw apprehension in the golden eyes. "I am your sister, Lauren." She slid her arms around Callie and hugged her. "I think we'll be great friends."

Callie was relieved and felt her nervousness melt away. "I do hope so."

Lauren's laughter was soft. "How could it be otherwise? We both love the same man."

Callie's laughter joined hers. "Tanner told me I would like you, and I do."

Lauren raised an eyebrow. "Let's present a united front. I'll need you close beside me when I face Clare."

"We didn't tell her you were coming, but your pa knows."

Lauren cocked her head to the side. "Ah, good. Then the element of surprise will be on my side."

Callie met Tanner's gaze, and he nodded approvingly. "Let's get on with it," he said, ushering them toward the door.

Lauren hesitated, staring at the door. She had a sinking feeling that once she entered that house again, her life would spin out of control.

Chapter Nine

Clare had just come downstairs, and she paused
on the last step with a look of stupifaction on her
face.

"Lauren?"

"Clare."

"So you have returned."

Lauren met her stepmother's gaze. "As you
see." She was incapable of pretending she was
happy to see Clare and unwilling to show any
warmth in her greeting.

Clare glared at Callie. "You didn't tell me Tanner had gone into town to get his sister. So that's
why you've been hanging around here all day. I
should have known something was up."

Callie shrugged. "It must have slipped my mind."

"Yes. Likely it did," Clare said heatedly. "Why are you here, Lauren?" she asked, looking her stepdaughter over carefully, and noting the astonishing change in her appearance.

"I should think that's obvious, Stepmother. My father wants me here."

Envy almost choked Clare as she noticed Lauren's fine gown and matching hat. She could barely conceal her hatred for Lauren, so she marched past the trio and headed for the door. Now that Lauren had come home unexpectedly, she had to think, and decide what her next move would be. Good Lord, the only other disaster that could befall her would be for Stone to turn up. And he probably would.

Lauren paused at the door, her hand trembling on the knob. She wanted to see her father, but she wanted him to be the way she remembered him, tall and strong. When she was a child, she'd thought there was nothing Tom McBride could not do. Now he was confined to his bed, his whole world his bedroom.

Suddenly the decision to enter was taken out of Lauren's hands. The door was wrenched open, and she stood at eye level with a thin, dark-haired man. He took in her appearance in a sweeping glance and nodded, backing away so she could enter.

"You must be Tiny. Tanner told me about you. I'm Lauren," she added unnecessarily. "I want to see my father."

Tiny nodded, then stepped around her, leaving her alone with her father.

The room was very dark, the curtains closed. The heavy atmosphere reeked of sickness and medicine. Lauren strained to see her father in the near darkness.

"Stop gawking, gal, and come over here," her father said in a weak voice, and then fell into a bout of coughing.

Lauren rushed forward, going down on her knees, and instinctively eased him to a sitting position. She hoped that the horror she felt at the sight of the frail, skeletal man did not show in her eyes.

This sickly man bore no resemblance to her stalwart father.

When Tom recovered, he fell back on the pillow and looked at her, thinking that the light was playing tricks on him. If this was Lauren, she looked very much like her mother when he'd first met her. He had almost forgotten the serenity his first wife had brought to his life. At the time he had not appreciated her. There had been plenty of time to think about that and other mistakes he had made. Emily had been soft-spoken and kind, and as different from Clare as two women could be. He tried not to think about that—not now.

"So," he said, blinking his watery eyes. "You've come home to grab up your inheritance. I thought greed would get you all here if nothing else would."

Lauren could hardly stand the sickening smell of unwashed flesh. "You delude yourself if you think I want any part of your money. I came home to see my brothers and to give you what comfort I can. I want no part of this ranch or anything else you have."

Tom was quiet for a long moment. "That fancy education did you some good. You talk like those damned Lassiters with their high-and-mighty ways." He seemed to have a burst of energy and even smiled. "Hell, they were gentleman farmers back in Virginia. If we'd lived there at the time, we'd probably have been working for them. They may have breeding and blue blood, but they're no better than me. Garret's been raised to stand up when a lady enters the room and remove his hat in the house. But scratch the surface of a Lassiter and you'll find he bleeds just like the rest of us."

She reached for the bedside table and turned up the wick on the oil lamp, noticing that her father's pale skin was now beet red. "I know you don't like the Lassiters; we certainly don't need to rehash that old argument."

"I like them well enough," Tom admitted grudgingly, watching her reaction. "The question is, how do you feel about Garret?"

"I don't see that this has anything to do with—"

"You turned out right pretty, gal. I'd never have thought it."

"Is that the way you see me, pretty? I'm told that I look like my mother and have my father's temper."

Tom's laughter became a shattering cough. His skin was again as pale as parchment paper, and his breathing was shallow. When Lauren bent forward to help, he waved her away. When he could catch his breath, he managed to say, "I'll wager you lose that temper a lot. Gave them a show of it in Savannah, I'll wager."

"I have learned to control my temper by using good sense, something you never learned, Papa. However, if I stay around you for long, I'll probably revert to my old ways."

Her father gave another deep laugh, which brought on another bout of coughing. Lauren felt pity wash over her and reached for his hand. "Is it always this bad, Papa?"

He could not speak but nodded as a strange calm settled over him. He had not given his daughter much thought until lately, and he should have. He felt pride in her, and he wished he had shown her more affection. He only hoped he had time to make up for his neglect. She would balk and rage when she discovered what he had in mind for her.

But her tantrums would not do her any good in the end. He knew what her weakness was, and he would use it to get what he wanted.

Lauren stood up and moved across the room. "For one thing, it's too hot and stuffy in this room. You need air, you need a bath, and you need your bed changed every day."

"Now, gal, don't you come here thinking you're gonna take over and change things."

She yanked the heavy curtains aside and raised the window, then went to the other side of the room and repeated the same ritual. "Now, that's better. Does this Tiny understand when you speak to him?"

"He can hear; he just can't speak."

"Good. I'll tell him what I want him to do."

Tom rolled his head from side to side, taking in clean gulps of air. "Clare thinks it'll do me harm if I'm bathed too often. And she says air isn't good for my lungs."

"Well, that's just too bad. You are going to have fresh air, and I want you bathed at once."

Tom watched her sail out of the room, and he smiled to himself. Damned if she wasn't going to liven things up around here.

He defied even Barnard Lassiter to produce such a daughter.

Lauren hurried downstairs and into the parlor. The room was just the same as it had been when her mother was alive. She wondered why Clare had not rid the house of everything that would remind her father of his first wife. Did she take some twisted delight in making a shrine to her husband's previous wife?

Lauren was never quite sure what went on in Clare's mind or what her motives were for what she did.

"So, you have come home like a vulture following the smell of death."

Lauren turned to face her stepmother, not bothering to hide her distaste for the woman. "You always did have a way of speaking that set you apart from everyone else, Clare."

Clare glared at Lauren, her gaze shifting to the exquisite gown her stepdaughter wore. She almost choked on her envy when she saw the strand of pearls around Lauren's neck and realized that they were real. There was a haughty, superior expression in Lauren's blue eyes that she had no doubt learned from her Savannah relatives. "Just what do you mean by that?" Clare demanded.

"Forgive me," Lauren said in a tone that did not show the least bit of contrition. "I was unfairly comparing you to my Aunt Eugenia, when I should have remembered you have not had the opportunity to learn how a *real* lady behaves. It's not your fault."

Clare, for the first time in her life, felt inferior to another woman. That skinny little redhead she'd sent off to Georgia had come back with confidence and poise. She reminded Clare of those high-stepping Lassiters, who always looked down their noses at her. "Is that meant to be an insult?"

Lauren feigned surprise. "Did it sound like one?" She picked up the glass figure of a bird, which had been her mother's favorite, and examined it closely so she would not have to meet Clare's eyes. She said in an insincere tone, "By all means, if I have offended you in any way, let me rush to apologize."

Clare's face reddened, and she clenched her fists so tightly that the nails cut into her palm. "Listen, little girl, don't use your fancy education thinking you can make me feel ignorant."

"Was I doing that? Clare, surely if a person feels ignorant, it is a situation of his or her own making." She clasped the blue glass bird and crossed to the door. "I'll just keep this in my room, since it was my mother's favorite."

Clare stepped between Lauren and the door, artfully calculating how she would handle her. "You've become the kind of woman I've always despised."

"Thank you. My Aunt Eugenia would be happy to know that her efforts have not been wasted. She strived to make me into a *lady*, as my mother was."

Clare had nothing to say in return. This little baggage was turning her own words against her. She tried another attack. "I heard you giving orders about your father's care. I'm his wife, and I'll make all the decisions for him."

"I understand that Doc Pierce will be here tomorrow, and I intend to ask him why my father's room is kept closed up and stuffy. The atmosphere in that room is enough to depress a healthy person, let alone one with my father's health problems."

"Don't get in my way, little girl," Clare warned, her voice threatening. "I got rid of you once. I can do it again."

"I'm not a little girl anymore, Clare," Lauren said coolly, shoving her aside and moving through the doorway. "And you can't make me do anything I don't want to do."

Clare rushed at Lauren, grabbed her arm, and jerked her around. "Don't be too sure about that. There are ways to get what I want, and I don't want you here. Mark my words, you'll be back on that stage for Savannah before the dust settles. I'll have you gone, and that milk-faced woman Tanner's married to as well."

Lauren was stunned by the venom in Clare's voice, and for a moment she reverted to the girl she had been, defenseless against such evil. She felt the coolness of the glass bird in her hand and thought of her mother. "I will only leave when I'm ready. And as for Callie, if she goes, Tanner will go with her. You wouldn't like that, would you? You always thought Tanner had a hidden passion for you when, in truth, he can't stand the sight of you. That must be hard for you to accept, Clare."

"You little bitch! Watch out that you don't push me too far. You won't like it if you do."

Lauren lifted her chin to a proud angle. "I'm quaking in my shoes, Stepmother. I'm so afraid, it will probably keep me awake tonight for at least five minutes." She gathered her gown and walked gracefully toward the stairs. "Excuse me. I want to see my father before I go to bed."

Clare watched Lauren disappear up the stairs. Something had to be done about her, and soon. She had to keep the girl away from Tom, but how could she do that? There was no wild stallion for Lauren to ride this time, but Clare would come up with something—she had to. That sassy little bitch was not going to ruin her plans. Clare had done things she did not even want to think about. She would go on doing whatever it took to get full control of the Circle M.

"Manuelo!" she cried, hurrying toward the back door. "Manuelo, I need you."

Lauren awoke early and dressed hurriedly, then lingered in her room because she did not want to see Clare. When she came downstairs, she was delighted to find Tanner and Callie having coffee and waiting for her.

"It's about time you got up, sleepyhead. We rode over to have breakfast with you and found you burning daylight, as Ma used to say."

She leaned forward and kissed her brother's cheek. "I've been up for hours, lingering in my room." She cast her eyes toward the stairs. "I didn't want to run into Clare this morning."

"She always eats late," her brother reminded her.

Lauren smiled at her sister-in-law. "Had I known the two of you were here, I would have come down sooner."

"Someone left you a bit of sunshine," Callie said, nodding at the plate laid for Lauren.

Lauren looked inquiringly at the rose beside her plate, thinking her brother had placed it there.

Callie laughed at Lauren's reaction. "It seems you have an admirer."

Lauren looked from her sister-in-law to her brother. "I can't think who."

Tanner took a sip of coffee and leaned back in his chair. "It seems Tiny wanted to make your first breakfast an occasion."

"Tiny? I didn't think he liked me."

Tanner wiped his mouth on a napkin and smiled as he stood. "Tiny never puts flowers by my plate." He kissed his wife and walked to the door. "Come out later, Lauren. Jeb should be back by now, and he'll want to see you."

As Tanner left, Tiny entered with eggs and huge slabs of steak heaped high on a platter. Lauren groaned inwardly, remembering the light breakfasts she had enjoyed at her aunt's house. She had

130

forgotten that Texans liked their beef, and in large quantities. "I'll just have coffee this morning, Tiny."

The dark-eyed man shook his head and proceeded to scoop two eggs onto Lauren's plate. He then held out a pan of biscuits to her.

Lauren gave a helpless sigh and took a fluffy biscuit. "Tiny, thank you." She raised the rose and inhaled the sweet fragrance. "And thank you for the rose."

He nodded his head, his dark eyes watchful.

"I will want to speak to you later about my father's care. But for now, could you get him two more pillows? It seems to me that he would be able to breathe better if he was propped up a bit."

Tiny nodded and left the room, his face red with pleasure.

So it continues, he thought.

"I believe you have made a friend for life," Callie speculated. "Tiny is a good man to have on your side."

"I want to talk to him about bathing my father daily. It doesn't have to be a tub bath; a sponge bath will do."

"You may have a fight on your hands with Clare. But with Tiny on your side, you have a powerful ally. He's the one who cares for your pa." Callie watched Lauren as she spoke. "I hope your pa will let you help him, Lauren. Most of the time, he refuses to even *see* Tanner, much less accept any help from him."

Lauren studied her new sister-in-law over the rim of her cup. Callie was beautiful and soft-spoken. It was easy to see why her brother loved her. "Papa will see me. I have no intention of allowing him to bully me."

Callie chuckled. "I can see that for myself."

"I'm glad Tanner has you, Callie. He's different with you, more . . . settled. I don't remember a time when he was so contented. The restlessness that was always in him is gone."

"Considering the circumstances under which we met, it's surprising we ever got together at all."

Lauren set her cup aside. "You did something no other woman ever did—you won his heart."

"Tanner was the last man in the world I wanted to fall in love with, but I did. Even Clare's lies and schemes to keep us apart didn't work."

"I can see we're going to get along just fine."

"Lauren, I'm glad you came, because I now have another woman in the house. Clare has been—"

"Did I hear my name mentioned?" Clare asked as she sauntered into the room, wearing a filmy pink housecoat that showed more of her buxom figure than it hid. A look of disappointment was clearly written on her face. "Tanner isn't here?"

Lauren met Callie's eyes. "As you see, he isn't."

Clare went to the sideboard and poured herself a cup of coffee. "I'm glad you're here, Lauren. I want to speak to you about something."

Lauren stood up, moving toward the door. "I must ask you to excuse me for now, Clare. I haven't seen Jeb yet." She looked past Clare to her sister-in-law. "I'm going to ride out with Tanner to look over the ranch. I hope you'll come with us."

Clare ground her teeth. "I said I wanted to talk to you, Lauren." She slammed down the coffee urn. "I have no intention of waiting while you go gallivanting about the country."

Lauren shrugged. "You'll just have to live with disappointment, Clare." She nodded at Callie, who was attempting to hide her amusement behind the napkin she held to her mouth. "When you're ready to ride, come on out. I'll be with Jeb."

Clare stared after Lauren and then turned her gaze on Callie. "That's what comes from indulgence. I can only imagine how her relatives in Georgia must have doted on her. Well, she won't get that treatment here!" She slid into a chair and stirred sugar into her coffee with such anger that the brew splashed on the table. "She can't get away with this!"

Callie stood. "Just what is she getting away with?"

"She thinks she's going to take over her pa's care. Well, I can tell you that isn't going to happen."

Callie moved to the door. "It's only her first

morning home, Clare. Just think how Lauren will stir things up when she's been here a week." Callie was barely able to contain her laughter until she got through the front door.

It was going to be such fun having Lauren home.

Chapter Ten

When Lauren entered the barn, she saw Jeb at the back hunched down beside a horse, examining its foreleg. She hurried toward him as if she could not get to him fast enough. She had forgotten how much she'd missed this gentle man who had always been a presence in her life.

Jeb heard Lauren approach and got to his feet. At first, he looked confused, as if he were seeing a ghost. Then a big grin spread over his crinkled face, and his arms opened wide for her.

Lauren propelled herself at him, and his arms closed gently around her.

"So," he muttered against her hair, "another prodigal returns home."

His arms tightened only briefly, and then he held

her away from him so he could look at her. "When I first saw you, I thought you was your ma. I thought she'd come back to life."

"I'm told I look a lot like her."

"From a distance you do, but up close those damned McBride eyes set you apart."

"How have you been, Jeb?"

"Passin' the seasons and keepin' busy. Waitin', mostly."

"Waiting? For what?"

"For all your ma's kids to come home."

She was struck, as she had always been, by how devoted Jeb was to her and her brothers. "You must think us all an ungrateful lot for not keeping in touch with you."

"That's not altogether true. You always sent me a Christmas present with an account of how you was doin' all year. I looked forward to that."

"You were my only link with the Circle M." She smiled. "But your Christmas cards were never very informative."

He stared at her. She would never know how much her communication had meant to him. He would always look after Emily's kids. Somehow, he felt as if they belonged to him, and he damn sure was going to do what was right by them, no matter whose toes he stepped on. "You know my writin's not too good. And I could never put my thoughts on paper."

"I'm happy to see you, Jeb."

"Now all we need is for Stone to come home."

"He may not come back, Jeb. You know Stone."

"He'll come." Jeb looked at her closely. "Tanner says he told you about Chase."

"Yes. I still have to sort out my feelings about him. I'm not sure I'll ever want to see him."

Jeb patted her shoulder. "You'll do what's right." He nodded toward the entrance. "Tanner told me you're goin' ridin', so I saddled your horse for you."

"Why don't you come with us?"

"Can't today. Got to ride to town for supplies." He steered her out of the barn and into the bright sunlight.

Lauren froze when she saw Manuelo leaning against the corral, sharpening his knife. She had a feeling he'd been there all along, eavesdropping on her conversation with Jeb.

Manuelo was thin and dark with a wiry gray mustache and thick eyebrows; his dark eyes were sharp and penetrating, and there was a sense of evil about him. He was Clare's watchdog, and everyone on the ranch knew it.

Manuelo spit on the whetstone and ground the knife against it. "Good morning, señorita," he said with a marked Spanish accent. "Welcome back to the Circle M."

Lauren looked past him to Tanner, who was helping Callie mount her horse. "Good day, Manuelo." She did not pretend to be happy to see him, because she was not.

Manuelo held his knife up as if inspecting it, and the sun glinted off the sharp blade. "Look after her, Señor Jeb. She is not accustomed to our ways. We would not want her to come to any harm."

Jeb placed his body between Clare's henchman and Lauren. "Don't you have somewhere else to be, Manuelo? Hadn't you better run see if Clare needs you to lick her boots?"

The man's eyes darkened even more. No one at the ranch ever gave him any respect, but that would soon change. When his señora had control of the Circle M, the others would be sorry for the way they had treated him. "Have a care, Señor Jeb. One day your words may dig your grave."

Jeb pushed Lauren forward, then turned to stare at Manuelo. "I'm supposed to be afraid of a gnat buzzin' around a horse's tail? Your threats don't mean much to me. But you'd better stay away from Lauren."

Manuelo shoved his knife into his pocket and moved away with jerky motions. "You do not take me serious. That will be your final mistake."

Lauren could feel the tension between the two men, so she tugged at Jeb's hand. "Did he threaten you, Jeb?"

"Yeah. It makes him feel like a big man, when in truth he's a shadow that only has presence if he's with Clare."

Lauren watched Manuelo disappear around the barn. "I never liked him. I just don't trust him."

"You're right not to trust him." Jeb gave Lauren a warning glance. "I don't ever want you to be alone with him."

Fear crept up Lauren's neck like the gathering of impending doom. "I won't. And I'm not going to let him spoil my day, either."

"Lauren," Tanner called out. "We're ready to ride—mount up."

She placed a quick kiss on Jeb's rough cheek. "I'd better go. You know how my brother hates to be kept waiting."

Jeb laughed. "Not so much since Callie came along. She's tamed him down nice and proper-like."

"You like her, don't you?"

"Yeah. I reckon I do."

"So do I."

Several days later Lauren mounted up once again, anxious to get away from Clare. She had to get out of the house or she would scream.

As she rode away from the barn, she felt the heaviness of her situation. It was becoming increasingly unsettling to live in the same house with Clare. The hardest thing to bear was coming to terms with her father's mortality. Then there was Chase McBride—what was she going to do about him?

For the first hour, Lauren rode aimlessly, not thinking about where she was going. The dappled gelding she rode had a smooth gait, and she felt as if she could breathe for the first time in days. She was startled when she realized that she had unconsciously ridden toward the old squatters' cabin where she and Garret had met just before she'd left Texas.

She dismounted, allowing her mind to go back to the past, to that day when Garret had broken her heart by telling her about the woman he was going to marry. Well, it had been her own fault. If she had not asked him to tell her about the woman, he never would have broached the subject.

If he was so much in love with the woman, why hadn't he married her?

Lauren could not imagine any woman rejecting a marriage proposal from Garret Lassiter.

She glanced at the crumbling cabin and frowned. It appeared that someone had been using the place for a campsite. She bent down to examine the remnants of charred wood and found it to be fresh. Perhaps some of the cowhands camped here, since Tanner and Callie had taken over the line cabin.

She stood up, shading her eyes and looking toward San Reanido. There was nothing but ghosts of the past here, and she did not want to revisit them—not today—not ever.

Making her way over the rocky ground, which

was littered with broken glass, she wondered what had ever possessed her to ride in this direction. She had been in such a hurry to leave the house, she had not taken the time to change her gown or put on her boots. The shoes she wore had two-inch heels and were laced ankle-high—most unsuitable for riding.

Lauren decided to leave and walked toward her horse. She stepped over a log, and her foot slipped, throwing her off balance. Thrown sideways, she managed to stay on her feet, but a sharp sliver of glass jabbed right though her shoe and buried itself deep in the tender arch of her foot.

She reached out and grasped the branch of the mesquite tree, trying to steady herself. Lauren could feel blood inside her shoe, wet and sticky. She had not known that a foot wound would bleed so much or be so painful. It was a throbbing ache that held her attention, so Lauren did not hear the rider approaching. She was startled when she saw Garret dismount.

He looked at her with a worried frown. "You've hurt yourself. Let me help you."

"I . . . yes, please." She felt foolish enough about her careless mishap without having Garret witness her misfortune. "I seem to have stepped on broken glass."

Garret took her arm and said, "Lean on me." He eased her down until she was sitting on a smooth, flat stone. Lifting her foot, he shook his head. "It

141

went in deep. I'm going to remove it now."

She nodded. "Just do it quickly, please."

He bent down beside her, quickly extracted the large shard of glass, and tossed it away. Then he began unlacing her shoe.

Garret's face was right next to Lauren's, and she was hardly able to draw air into her lungs. She breathed in his scent, the very essence of him. She was so aware of him as a man that she forgot about the pain in her foot.

He removed his hat and smoothed back his thick black hair. "Don't move. I'm going to get my canteen so I can wash the wound."

"I'm not going anywhere," she managed to say, wondering how he could appear so calm when her heart was beating so erratically.

He was beside her again, and Lauren's mouth went dry when he shoved her gown up to her knee and lifted her leg, cradling it gently.

"You're hardly dressed for riding," he said.

"I know. I just had to get away from the house."

Lauren gasped when Garret's hand went higher and he deftly unhooked her blood-soaked stocking, sliding it downward.

"I see you don't have any trouble dealing with laces and hooks. It would seem you have done this before."

Garret looked up at her, pausing in his task. "I don't suppose it would do any good to deny it."

"No."

He bent his head again and examined her wound, grinning. "Then I'll save myself the trouble." His touch was impersonal, but just the feel of his hand on her skin sent waves of heat through Lauren. As he washed away the blood, she kept her eyes focused on his jaw, not daring to go any higher or any lower.

Garret stood up, jerked his shirttail free of his trousers, and ripped a strip from the bottom. She bit her lower lip to keep from crying out when he bound her foot, pulled the wrapping tight, and tied it.

"I'm sorry. But it's necessary to bind it to stop the bleeding. I think I should take you into town so Doc can look at it. You may need stitches."

"That won't be necessary," she said, wishing anyone but Garret had come upon her. "The doctor will be looking in on Papa this afternoon. I'll have him examine my foot while he's there."

Garret pulled her gown down. "He'll probably advise you to stay off it for a few days." He took her hand. "Do you think you can stand if I help you?"

"Yes. Of course I can."

He smiled at her. "This reminds me of when you were a little girl, always getting your knees skinned."

"I'm not a little girl any longer."

His eyes flashed with a dangerous light, and his hand tightened on hers.

"No. You're no longer that adorable little girl I once knew."

She freed her hand from his and clasped it behind her back so he would not see how it was trembling. She was having a much stronger reaction to him than she had had as a young girl. The yearnings he was stirring in her body at the moment were those of a woman.

After taking several gulps of air, Lauren was able to breathe normally until she met Garret's gaze and saw the storm brewing in those dark eyes. Then her throat tightened, and she could not have uttered a word even if she had been forced to.

His gaze swept slowly upward until their eyes met. Lauren did not see it coming—she should have. Garret took her arm, pulled her to him, and gathered her close. His mouth took hers in an all-consuming kiss, and she could no longer feel the ground beneath her feet. He pressed his body against her, and she felt her world tilt and then spin out of control yet again.

Lauren's heart hammered, and her blood burned a heated path through her body. Nothing had changed in her reaction to Garret except that her feelings were now more intense. She wanted him to go on kissing her and never stop. She knew that she could find comfort in his strong arms, and much, much more.

Garret broke off the kiss and nuzzled her ear,

sending shivers of delight down her neck. "I've wanted to do that for a long time. I only had that one taste of you, and it left me craving so much more." His mouth slid across her face, and she clung to him. "I want so much more, Lauren."

This was the last thing she had expected to happen. She did not want Garret back in her heart—she did not want to see or speak to him, lest he break her heart again. She had built a safe little world where she had kept everyone from getting too close to her. Tears welled in her throat, and she choked them back as she shoved against his hard chest.

"Don't ever do that again!"

He continued to support her weight, but when she pushed against him, he released her and stepped back a pace.

"It feels right between us, Lauren—you know it does."

She could not deny it. "I'm not in the habit of allowing men to kiss me."

He glanced at the heavens as if for divine guidance. "I'm glad to hear that."

She touched her lips. "Why did you kiss me?"

He stepped away from her so quickly that it took her by surprise. "I didn't intend for this to happen—not yet."

The dark eyes that moments ago had been swirling with passion now seemed cool and detached. "Will you allow me to take you home?"

It was ironic that he had once demanded to take her home on that very spot. "No. I don't need your help."

"Very well." He scooped her up into his arms and carried her to her horse, where he deposited her on the saddle. He placed her shoe in her hand and stepped back. "If you'd been wearing proper boots, this wouldn't have happened."

She watched as he walked away, wanting to call him back. "Thank you for your help."

Garret wedged a booted foot in the stirrup and with a creak of leather, hoisted himself onto the saddle. "This isn't finished between us," he said softly. "You know it, and I know it."

Through a blur Lauren watched him ride away. He did not glance back but dug his heels into his horse's flanks and soon disappeared over the rise, leaving only a cloud of dust that soon settled to the ground.

Lauren suddenly felt the throbbing pain in her foot. She turned her mount toward home, feeling every bit as devastated as she had that tragic day so long ago when Garret had shot Raja.

Chapter Eleven

Lauren had just come downstairs when Tiny approached her and signaled that her father wanted to see her.

She caught his hand and smiled. "I have been wanting to tell you how grateful I am for the way you take care of my father. I really appreciate all you do."

Tiny watched Lauren's mouth, reading her words as they formed. He nodded his head, wishing he could tell her how much sunshine she had brought into the house since she had come home.

She released his hand but continued to smile. Every morning she would find flowers waiting for her at breakfast. Sometimes there would be a rose, or even a clump of wildflowers. It was the most

Constance O'Banyon

charming act of kindness anyone had ever shown her.

"Thank you for the flowers. I find myself looking forward to them every day."

The joy of her words spread all through Tiny. He merely nodded and turned toward the kitchen. He did not approve of what Lauren's father was about to force her to do. But Thomas McBride thought it would be right for Lauren, so that was the way it would be.

Lauren straightened her father's cover and plumped his pillow before handing him a glass of water.

"Why're you limping, gal?"

"I cut my foot on a piece of glass. It's all but healed now."

"Did you have Doc look at it?"

"Yes." She began rearranging the medicine bottles on his bedside table. "Last week. He said it was fine."

"Dammit, Lauren, will you stop fussing about my bed! I won't have you fidgeting all the time."

"Papa, you shouldn't excite yourself. You know Doc wouldn't like it."

"Lauren, just sit down and listen to me without interrupting. It takes a lot out of me to talk."

"Papa, save your strength," she told him, pity creeping into her voice. "Anything you have to say to me you can save for another time. I'll be here when you feel stronger."

He shook his head just the merest bit. "Why are you calling me Papa when you used to call me Pa?"

"I had a French teacher who would rap my knuckles with her ivory fan if I didn't speak just as she said." She smiled as she smoothed the sheet about his chest. "I was more afraid of her than I ever was of you. She was a tyrant and would have gone on whacking my knuckles if Aunt Eugenia hadn't caught her at it one morning."

"Eugenia sent her packing, did she?"

"Bag and baggage."

Tom chuckled. "I kinda like it—gives me a certain stature, don't you think? It makes me feel like one of them damned Lassiters, you saying Papa with a French accent."

She reached down and planted a kiss on his brow, bringing a startled glance from him. "I don't think you need anyone to give you stature. You were always a giant in my eyes."

"Was I?" he asked, looking pleasantly surprised. He drew his gaze away from hers as if he could no longer look into her eyes. "Now, let's talk truth here. We both know I won't get better." His hand moved across the patchwork quilt to cover hers. "But, since you came, I do feel stronger. And you were right about airing out my room. And," he admitted grudgingly, "I do feel better after a bath. Doc says it's the steam that opens my lungs up."

She laced her fingers through his. "Oh, Papa. If only—"

He cleared his throat, which brought on a hacking cough. Lauren raised him to a sitting position, aware of the frailty of his body. When the spasms ceased, she eased him back onto his pillows.

"You must rest—"

He held up his hand to silence her. "Lauren, sit down. I don't like to have you hovering over me."

First she slid her arm behind him and raised him up enough so he could take a sip of water. Then she drew the chair close to the bed, sat down, and folded her hands in her lap, knowing he was going to have his say, one way or another.

"There's no other way to tell you what's on my mind other than just to say it outright. I'm going to settle the Cedar Creek property on you. There isn't a lot of land, but the creek's never dry, even in the years of our worst droughts. That makes it some of the best land within hundreds of miles. Of course, if the Circle M ever needs water in bad years, I'll expect you to grant that right."

"I don't want—"

"Lauren!" His voice was surprisingly strong. "Just be quiet until I finish. Then you can have your say. You can't come to a dance late and expect to know the steps unless someone teaches them to you—that's what I'm trying to do now."

"Oh," she said with a teasing light in her eyes.

"Is that what this is all about? You want to teach me to dance."

He was losing patience. "Lauren."

She settled back reluctantly. "All right, Papa, I'm listening."

"I'm giving the property to you," he went on, "as a wedding present."

"Then you're wasting your time. I don't intend to get married in the near future—maybe never."

"Gal, are you going to let me talk or not?" His voice was raspy, and she wanted him to conserve his strength.

"Go ahead. But when you talk like that, it's hard for me to take you seriously."

"You *are* getting married, daughter. It's all settled."

Her eyes widened, and she surged to her feet. "I-am-not! What are you saying?"

Tom stared at the ceiling for a moment as if gathering strength. When he looked at her, moments later, his voice was strong and steady. "There are two conditions attached to your getting the property."

Lauren stared at her father with a sinking feeling in the pit of her stomach. Thomas J. McBride never did anything without a reason. He was up to something. Even on his deathbed, he wanted to control her life.

"Secondly," he continued, "if you *don't* comply

with my wishes, the Cedar Creek property goes to Clare."

"And first? You forgot first."

"I'm getting there," he told her in an irritated voice. "If you don't fulfill the terms I lay down for you, I'll cut your brothers off without a cent."

"What?"

He sank into his pillow, coughing. And in that moment, Lauren realized that he could make himself cough whenever it suited his purpose. He had always used whatever means were at hand to get what he wanted, and at the moment he was using his illness to trap her.

And her brothers.

He nodded the merest bit. "It's my wish—"

"You mean your demand," she said, her anger rising.

A rare smile curved his lips. "Damn, what a daughter I have me." There was pride in the faded blue eyes, but there was determination as well. "You're right, though, I do demand this of you."

"I'm sorry, Papa, but you can save yourself the trouble. I won't bend to your demands like I once did."

"I think you will when you realize you have no choice," he retorted, enjoying her sharp wit. She was certainly his equal, he thought with pride.

Suddenly he was overcome with another coughing spasm, and this time it was not within his control. His body shook from the violence of the attack, and sweat popped out on his forehead. Lauren wet a cloth and wiped his face, and he dropped back, exhausted.

She gave him a spoonful of the mixture she had made of honey and whiskey. It was a remedy her aunt had used, and it seemed to soothe her father's cough.

"Death stalks me, gal, and it's gaining on me every day," he said in a choked voice.

"You've talked enough for one day," she said with authority. "I want you to rest."

He gripped her arm with renewed strength. "This has to be said—today!"

"As you wish," she replied, sinking back onto the chair. "But you must listen to me first."

He nodded. "Have your say; then I'll have mine."

"First of all, there is no one I want to marry, and secondly, I don't want anything from you. Neither does Tanner, and I'm sure Stone doesn't either. I haven't met Chase yet, so I don't know what he wants."

"So you know about him."

"Did you think I wouldn't?"

"Let it be, gal. He's my son the same as Tanner and Stone."

"I choose not to comment on how I feel about that situation."

Lauren saw his eyes take on a cagey expression.

"So let's talk about your brothers and how

they'll lose everything if you don't do just like I say."

"You can't use them to bully me. It won't work."

He knew just how to get her riled. "You don't want your stepma to end up with everything, now do you?"

The thought of Clare inheriting land that should go to her brothers was infuriating, but no more so than the idea of her father trying to bend her to his will. "You married her—let her have it all. I don't care, and neither do my brothers."

His voice hardened. "You care, and don't pretend otherwise. Have you asked Tanner how he'd feel if Clare got everything?"

That thought was sobering. Although Tanner had said he did not want the ranch, he would not want Clare to have it either.

Lauren reached for a water glass and held it so he could drink. "I suppose you have a husband all picked out for me."

Although her statement had been made in jest, her father was not laughing. He took a sip of water, keeping his gaze on her all the while.

"Yeah—I do."

She smiled, unable to take him seriously. "And just who is this man I'm supposed to marry?"

"I've had a lot of time to think just lying here, and I have some regrets about the past. I'm trying to set things right for you."

"You have regrets? Papa, don't think you can hook me with that kind of stratagem. You have never regretted anything you've done in this life. If you had a second chance, you'd do it all again, and you'd do it the same way."

"Not everything. I would've appreciated your ma more." He was thoughtful for a moment. "And I would've taken better care of my children."

There was a look of sincerity in his eyes, but she was suspicious of him all the same. "So if you had another chance, you would be a better husband and father. But you don't have a second chance— none of us do."

"That's not true. I'm giving you back the chance I took from you."

She was confused. "What are you talking about?"

"Garret Lassiter."

As he spoke the name, the memory of Garret kissing her flashed through Lauren's mind. "What are you trying to say?" She jerked to her feet with the suddenness of a bullet fired from a gun. Her chin tilted stubbornly. "Don't play games with me, Papa. We both know you hate Garret."

"People change."

Her eyes iced and then filled with heat. "You don't."

"I'm serious about this, Lauren. I will see you settled in Texas near your brothers and married to Garret before I die."

"I refuse even to consider it, and you can be sure that you won't be able to maneuver Garret into marrying me. You can't bully him, Papa."

"How would you answer if Garret wanted to marry you?"

"And he leaves you to do the asking? I don't think so."

"I'm serious. What if he wants you?"

Humiliation washed over her like tidewater on a beach as she imagined her father trying to bend Garret to his will. "I thought you no longer had the ability to hurt me, but you do. I don't understand why you would do this to me. Tell me you haven't said any of this to Garret!"

There was a tone of urgency in his voice when he said, "Let me go on so you'll understand."

"No! You've said quite enough."

His color turned grayish, and he was obviously having a difficult time breathing. "You once cared about Garret Lassiter. I knew it then, and I know it now."

"A young girl's daydreams, nothing more."

"I made a mistake about Garret. He's a fine man. I'd like to think of you married to him when I'm gone. He's the kind of man who'll take care of you, Lauren. I won't have to worry about you if he's your husband."

She shook her head. "This is just too ridiculous to discuss. Garret doesn't want to marry me any more than I want to marry him." She swallowed hard. "He loves someone else."

"He wants you."

Her past experiences with her father had taught her to be wary, and a sudden light went on in her mind. "I see it all now. You offered Garret the Cedar Creek property like you'd dangle a carrot before a horse. Oh, Papa, how could you? I'll never be able to face him again!"

"There's a lot you don't know, Lauren. But that's for Garret to tell you. He's been paying me regular visits, and I've come to respect him—you know I don't respect many men."

"If you respected him, you wouldn't have involved him in such a loathsome scheme."

"Lauren, hear me out, gal. If you walk away from this, your brothers will be left with nothing, I can promise you that." His eyes became hard, and he resembled the man she remembered, the man who rode roughshod over everyone who got in his way. "The fault will rest on your shoulders if your brothers lose everything."

"I'm a different person now, Papa. Your high-handed tactics just won't work with me anymore."

"The hell they won't."

She began pacing back and forth. "Do you think Tanner or Stone would take anything from you under these circumstances? You know they wouldn't."

"They aren't going to know anything about it.

What's said here today stays in this room, because if your brothers knew, they'd do the noble thing and leave. Then Clare would get it all."

She sank down in the chair. "How could you do this to us? You know I'll never agree to it. I can't believe Garret would either."

"You just think about what I said. Talk to Garret and feel him out. You'll come around."

"No—I won't! Never!"

His eyes suddenly dimmed. "Never is not a word that means much to me. I was *never* going to die, dammit."

Chapter Twelve

Rushing down the stairs on her way out the door, Lauren brushed past a startled Clare.

"And where are you going in such a hurry? I wanted to talk to you about your pa."

"I don't have time. I'm going for a ride." Lauren had made up her mind that she would go straight to Garret that very day. He certainly deserved an apology from someone in her family. He must have felt humiliated when her father had put his absurd proposition to him.

"The way you came hurtling down the stairs, I was sure something was wrong with your pa."

Lauren turned to her stepmother. "Are you a party to this odious scheme between Papa and

Garret? It sounds like something you would suggest to get rid of me."

Clare looked puzzled and then angry there was something going on that she had no knowledge of. "What scheme?"

"Don't pretend you don't know." Lauren jerked the door open. "Well, it won't work, Clare." She stalked out the door and headed for the barn. It would be hard to face Garret, but it had to be done.

What must Garret think of her?

Clare sailed into her husband's room, her lips tight, her heart pounding. What had Tom been up to that she did not know about? "Your daughter's acting like a crazed woman. She just accused me of plotting with you to get rid of her. She mentioned Garret Lassiter. What do you suppose she meant by that?"

Tom opened his eyes and looked at his wife. "Lauren is not herself these days."

Clare drew closer to Tom's bed, her eyes sly. She saw that he was no longer so pale; he seemed to be doing better these days. "What did you and Lauren talk about?"

"Don't concern yourself about it," he said, yawning. "I'm too sleepy to go into it right now. That gal of mine just plumb wore me out."

"How dare you shut me out like this!" she cried

angrily. "You are keeping secrets from me, and I won't have it!"

"Calm yourself, Clare. If there are any secrets, you will soon know all about them."

She paced the room, ranting as she went. "You aren't going to tell me what happened between you and Lauren, are you?"

Tom closed his eyes. "No. I'm not."

She moved closer to his bed, secretly hating the sight of him. "You don't love me anymore," she cried, using a ploy that had worked many times in the past. "If you did, you wouldn't keep things from me."

He said wearily, "I need to rest, Clare."

She sat down on the edge of the bed and brought her face level with his. "You're hateful and mean."

He patted her cheek. "I'm all that and more." He was having a hard time breathing as she leaned over him, pressing down on his chest, cutting off his air. "Please move," he gasped.

She pressed down harder. "Not until you tell me what you've cooked up."

Tom's ears began ringing, and everything went black as he gasped for air. He tried to push Clare away, but he did not have the strength.

Suddenly he felt the unbearable weight lifted from him, and he took big gulps of air. When he could focus his eyes, he saw that Tiny had pulled

Clare off him and she was struggling with him and clawing at his face.

"You stupid mute! Do you think you can come between me and my husband?" she raged. "Tell him to let me go, Tom!"

Tiny kept his grip on her wrist and shoved her across the room. Then he pushed her into the hallway, closed the door behind her, and locked it.

Clare was pounding on the door and screaming loud enough for everyone to hear. "You'll be sorry! You'll be sorry!"

"She's getting more unsettled," Tom observed between coughing spasms.

Tiny nodded.

"Watch her, Tiny. I don't want her hurting Lauren."

Again Tiny nodded.

Lauren rode the dappled gray through a red dust gully higher than her head. Sliding her boots out of the stirrups, she swam the horse across Cedar Creek. Moments later, she rode up the other side, putting her heels to the horse. She did not slow the animal's pace as she rode through the gates of San Reanido.

She had never been on the ranch before, and she looked around with interest. There were spirited horses frolicking behind whitewashed fences, and several barns, a stable, and bunkhouses in the distance. The huge house loomed above all the rest—taking her by surprise. Lauren reined in her mount and stared at it in amazement.

Garret had once told her that his father had built the house in Greek Revival style to resemble their home back in Virginia, but she had not expected anything so magnificent. The white structure gleamed in the noonday sun. Ten wide columns rose above the windows of the second story. It was grander than Aunt Eugenia's home in Savannah; in fact, Lauren had never seen a house to rival it.

Her confidence waned a bit as her horse galloped forward. The horse's hooves resounded on stone as she rode to the front of the house.

A Spaniard appeared from nowhere to take the reins of her horse when she dismounted. The dark gaze the man settled on Lauren was chilling. She could not understand the uneasiness she felt about him. Sudden fear was like a living thing, hard and evil, cutting off her breathing.

The Spaniard touched his hat, and said presumptuously, "I am Estaban Velasquez. Remember that name, Señorita Lauren."

"You're unfamiliar to me."

"You will know me." Estaban's eyes shifted away from Lauren, and she felt a rush of relief. Who was he? Why had she felt such fear when he spoke to her?

"I will give your horse water and hay, señorita," he assured Lauren, leading the animal away with such ease that she thought she might have imagined the whole thing.

Lauren shook her head trying to rid her mind of the uneasy impression. She moved up the steps and was about to knock when the door opened, and a cheery-faced woman with an Irish brogue greeted her. "You'd be Miss McBride. I was told you might be expected."

Lauren was shocked. "Who is expecting me?"

"Why, Mr. Garret, miss. Come in, come in," she said, opening the door wider. "He's in the study. It's down the hall and on the right. It'll be all right if you announce yourself."

Lauren's footsteps echoed across polished wooden floors that shone so brightly she could see her own reflection. The ceiling was high in the entry, and sunlight burst through in a rainbow of light from the stained-glass window overhead.

She stopped at the wide mahogany door, almost losing her nerve. Swallowing her uncertainty, she rapped softly.

"Enter." It was Garret's voice.

She turned the brass knob and stepped inside a huge room with bookcases on three walls and floor-to-ceiling windows on the outer wall. Garret sat at a mahogany desk; he rose to his feet when he saw her.

"Lauren. You're here."

"Yes." She almost lost her nerve again as Garret stared at her. "I was told by your housekeeper that you were expecting me. How did you know I would come?"

"I didn't know when, but I knew you would be here after your father spoke to you about me. He must have told you today."

"So you know. I'm so ashamed of what my father did. I need to explain it to you, Garret."

He made a wide sweep with his hand, motioning her toward a high-back chair. "Then make yourself comfortable. Would you like something cool to drink?"

She stood in the middle of the room, her heart slamming against her chest. Garret seemed different in these surroundings—so formal. "No. Thank you. I want nothing."

What she wanted to do was leave.

"Then please be seated."

This was not the man she had always known. His hair was neatly groomed, and he wore dark trousers and a crisp white shirt, the sleeves rolled up to his elbows. She drew in a deep breath to steady herself and blurted out, "Let me apologize for my father's actions. You must have been as humiliated as I was by his odious plans."

"I was more intrigued than humiliated."

A tightness formed in Lauren's chest as she envisioned herself married to Garret. That was what she had once wanted above all else. If she was truthful with herself, it was what she still wanted. "You have to understand, my father isn't himself.

His illness has surely affected his mind."

"I found him to be perfectly lucid."

"You don't have to be a gentleman. I know how all this must have embarrassed you. You have my assurance that no one will hear of it from me."

"I understand your feelings on the matter. And you can be assured of my discretion as well."

"After today, we will never speak of this again." She circled the chair. "But before I leave, I must know how it all came about. We both know how much my father disliked you. Now I find him heaping praise on you."

"No one could have been more surprised than I was when, about six months ago, Jeb came to the house with a message that your father wanted to see me."

She sank down in the chair and folded her hands in her lap. "Extraordinary."

"Wasn't it? Considering, as you say, how emphatically your father disliked me."

"You went to see what Papa wanted. That was your mistake. You should have ignored him."

"I admit to being curious."

"I'm still trying to understand it myself. So he just threw the idea out to you?"

"Not right away. I was shocked at first, because he was so cordial toward me. I could see that he was ill and having a difficult time breathing. At the time, I imagined that he was suffering from some kind of mild chest infection." Garret lowered his head. "I know now that was not the case."

"Just how did he get around to bargaining Cedar Creek for the hand of his daughter?"

Garret watched her silently for a moment before he replied. "You know your father—he just said it right out. Asked if I would be interested in marrying you."

Lauren could not help noticing how well his tight trousers defined the shape of his magnificent body. She stood up and began to pace, trying not to think about the effect he was having on her. "I can only imagine how you must have reacted to my father's insult."

His voice was deep. "Can you?"

"Of course. Surely you realize that I had nothing to do with this." She turned to him. "Please believe me."

"I know."

She took a relieved breath. "I'll just be going, now that this is settled."

He caught her hand and turned her to face him. "What if I want the marriage, Lauren?"

She thought he might be teasing her as he used to, but he was not smiling. "Surely you jest?"

"I can assure you that you must take me at my word."

"You are a gentleman and want only to spare my feelings," she reasoned.

He bestowed an incredulous look on her. "Do

you think I would marry you just to save your feelings?"

She met his eyes as humiliation tinged her cheeks. "I just came here to apologize for my father and to tell you that this was none of my doing."

"I know it isn't your doing." Garret paused and folded his arms over his broad chest. "It's my doing."

She did not know if she should laugh or be angry. "You want to marry me?" She thought of the woman he loved. "I know that . . ."

Garret waited for her to continue, but she had fallen silent as if she did not know what to say. "Would marrying me be such a hardship for you?" He watched her closely as he asked the next question, "Are you interested in someone else?"

Through the years, she had dreamed of what it would be like to be Garret's wife, of lying beside him, of having those strong arms around her. She could still feel the way his demanding mouth had taken possession of hers just a few days ago. Her voice was no more than a whisper when she said, "I don't understand."

"You're a very desirable woman, Lauren, and just the kind of lady I want for my wife."

Her eyes rounded, and she stared at him for a long moment, trying to decide if she had heard him correctly. Understanding seeped through her mind, slowly at first like dripping water, then swiftly like a flooding river. "You want Cedar Creek."

Lauren felt as if all the air had been sucked from her body when she saw the truth in his eyes. Her father had bought her a husband. At that moment, she felt sick inside and feared that she might lose her breakfast right in front of Garret.

"The creek is part of my reasoning, but I can assure you, not the most important part."

"Just how badly do you want that property?"

"San Reanido uses a lot of water. We have been hauling water from Panther Creek, but we can't haul it fast enough to meet our needs."

She doubled her fists, wishing she could pound his chest. She turned her back to him so he would not see her distress. "I beg you to reject me to my father's face, Garret. That's the only way he can be stopped. I promise you he can rule all our lives from his sickbed. You don't know what he's capable of."

"I'll never reject you, Lauren." He turned her to face him. "Why would I want to do that?"

She shook her head, and red-gold hair swung about her face. "Then you are as mad as my father is."

"Perhaps. But have you considered that I might want you for more than just the land?"

"No. Not for one moment."

He hardly spoke above a whisper, but his words

wounded her just the same. "I need a wife, Lauren. And you will do very nicely."

"I hold a higher regard for myself than to be traded in marriage for water rights." She stepped away from him. "I have nothing further to say to you. Good day, Garret."

He took a step that brought him almost against her, so near that she could see her own reflection in the brown irises of his eyes.

"Consider very carefully before you reject me, Lauren."

"How can you do this to me?" She felt crushed. "I thought we were friends. You used to like me."

"I still do."

"If you only knew what my father is using to force this marriage, you wouldn't be a party to it."

"I do know. He's making you responsible for your brothers' inheritance, isn't he?"

"And he has made you a party to this . . . this treachery." She felt as if her mind were splintering. "Do you understand that if I refuse to go along with this, Clare will get everything and my brothers will get nothing?"

"I do."

"And you don't care?"

"I do care, Lauren. I would like to throw your father's offer back in his face. I know I am being used the same as you. But I am willing to be used if it will get me what I want."

"Cedar Creek," she said with disgust. She

moved across the room and grasped the door handle. "You will never see the day that I'll agree to marry you, Garret. Never!"

He just stood there looking at her as if expecting something more of her. "I'll be waiting for you, Lauren."

She rushed out of the house and across the yard toward the barn. Had the whole world gone mad?

She did not spare her horse as she rode back to the Circle M. Her heart felt trampled and bruised. She had always thought she would be worth something to the man she married, not just a pawn in a game her father was playing.

It was early morning when Lauren approached the hill where her mother was buried. She saw a familiar figure standing there, his hat in hand, his head bowed.

"Tanner."

Tanner did not look up as Lauren approached but took her hand in his. Silently, brother and sister stood there. There was no need for words. They had somehow always sensed what the other was thinking.

At last Lauren spoke. "Do you ever wish you could talk to Mama and tell her about your life and ask her advice?"

"Not in a long time. But I once did." His gaze clouded. "I didn't come home so I could inherit any part of this land, but this morning everything seems so clear to me. This is where our ma worked, lived, gave birth to us, and died. I don't want Clare to have any part of it."

At that moment there was a stirring among the high branches of the cottonwood tree that shaded their mother's grave. Lauren blinked her eyes in disbelief and held her breath as a mockingbird gracefully perched on her mother's gravestone and broke into song.

Lauren pressed her hand over her mouth to hold back the dry sobs that were rising up inside her.

Lauren knew what she must do. "Clare won't get her hands on the Circle M if I can stop her."

Tanner only half heard what Lauren had said. He was staring at the bird that boldly serenaded them. "Do you remember that Ma liked mocking-birds? This one isn't even afraid of us," he said in astonishment. "I know Ma isn't really there, but I hope she still hears that song."

"She hears," Lauren said softly.

Tanner watched the bird take flight. "I never knew until now how I felt about this land. I guess it doesn't matter, because Clare will probably get it all."

"No, she won't." Lauren knew that she had it within her power to protect Tanner's inheritance.

She would agree to marry Garret if he still wanted her.

Chapter Thirteen

When Lauren rode up to San Reanido, she saw that several cowhands had gathered around the corral. "Where is Mr. Lassiter?" she asked the older man who came forward to take her horse. She was glad it was not the Spaniard who had taken her horse before.

"I'm Charley, Miss McBride. The boss is down at the corral. He's breaking a two-year-old."

Lauren thanked the man and walked toward the barn, her footsteps unhesitating. When she reached the fence, a cowboy tipped his hat and moved aside to give her room.

Garret had not seen Lauren yet, so she watched him pull on his leather gloves, climb over the fence, and drop to the other side. The chestnut quarter horse whinnied, lowered its ears, and pulled back as he approached.

Lauren was reminded of how handsome Garret was. He wore rough-out chaps that emphasized his tall, lean body. The sleeves of his blue shirt were rolled up to his elbows, and she could see the black hair on his arms. Lauren's stomach tightened as Garret spoke softly to the animal. She could imagine him using that same tone with a woman he wanted to make love to.

"Easy, girl." He stepped closer, keeping his tone even. "Gentle down, because I am going to ride you."

With one quick motion, Garret jammed his boot into the stirrup and swung his long leg across the saddle. Before he was seated, the animal was airborne. His muscled legs clung to the quivering sides of the animal as it bucked and twisted. It soon became apparent to everyone watching that the man would master the horse.

The spirited chestnut was no match for Garret. Not once did she unseat him, and at last, with her sides quivering and lathered, she gave one final defiant toss of her head and trotted around the corral as docile as a newborn colt.

Garret saw Lauren and dismounted, tossing the reins to Charley. Removing his gloves, he strode toward her, his expression unreadable. He dabbed sweat on his shirtsleeve. "Hello, Lauren."

Her pulse throbbed in her throat. "I need to talk to you."

He swung over the fence and dropped to the other side. His eyes searched her face. "Are you all right?"

"How can you ask?"

Will poked Charley in the ribs and whispered, "The boss has always wanted that little filly. Do you reckon he'll get her?"

Charley gave the cowhand a sharp look. "Don't ever let me hear you call Miss McBride a filly again. And as for what the boss'll get or not get, it's not our business."

Will shuffled his feet. "I was just wonderin'."

Garret unbuckled his chaps and slung them over the fence, then glanced down at his dusty pants and shirt. "Excuse my appearance. I'm hardly fit to receive a lady."

Lauren noticed the cowhands were watching them. "Where can we talk?"

"Come with me." Silently he led her into the house and to his study. If she had not known better, she would have thought he was nervous.

He touched her arm. "Will you be seated?"

She shrugged his hand away. "I won't be staying that long."

His dark gaze settled on her. "You have changed your mind."

Lauren wrestled with her dilemma even now, trying to think of a solution, but there was none.

Her father had planned everything so well, leaving her no way out.

Her shoulders slumped, and she said in a whisper, "I will want my own bedroom."

Garret let out his breath and closed his eyes for the merest moment. "That," he said, finding his voice, "is no way to begin a marriage, Lauren. You will share mine."

He was going to leave her no pride—nothing. There was a burning sensation behind her eyelids, but she would not give in to tears. "Will you insist on that?"

He stepped away from her. "Yes, but I want you to be happy."

"Happy," she said heatedly. "Is that another requirement you expect in a wife?"

"It isn't a requirement, it's something I want to give you."

She met his gaze and thought she saw uncertainty in the dark depths—but there could be no weakness in a man with Garret's strength. "One of the things my father taught me was to know when to walk away from a fight." She lowered her gaze. "But we McBrides have a way of winning in the end."

"If it's within my power, I'll help you win."

"I have some conditions that I would like you to agree to."

His tone was even as he asked, "And they would be?"

176

"I will expect you to honor our marriage vows, and never to shame me. That's the most important part to me."

He frowned. "In what way, Lauren?"

"I will not have a husband who seeks out other women. I have seen what my father's faithlessness did to my mother, and I will never live like that. If you are like that, then tell me now."

"I am not like your father. You'll be the only woman I'll ever want."

Garret appeared restrained, as if he wanted to say something more, but she held up her hand.

"When will the marriage take place?" The situation was so unreal that Lauren felt like an actress in a play, saying words that were not her own. "I suppose you and my father have already decided on a date."

"No. I was not so confident that you'd have me."

"You decided everything else."

"Lauren, this is not the way I wanted it to be between us."

She was ready to do battle, but she had no weapons. "You have won," she shot back. "Enjoy your victory."

"I'm not enjoying myself much at the moment, Lauren." His gaze moved slowly down her body, and he made no secret that he liked what he saw. "Are you ready to listen to me? I want to explain about us."

177

She swallowed twice before she could answer. "There is no us."

"The hell there isn't." He reached for her and brought her against him. "There has always been us."

She shook her head, feeling the pull of his sensuality and the power of his passion. Even now, as angry as she was, she wanted to lay her head on his shoulder and let him hold her. "Why did you so willingly fall in with my father's plans?"

Garret could have told her that there had never been anyone else in his heart but her. He could have told her that if she had not come home he would probably have waited for her until he was an old man. His lips were close to her ear, and when he spoke, his breath stirred her hair and touched her cheek. "Because I wanted you at any price."

She backed away from him, already falling back into the world she had left behind when she had fled Texas four years ago—falling back into loving Garret. He was the sun, and she was the moon that worshiped his brightness. All those years away, all the polish and manners she had been taught in Savannah, had not changed her inside. She still loved him desperately.

"Will you come with me to tell my father the news?" he asked. "He always liked you and will be happy about our marriage."

"What about your mother?"

Garret lowered his eyes. "She's dead, Lauren. I thought you knew. She died not a week after you left for Savannah."

"I'm so sorry. I didn't know." She saw the pain in his eyes and felt an overwhelming need to comfort him, but she stood stiffly as she asked, "How did it happen?"

"A senseless accident. She had gone into town with one of the hands." He paused. "She was crossing the street and a runaway buggy ran her down."

"How could such a thing happen?"

"I don't know. It was Doc Pierce's buggy, and he swears he tied it securely to the hitching post."

She placed her hand on his. "I am so sorry. I know what it feels like to lose a mother. My mother died in the same kind of accident."

He walked with her to the door of his study as if he wanted to dismiss the subject. "Shall we find my father and tell him about the marriage?"

"Please excuse me, but not now. I have to tell Tanner, and I don't know how he'll take the news."

"Would you like me to ride over to the Circle M tomorrow so we can tell him together?"

Lauren turned the handle and paused in the doorway. "Not tomorrow. Give me until the end of the week before you tell anyone. As for Tanner, I'll tell him myself." Without looking back, she left the house, mounted her horse, and rode home.

If someone had told Lauren four years ago that she would be Garret's wife, she would have thought her fondest dream had come true. But to marry him under these circumstances was more painful than living without him.

Garret found his father in the stable, hand-feeding a mare that had colic. Barnard Lassiter was tall like his son and had the same dark eyes. His hair had once been dark, but was now mostly gray.

"I saw Lauren ride up."

Garret opened the half-door and stepped into the stall with the mare. He removed the blanket from her back and began sponging her with cool water. "Yes. She left a few moments ago."

"And?"

"She agreed to marry me."

"Did you take my advice and tell her you loved her?"

"Lauren is different from other women—she would not have believed me. Too much is wrong between the two of us at the moment. I will have to win her love and confidence slowly."

"You're making this more difficult than it has to be, son. I never left your mother in doubt of my feelings for her."

"My relationship with Lauren is difficult right now. At first, I had to wait for her to grow up; now I have to wait for her to accept my love when she thinks I have betrayed her. I wouldn't blame her if she detested the sight of me."

"You could have thrown Tom's offer back in his face."

"I can't begin to understand why Tom McBride made such an offer to me. But I had to take him up on it because I was afraid that if I didn't, he'd only bargain her off to someone else. I could never have allowed that to happen, the bastard."

"You could explain it to her like you just did to me."

Garret dipped the sponge into the bucket of water and continued to sponge the mare. "She's not ready to hear the truth from me. And how can I tell her what a bastard her father is when he's dying?" He drew in a deep breath. "I have been patient for a long time. . . . I can wait a while longer."

Lauren dismounted in front of the sheriff's office. Tying her horse to the hitching rail, she lingered for as long as she could. She was not going to lose her nerve now that she had ridden all this way. She had come to meet her half-brother, and she would not leave town until she had done just that.

Climbing three steps, she opened the door and entered. The room was larger than it looked from the outside. There were the usual wanted posters on the wall, a chipped desk and three chairs. The papers on the desk were neat and tidy, but the older man behind the desk was not Chase McBride.

"I would like to see the sheriff," she said. "I'm Lauren McBride."

She noticed that the hefty man with a shock of white hair was wearing a deputy badge. He rose to his feet. "I know who you are, Miss McBride. But it's been a long time since I've seen you."

The man looked familiar, but she could not put a name to the face. "Do I know you?"

"Sure you do. I'm Bud Sanders, Miss McBride."

She was taken by surprise. Bud Sanders had been the butt of many jokes in Sidewinder. He had been the town drunk.

He stood, hiking his gun belt over his ample waist. "I know what you're thinking, but I don't drink no more. Chase . . . er, Sheriff McBride, he gave me a chance to better myself. I haven't had me a drink in over a month. Haven't even wanted one."

Lauren did not know what to say to the man. "I'm glad, Bud. Where can I find the sheriff?"

"He'd be over at the Roundup Saloon. They had a little ruckus there, but nothing he can't handle. I 'spect before too many days pass, he'll clean the place up so decent folk can feel safe when they come to town."

It was hot, and Lauren was weary and disheartened. She wished she could get on the first stage heading for Savannah. Barbara must have had her baby by now, and Lauren did not even know if it was a boy or a girl.

"Do you know how long he'll be?"

"Could be quite a spell." He looked into her McBride blue eyes, recalling the secret of the sheriff's parentage. "The sheriff's a good man, Miss McBride." The look in the old man's eyes dared her to deny it.

"I'm sure he is, Bud." She walked to the door. "Tell him I was here."

"You oughta wait for him. I'm sure he'd like to see you."

"Some other time."

Lauren rode down the street and dismounted in front of Annabelle Chapin's boardinghouse. There was a Mexican woman washing the windows, and Lauren nodded to her. "Good day," Lauren said, removing her gloves and tucking them into the waist of her skirt.

The short, dark-haired woman dropped her scrub brush in a bucket and wiped her hands on her apron. "Good day to you, señorita."

Lauren moved to the door of the boardinghouse. "Is Annabelle here?"

"Sí. She was just a moment ago. Try the parlor."

The inside of the boardinghouse smelled of good cooking and lemon wax. Annabelle Chapin was busily polishing a massive breakfront; she paused and turned to stare at Lauren.

"How are you, Lauren?"

Annabelle was tall and slender with wheat-colored hair and wide-set eyes. Although Lauren had known her all her life, she had not known her very well. Annabelle had always taken care of her elderly mother and had rarely socialized.

"I'm fine, Annabelle. How is your mother?"

Annabelle went back to her polishing. "My mother has passed on."

Lauren felt a blush stain her face. "I'm sorry, Annabelle. I didn't know . . . no one told me." She had been away too long. She had not known about Garret's mother, either.

Annabelle shrugged. "Death comes to us all." She laid her polishing cloth aside. "What brings you to town?"

"Personal business. But I wanted to ask you about Molly and Albert. Did they get on their stage without any trouble?"

"Of course. They only stayed two nights with me."

"I would have come to see them off, but everything . . ." Lauren shrugged. "I just wanted to make sure they caught the stage."

Annabelle could see sadness in Lauren's eyes; the girl was carrying a heavy load. Annabelle knew what it felt like to take care of an ailing parent, so her voice was softer when she asked, "How are you managing out at the ranch?"

"I . . . it's very difficult at the moment."

"I know—I know it is."

"Tanner has settled into a happy life," Lauren said, trying to think of something to talk about. "But I still haven't heard from Stone."

Lauren did not see Annabelle stiffen when she spoke of her older brother. "I wish Stone would come home. We need him—I need him."

Annabelle picked up her polishing cloth and began shining the wood with hard round strokes. "I doubt you'll see him," she murmured.

"You're probably right." Lauren smiled, feeling the awkward silence. "I must be going."

Annabelle watched Lauren leave, not wanting to think about Stone. She walked to the window and tapped on the glass, motioning for the Mexican woman to come in. It was time to set lunch on the table for the guests.

Lauren had already ridden to the edge of town when she thought better of her decision to leave. She must see Chase. If she did not meet him today, she might lose her nerve. She turned her horse around, rode up to the Roundup Saloon, and dismounted. Stepping inside, Lauren was surprised at how brightly lit it was. She had never been in a saloon before and almost backed out the door when she realized that everyone was staring at her. Even the piano player had stopped playing and turned his attention to her. Her gaze moved over the room and momentarily settled on the woman at the bar, who stared at her with insolent eyes.

The woman's face looked as if it had been painted on, and the gown she wore did little to cover her.

No one moved until a man sitting at one of the tables scooted his chair back and walked in her direction.

Ace Bellamy, the owner of the Roundup, smiled at the beautiful redhead. "I don't think you want to be in here, ma'am."

She clutched her hat between her fingers. "I'm looking for someone."

"Why don't you just tell me who you want and go outside. If he's here, I'll send him out to you."

"The lady was just leaving," a deep voice said just behind Ace.

Lauren's eyes collided with Chase McBride's cold gaze. He gripped her arm and steered her toward the door. When they were standing outside in the sunshine, he released her arm and continued to stare at her.

"What were you doing in the Roundup? It's no place for you."

Lauren blinked her eyes. That was exactly what Tanner or Stone would have said if they had caught her in such a place. She glanced about, noticing that they were quickly becoming the objects of curious stares. "I went there to find you. I wanted to talk to you."

Onlookers stared at them, and several people from the saloon were gazing out the window at them. "Could we go somewhere so we can talk privately?"

Chase had been expecting Lauren, and he knew why she had come. It certainly was not to welcome him to the family. She was a beautiful woman—stunning, in fact. He had met her kind before. A half-breed such as himself would be beneath her contempt. He would hear what she had to say and send her on her way.

"We can talk in my office." He nodded at the hitching post, where he noticed a horse with the Circle M brand on its rump. "Is that your mount?"

She nodded.

He gathered the reins of her horse and led him toward his office. Lauren walked beside Chase, wondering if she had done the right thing in coming. He was cold and unapproachable. What would she say to him?

Chase tied Lauren's horse to the hitching rail and ushered her into his office. Bud stood when they entered.

"I don't think there'll be any more trouble, but go on over to the saloon and make sure everything stays friendly," Chase told his deputy.

Bud nodded, grabbed up his battered hat, and edged his way to the door. "I'll just do that very thing."

Chase's voice was without warmth when he

turned his attention to Lauren. "Why are you here?"

"You know who I am?"

"Of course I do."

She sat down in a hard-back chair and leaned forward, gazing up at him. Not only did he have the McBride eyes, he also had many of her brothers' features. His hair and skin were darker than theirs, but that was because his mother was an Indian. There was an air of suspicion about him, as if he did not trust her. And something else, too—he expected her to reject him.

Lauren made a small gesture with her hands. "I tried to think what I'd say to you when we met, but it's very difficult for me. I hope you can understand that."

"Yes. It can't be easy with a bastard brother turning up to shame you before all your friends."

"I don't mean that at all. I mean . . . my father . . . our father—"

"Your father. I want no part of Tom McBride."

She wished he would sit down, so she did not have to look up at him. "I can understand your feeling that way. I feel that way about him most of the time myself."

Chase saw the hint of tears in Lauren's eyes. He had expected anything but that. His voice was kinder as he asked, "What do you want to say to me?"

"You can deny our father, but I would like for

you to consider me your . . . sister. I want to make up to you for some of the hurt our father caused you. I hope you'll let me."

Chase felt a tightening in his throat. He had not expected Lauren to accept him, and he certainly did not expect her to reach out to him in this way. "It's not for you to make anything up to me."

"I understand that you have a wife. I would like very much to meet her."

He was still suspicious of Lauren's overtures. She could be up to something. He certainly was not going to have Faith meet Lauren until he understood her real reason for approaching him—Faith had been hurt enough. "I'll tell her you said so."

"I'm getting married," Lauren blurted out. "I would be happy if you and your wife would attend the wedding."

Chase watched Lauren rise to her feet, and he stepped back a pace when she moved closer to him.

"I want all my brothers to be at my wedding. I wish Stone would come home so he could be there, too. I don't know the exact date, but I'll send you word later. I suppose it'll be held at the house so Papa can be there."

Lauren had taken him completely by surprise. Chase prided himself on being able to read people, but he certainly had misread her. There was no trickery in her . . . She had meant every word she'd said. It could not have been easy for her to seek him out in a saloon.

"Do you know what you're doing by coming here today, by inviting me to your wedding? The whole county will gossip if you acknowledge me as your brother. There's already talk, of course, but now you'll be at the center of it."

Lauren reached out and touched his hand, feeling affection for the man she had not even known existed three months ago. "Let them talk. We're family. The sooner everyone realizes that, the better it will be for all of us."

Chase felt a catch in his throat. "I'll be at your wedding, and so will Faith. But who is the bridegroom?"

"Garret Lassiter. Do you know him?"

He remembered seeing Garret and Lauren the day she arrived in town. She had not seemed too glad to see Lassiter that day. "I'm not acquainted with him, but he's well respected hereabouts. Does he know about me?"

"I don't know. But he will. I want everyone to know that I have three fine brothers."

Lauren took Chase by surprise when she stood on tiptoe and kissed his cheek, sliding her arms around his shoulders. He stiffened at first, and then his arms went around her. For a long moment, neither of them spoke.

At last he said, "Do you really want me to treat you like my sister?"

She moved back and saw that he was smiling, and it made him even more handsome than he already was. "Of course I do."

"Well, then, as your brother, I'm going to demand that you never set foot in a place like the Roundup Saloon again."

She returned his smile. "Did that woman really have paint on her face?"

"Paint, and very little else. It's not the sort of place for you."

"I'll remember that." She touched his dark cheek. "I'm glad you are my brother, Chase McBride. Tanner and Bud were right: You are a good man."

Chase watched Lauren leave, amazed by what had just happened. Tanner and Lauren had reached out to him, and he was beginning to know what it felt like to have a family. It was a good feeling, a steadying feeling—something he had never had.

Chapter Fourteen

During the night, Tom McBride had taken a turn for the worse. Lauren had sent Jeb after Doc Pierce and to let Tanner know. Doc was in Tom's room now, and she was afraid her father might be dying. She sat in a chair outside his door, afraid to leave because he might ask to see her.

Just as the sun lit the darkened hallway, she heard footsteps on the stairs. She was relieved to see Tanner and Callie.

Tanner caught Lauren's hand. "Jeb told us Pa's bad off. How's he doing?"

"I don't know. Doc's been with him for over an hour. I've been waiting for him to come out and tell me something."

"Have you been sitting here all night?"

"Just since midnight when Tiny woke me." Lauren stood and stretched her aching muscles. "I'm going to help Tiny get breakfast for the men. Let me know if there's any change in Papa's condition."

Tanner watched the door where his pa struggled for life. "This could be it, Callie."

Callie slid her arms around him. "I know."

When Clare heard Tanner's voice, she opened her bedroom door and walked toward him. Positioning herself beside him, with her back to Callie, Clare placed her hand on Tanner's arm.

"Your pa's probably not going to recover from this attack."

Tanner shrugged Clare's hand off his arm and pulled Callie beside him. Clare's touch left him feeling as if a spider had been crawling on him. His gaze was cold as he looked at Clare. "Why aren't you at your husband's side if you think he's dying?"

"Sick people depress me," she answered. "Tanner," she said, changing the subject, "do you know of anything going on between Lauren and Garret Lassiter?"

"No, I don't," he said in a tone that implied he would not tell Clare even if he did know something.

Clare's lids swept across her eyes, and she took on a helpless expression. "Actually, I'm glad you're here. I have a drawer that's stuck, and it won't budge no matter how I tug and pull. Will you see if you can open it for me, Tanner?"

He was about to refuse when Callie spoke up. "Go ahead. I'll wait here in case there's any change in your pa's condition."

Clare could not believe her good luck, the simpering wife giving permission for her to be alone with Tanner. She moved sensuously at Tanner's side and, once inside her bedroom, she turned into his arms.

Before Tanner could untangle himself, her hot lips were on his, and he felt suffocated from the smell of her heavy perfume. He closed his mouth when she tried to wriggle her tongue inside. Feeling revulsion, he gripped her arm, his fingers digging into her flesh as he flung her away from him.

"Your drawer isn't stuck, is it?"

"No. That was the only excuse I could think of to get you alone. I never see you anymore. You're always with that milk-faced woman you married. How can you stand her?"

"You just don't get it, do you, Clare?" His hard mouth curved in disgust. "You're the one I can't stand."

She reached out to him in desperation. "That's not true. You've never given us a chance." She advanced toward him, her hand sliding up his arm. "If you'd let me, it would be so good between us."

"Go to your husband," he said angrily. "Sit by

his side and tell him how much you love him. Maybe you can make him believe you, but no one else does."

She seemed to slither up his body, touching him as she went. "You're the only one I care about. I'll give you something to remember me by." She moved toward his lips, her sharp teeth biting into tender skin.

Pain shot through Tanner, and he flung her away so forcefully that she landed on the floor. Touching his lip, he found it was bleeding. "Bitch."

Clair stared back at him, her poisonous smile in place. "Go and explain that to your wife, if you can."

Tanner walked toward Callie with anger in his stride, and Clare stalked right behind him. Callie detested the way that woman always hung on to her husband. But she had learned early on that the best way to defeat Clare was not to take her seriously—Clare could not stand that.

Callie swallowed her anger and managed to smile, even when she saw his cut lip. Taking a handkerchief from her pocket, she dabbed at the blood. "Has Clare been up to her usual tricks?" she asked, when what she would really like to do was drive her fist into Clare's face. Probably some day she would do just that.

Callie glanced at Clare and forced a laugh. "You

need to understand that Tanner loves me. He doesn't even like you."

Clare glared at Callie, fury churning inside her. "Are you laughing at me?"

"You make it so easy, Clare. You're just so predictable. My poor husband is forever dodging your advances."

"Are you sure he doesn't lie to you about us?" Clare asked in a silken voice that hinted Tanner might be deceiving Callie.

Callie looked at the door to Tom's room. "This is not the time or place to be having this conversation. But since you asked, I *know* how my husband feels about you."

Clare's eyes were cold and filled with hatred. She turned away and practically ran to her room, slamming the door behind her.

Callie now turned her anger on her husband, shoving her handkerchief at him. "You can just clean up your own blood."

Lauren removed a pan of biscuits from the oven and turned them out into a bright blue bowl, covering them with a towel to hold the heat in. She worked companionably beside Tiny as he served the ranch hands their breakfast.

An hour later, when the cowhands ambled out to do their morning chores, Lauren was up to her elbows in dishwater. She handed Tiny a coffee cup to dry.

"Are you aware that Papa planned my marriage to Garret Lassiter?" She was sure he was—Tiny seemed to be aware of most things that went on at the ranch.

Tiny nodded as he concentrated on drying the cup.

"I have accepted Garret." She sighed. "I had to. There was no way out of it."

Tiny set his dishcloth aside and reached for paper he kept tucked beside the sugar jar. He quickly scribbled something on it and handed it to Lauren.

She read the note. "How am I holding up?"

Tiny nodded.

Her voice trembled when she answered. "About how you'd expect under the circumstances. My father is dying, I found out about a brother I never knew existed, and my father has hatched this crazy scheme that forces me to marry Garret."

Tiny wrote something else and handed it to Lauren.

"Do I love him?" She was quiet for a long moment while she considered her feelings for Garret. She had admitted to herself that she loved him, but not to anyone else. She looked into Tiny's inquiring eyes and nodded, deciding to tell him the truth. "I have never loved anyone but Garret. But he does not feel the same way about me."

He smiled sadly.

"Thank you," Lauren told him. "It helps to tell someone how I feel. I told my brother Chase about

197

the wedding, but you are the only other person who knows."

His face was bright with silent laughter as he scribbled again.

Her laughter bubbled out when she read what he had written. "Yes. It is wise of me to tell someone who can't repeat what I say."

Tiny reached up his sleeve and, as if by magic, produced a slightly crushed red rosebud. He held it out to her.

Lauren took the flower and smiled. "I seem to always be thanking you, Tiny. Although we haven't known each other very long, I believe we are friends."

Tiny placed his hand over his heart and nodded his head.

Doc Pierce's bushy eyebrows became a straight line across his nose as he advanced into the hallway. To Lauren, he looked tired and worried. She was afraid to hear what he had to say about her father.

"Your pa's gonna be all right. He's weak and needs peace and quiet. I'm insisting that he have no visitors, and that includes family, for at least two days."

"I need to see him for just a moment," Lauren said. "I promise you, I won't upset him. In fact, what I have to tell him will probably make him feel more at peace."

The doctor nodded. "All right, Lauren. But just for five minutes and no longer."

"I want Tanner to come with me."

"Go with your sister, Tanner. But you both stay calm and don't tell him anything upsetting."

Tanner cast a quizzical glance at his sister as he opened the door and followed her into their father's room. Tom's eyes were closed, and his chest rose and fell in a jerky motion.

With Tanner at her side, Lauren approached the bed and went down on her knees, taking her father's hand in hers.

"Papa, can you hear me?"

His eyes fluttered open, and he stared at her blankly.

"I just wanted you to know that I'm going to marry Garret."

His lips curved the merest bit, and he sighed, closing his eyes. "Make it soon," he said in a weak voice.

It seemed to Lauren that his breathing was easier.

Tanner drew Lauren up beside him and then accompanied her out of the room. He had no sooner closed the door than he gripped her shoulders and turned her to face him. "What was that all about?"

"Let's step away from the door," Lauren cautioned. She went down the stairs, with Tanner dogging her steps.

"Now," he said, planting his feet wide apart and placing his hands on his hips the way their father had once done. "What's this business about you marrying Garret Lassiter?"

"I meant to tell you—I would have if Papa hadn't gotten worse." She wanted so badly to confide in Tanner, but he must never know the circumstances that were driving her to marry Garret. So Lauren told a half-truth. "I love Garret. You know that."

"I understand that you fancied yourself in love with him when you were young. What I *don't* understand is why you thought it was so important to tell Pa at this time. You said it would calm him, and we both know he hates the Lassiters."

"Papa approves of Garret now. I don't know why he'd changed his mind, but he has."

Tanner looked confused. "There's something going on here you're not telling me."

She moved to the door, needing to get out of the house and go for a ride. "I love Garret, and I'm going to marry him."

Lauren felt hollow inside. She needed to be alone so she could gather her thoughts and call on her reserved strength. As she rode along the banks of Cedar Creek, she felt resentment toward the mud-colored water that had bought her a husband. When she reached a grove of pecan trees, she dismounted and sat on the bank beneath their wide shade.

"I've seen an ocean," she mused aloud, "and I've seen rivers big enough to swallow you in." She tossed a pecan hull into the water and watched a small ring grow larger. "What's so special about you? You're nothing but a muddy little creek."

She heard a rider approaching, and it was too late to leave when she saw that it was Garret. She watched him dismount and stride toward her.

"Come to inspect your creek?" she asked guilelessly. "Or perhaps you'd like to inspect me." She opened her mouth. "Do you want to check my teeth? I have all of them."

He grinned. "Jeb told me I'd probably find you here, and I've seen your teeth—they're perfect."

She turned her back to him. "I'm glad they meet with your approval."

"Want to talk about what's bothering you?"

She glanced at him over her shoulder. "You're what's bothering me."

"Lauren, I need to explain some things to you, and I want you to listen to me without judging me just yet."

She leaned her back against the tree trunk and folded her arms across her chest. "I'm listening."

"I told you the day you arrived that it was no coincidence that I was in Sidewinder."

"I remember. Thinking back on it, I assume you

wanted to see what you had bargained for in a wife."

"No, that's not it. I came to town because I had to see you." He paused a moment, allowing his words to penetrate her mind. "I could hardly breathe when you stepped to the ground. I hadn't thought that the years would change you so much. In my mind, I still expected a cute, freckled-face imp to get off that stage. But instead, a beautiful young woman came home. I looked for that young girl who loved life and reached out for it. But there was only sadness in your eyes that day. I want to make you carefree and happy again."

"We all change. You have. How quickly you turned away from the woman you loved—to replace her with me."

"What are you talking about? What woman?"

"The one you told me you loved, the one who was perfect for you in every way." She let out her breath. "You don't hold on to love for very long, do you, Garret?"

Garret glanced up at the branches. His own words had now come back to haunt him. How could he convince her that she had been the one he had spoken of that day? If he told her now, she certainly would not believe him.

"I've waited a long time for you, Lauren. I was so damned afraid that you were going to marry some man you met in Savannah and not come home at all." He searched her face. "Is there some man I should be worried about?"

"I knew many gentlemen in Savannah."

"Was there one man who stood above all the others?"

She looked at him—he stood above all the others in her heart. "What does it matter?"

He looked into her sultry blue eyes, and it was as if he'd been yanked back to the past. He could not remember when he had first begun to love Lauren. It just seemed as if the love had always been there. He had not felt alive the whole time she was away, but she would not believe that—not yet. He had lost her respect, but he was damned sure going to get it back. Then he would win her slowly.

She reached up with both hands, grasping an overhanging branch, not realizing that the gesture made her breasts push enticingly against her blouse.

But Garret noticed. His body felt as if it were on fire.

"Papa had a bad spell last night."

"I'm sorry," he said, trying not to look at the lips that begged for a man's kiss. "I hope he's better now."

"Doc says he is." She snapped off a narrow twig and shredded the leaves, allowing them to sift between her fingers. "I would like to wait to be married until my aunt and her family can come from

Savannah. But Papa wants us to marry right away."

"How soon?"

"I don't know. I wish Stone could be here, but he probably won't come home at all." She looked into Garret's eyes. "It will have to be real soon, for Papa's sake."

"How about next Wednesday?"

"No, not that soon."

"Friday, then?"

"No, not Friday. Perhaps two weeks from this Saturday."

Hell, he wished she were already his wife so he could hold her against his body. He wanted to kiss her breasts, to touch her naked. His voice came out in a deep whisper. "Should we wait that long?" He did not want to wait another day.

She relented, but just a bit. "Next Saturday, I think. Yes, Saturday will be fine."

The irony of it hit Lauren. She was discussing her wedding as if it were an everyday happening in her life.

"Will you come over and see my father, Lauren? He wants to talk to you."

"I can't say for sure. I don't want to be too far away from Papa until he's stronger."

Garret took her arm and pulled her resisting body toward his. "Lauren, Lauren, there is so much unsaid between us. Will you ever again look at me with the trust you had when you were fifteen?"

"I'm not fifteen." She felt his hand move slowly up her arm to rest against her shoulder. "I don't ever want to be that young again."

He lifted her chin and looked deep into her eyes, his thoughts in a turmoil. "Just touching you makes me tremble inside. I can't imagine what I will feel when I actually make love to you."

Lauren closed her eyes as Garret pressed her closer to him. "I don't know how it will feel, Garret. I have never been with a man."

His lips touched her eyelid and remained there. He would be the first to take her. She would respond to him—of that he had no doubt. Even now, he could feel her reaction to him, as her breathing came out in a sigh.

"I look forward to the day when you will come willingly into my arms."

Lauren wanted to stay in his arms, to listen to the words that made her insides ache. But Garret knew all about women, and he knew how to stir their blood, just as he was stirring hers at that moment. He was dangerous, and she had to get away from him. She wiggled out of his arms. "I have to go now."

"Must you?"

She hurried to her horse, picked up the dangling reins, and thrust her scuffed boot into the stirrup, mounting. "And let me make this clear to you,

Garret Lassiter. It will be a cold day in hell before I go willingly into your arms."

Stepping close to Lauren, Garret patted her horse's neck. "Get ready for hell to cool down, Lauren. Because the time will come when you surrender to me willingly. You will welcome my touch."

Just the sound of his voice and the sensuous words he was saying made her ache inside. "I'll go to your marriage bed, and I will lie down for you, but you will not like me that way. You may take me, but you'll never make me go to you freely."

"Yes, you will, Lauren. You will come to me, you will beg for my kisses, and you will like what I do to you."

Her mouth opened, and her head jerked up. "I don't think so."

He lifted her off her horse and held her in his arms, pressing her softness against the hardness of him. He bent his head until his lips were almost touching hers. "Do you feel what I feel when our bodies are this close? Does your heart beat so fast you can hardly breathe, like mine does?"

Lauren felt her flesh tremble. Yes, yes, she felt that way. Garret was going to kiss her, and she wanted him to.

He touched his lips to her ear, and she almost cried out. Softly at first, his lips touched her, tasting, testing, causing a feeling so exquisite that her breath came out in a soft moan.

With the age-old knowledge that a woman possesses, Lauren wanted him to make love to her. She wilted against him when he cupped his hands just below her breasts, teasing but not touching. Her lips opened, begging for more, inviting him to take what he wanted.

Garret suddenly broke off the kiss and forcefully put her back on her horse, then stepped away from her.

His voice was raw; his eyes held an unfathomable glow as if he were looking into the future and seeing something she could not. His laugh was rich and deep, and it sent a thrill through her. "You *will* like what I do to you, Lauren. I can promise you that."

Lauren watched him mount his horse and ride away, disturbed by her reaction to him. She had wanted him so much, she would have taken her clothes off right there if he had asked it of her.

She had always had a passionate nature, but knowing that about herself had not prepared her for the desperate yearning Garret had coaxed to life within her.

Each time they met, Lauren's feelings for Garret grew more intense. She felt something wild and wonderful building inside her, like a crashing tide. Even now, she burned for his touch.

How much more powerful would her feelings for Garret be once she actually became his wife?

Chapter Fifteen

Lauren slipped her mother's wedding gown over her head, and the ivory satin drifted down her body like a soft kiss.

"I need you to stand on that chair so I can measure the hem," Callie mumbled, her mouth full of pins.

Lauren felt like crying as she touched the soft satin. "Isn't it lovely? I used to take this out of the trunk and touch it, trying to imagine how my mother looked when she wore it to marry my father."

"Hold still," Callie cautioned, going down on her knees and using the measuring stick. "Umhum. It won't take much to make it a perfect fit."

Lauren's eyes were sad as she glanced at her

image in the mirror. She could still say no to Garret. She shook her head. She did not have the choice of walking away from this marriage.

Callie finished pinning the hem and stood back speculatively. "I'll need to take in the waist a bit."

Lauren wondered if her mother had been as frightened as she was when she had been fitted for this gown. "I never realized that I'm taller than my mother was."

"Yes, you are. By a good four inches. It's fortunate that the gown has a wide hem."

Lauren felt her mother's presence as the softness of the gown swirled about her, and her eyes became bright with tears. "I hope my marriage won't be as miserable as my mother's was."

Callie looked at Lauren, startled. "You aren't going into this marriage expecting to be unhappy, are you?"

Lauren could not meet her sister-in-law's eyes. "Every woman thinks . . . hopes her marriage will be right in every way."

Callie's honey-gold eyes took on a look of concern. "Lauren, come down off that chair. I want to talk to you."

Lauren stepped down, swallowing with difficulty. "Thank you for helping me. I'm absolutely helpless with a needle and thread." She knew Callie was watching her with a troubled expression. "What did you wear when you married Tanner?" she asked, wanting to distract her sister-in-law.

"Lauren, what's wrong? This should be the happiest time of your life, yet you are definitely unhappy. Why is that?"

"Well, Papa is dying."

"It's not that. Forgive me if I'm poking my nose where it doesn't belong, but I care about you. Tanner is worried that something's not right, and so am I."

Lauren sighed and sagged onto the chair. "I can't tell you what's bothering me, Callie, because I don't want Tanner to know."

Callie bent down beside her. "Anything you tell me here today won't go any further than my ears. I won't tell Tanner or anyone else if you don't want me to."

Lauren's eyes filled with misery. "Papa wants this marriage. If I don't marry Garret, Papa will leave the Circle M to Clare, and my brothers will get nothing."

Callie shot to her feet. "That's terrible! Tanner would never let you sacrifice yourself for him, and I'm sure, from what I've heard of Stone, he wouldn't either. You already know that Chase doesn't want anything to do with the Circle M."

Lauren shook her head. "None of my brothers must ever know about this arrangement." She looked into Callie's eyes. "You promised you wouldn't tell—you won't, will you?"

Callie let out an angry breath. "I am furious with your pa and even madder at Garret Lassiter. Why would a man like him do this to you?"

"Papa is settling Cedar Creek on me as a wedding present. Garret needs the water."

"I can't believe a man like Garret would go along with such a plan just for water. No, he must love you."

"Callie, you know how important water is out here."

"Yes, I do. And I have also seen the Cedar Creek property. It's hilly and unfit for grazing. Tanner told me that even a family of squatters deserted their cabin and moved on because they couldn't make a living there."

"So that's why the squatters left. I never knew. I thought Papa might have run them off."

"The way Tanner tells it, your pa left them alone, hoping they could develop the land for him."

"But Cedar Creek is important."

"Please don't do this. Tell Garret you can't marry him."

"I can't."

Callie had only known Lauren for a short time, but she had already seen how determined she could be when her mind was set on something. Lauren was a true McBride, and no one could sway her from her course, so Callie did not even try.

"Lauren, I have only seen Garret Lassiter from a distance, but I could tell that he's a very handsome man. Any woman in town would be flattered if he even looked at her. I have heard his family is very wealthy. Why would he marry you just to get Cedar Creek?"

"I don't know."

Callie saw the anguish in Lauren's eyes. "The important question is how you feel about Garret."

Lauren looked at her sister-in-law with misery in her eyes. "I love him. I always have."

"And he loves you."

"No, he doesn't. He told me once, when I was only fifteen, about the one woman in the world for him—it wasn't me."

"Then who?"

Lauren shrugged. "I don't know. He didn't say."

"But he's marrying you."

Lauren gazed out the window and said in a trembling voice. "Yes. I will be his wife, and every time he takes me in his arms, he'll be remembering that other woman and wishing I were her."

Callie shook her head. "Don't think so little of your own worth, Lauren. You have many admirable qualities, and you are very beautiful. If Garret Lassiter isn't already in love with you, he soon will be."

Lauren stepped back onto the chair. "Let down four inches at the hem and take it in at the waist. Then everything will be perfect."

The door opened a crack, and Clare stuck her head in. When she saw Lauren in the wedding gown, she pushed the door back so hard it slammed against the wall. "What are you dressing up for, a costume party? And why wasn't I invited?" she asked in a snide tone.

Lauren met Callie's eyes. "I'm dressed for a wedding, Clare, and you *are* invited."

Clare's jaw went slack. "Why are you in that dress, and who's getting married?"

"Why, I am." Lauren smiled at Callie. "Clare, do you remember you once told me that if I went to my aunt's, she might make a lady out of me and Garret Lassiter might then show an interest in me?"

"What are you saying?" Clare asked, her complexion paling.

"Well, Stepmother, you were right. Garret has asked me to marry him. The wedding's in four days."

"That's not possible!"

"I can assure you it's true. I never imagined you would be so upset about my leaving the Circle M."

For the first time since Lauren had known Clare, the woman was speechless. With anger flaming in her eyes and her jaw set tight, she sailed out of the room, slamming the door behind her.

Joining Callie's laughter, Lauren sat down, fearing she would topple off the chair. "You have to say this about Clare—she knows how to enter and leave a room in the most dramatic fashion."

Callie wiped tears from her eyes and said between gales of laughter, "Did you see the look on her face?"

Lauren leaned back and tried to suppress a giggle. "That scene made it all worthwhile. Can you imagine, Clare rendered speechless." Lauren took Callie's hand. "I needed to laugh. We were getting entirely too serious."

Callie felt affection for her electrifying sister-in-law. How could any man not love Lauren? She could not believe that Garret Lassiter would marry Lauren just to get his hands on Cedar Creek. The man had to be in love with her!

The day before Lauren's wedding, she entered her father's bedroom. She had not been in the room since the night he had been so ill, so she was surprised to find him sitting up in bed, feeding himself.

"You look wonderful, Papa. Apparently, you're feeling much better."

He grinned. "Women always tell me I look wonderful."

She sat down in the chair by his bed. "I bet they did, at that. You must have been something—bet you swept Mama right off her feet."

He paused with the spoon halfway to his mouth. "Your ma, she was a pretty one. Had most of the men in Savannah after her. But when she saw me, they didn't stand a chance."

"The wedding's tomorrow."

"I know. That's why I'm getting my strength back. I'm going to be at that wedding or die trying." He burst out laughing. "I'd rather not die just yet, though. Not until I see you settled, and Stone back home."

Lauren thought it was best not to talk any more about the wedding. She was still too angry, but she could not let it show. If she spoke her mind, her father would surely have a relapse.

When she glanced at him, he was smiling. "You look as if you're thinking about something pleasant, Papa."

"Catfish. I was thinking about fried catfish," he said wistfully. He looked down at his bowl of thin broth and shoved it aside. "Gal, I used to love the way your ma made catfish. No one was a better cook than she was. When we were first married and didn't have much money, I'd catch a string of catfish and we'd feast that day." His eyes softened. "Funny how I forgot about those good times."

"Your second wife doesn't cook," Lauren reminded him.

He made a gesture of disgust. "Well, we'll not go into that."

Lauren stood and kissed him on the cheek. "Are you finished with your lunch?"

"Yeah. Take it away."

Lauren lifted the tray. "Get some rest."

Moments later, Lauren found Tiny in the kitchen. She placed her father's tray on the table and looked thoughtful for a moment. "Tiny, do you know how to fish?"

He gave her a puzzled nod.

"Will you take me fishing?"

He nodded and looked inquiringly at her.

"Papa has it in his head that he wants catfish. And I want him to have some."

Tiny took his paper and scribbled to Lauren.

"Yes," she replied. "Cedar Creek would be the best place. I'll change, and we can leave."

He nodded.

"I'll meet you at the barn," she told him, hurrying out of the kitchen.

The house was quiet as Lauren stepped out on the front porch. She had just finished a letter to her aunt, telling her about her marriage. Her aunt was going to be shocked and would not understand why Lauren was getting married so soon after returning to Texas.

She sighed and leaned against the porch railing, watching tattered clouds play peekaboo with the full moon. Tomorrow night she would be a bride. She closed her eyes and imagined Garret touching her, kissing her—she imagined him—

"Good evening, Lauren. Dare I hope it was me you were thinking about with such a soft expression on your face?"

Her eyes flew open. "Garret," she said, blushing

as if he could read her thoughts. "I didn't expect you tonight."

He climbed the steps and stood beside her, following her gaze to the moon. He could smell her scent, and it made his stomach tighten into a knot. "I know tradition dictates that a groom isn't supposed to see his bride the night before the wedding, but I had been doing some business with Jeb and saw you standing here. Do you mind if I join you for a bit?"

She eyed him disdainfully. "Of course not."

"I have been here since early afternoon. Tanner told me you'd gone fishing. I had a difficult time picturing you baiting a hook."

"Papa wanted fried catfish. Tiny and I caught five." She lowered her lashes. "Papa could only eat a few bites." She shrugged. "I get my hopes up on his good days, but I know he's getting weaker all the time."

"I know it must be difficult for you."

"Jeb says it'll rain tomorrow night."

Garret knew she did not want to talk about her father anymore, because it was too painful for her. "If Jeb says it'll rain, then it will."

"I hope it waits until after the wedding."

He stepped closer to her. "Everything has happened so fast, we haven't had much of a chance to talk, Lauren."

"We talked!"

"No. We sparred. What I meant is . . . for instance, will you want to redo the house? Is there anything about it you'd like to change? Would you like to go on a honeymoon, perhaps aboard ship to some island or even to Europe?"

"You know I can't leave with Papa so ill. And I haven't seen much of your house—even if I had, I wouldn't presume to change it."

"Of course, I know you can't go away with your father ill. I was speaking of later. And as for my house, I want you to think of it as your home. It hasn't had a woman's touch since my mother died. I want you to change anything you don't like."

"I liked your mother, Garret." She glanced back at the moon. "I always wanted to be like my mother, but unfortunately, I'm nothing like her."

Her long lashes made shadows on her cheeks as he watched her. "You look very much like your mother, but you are your father's daughter. You once told me that your brother Stone was like your father, but it's you who is most like him."

She moved to the steps and sat down, not altogether pleased that Garret had compared her to her father. "In what way am I like him, aside from my eye color?"

"Your pride, your stubbornness, your tenacity." His mouth curved into a smile. "I see a fiery redhead who's ready to battle the world if it happens to step in her path."

"Now, there you have me. I would have to say, if I'm being honest, that I'm quick to anger and slow to forgive." She lowered her lashes. "I have a terrible temper."

He crouched down beside her, his thigh brushing against her leg. "I hope you aren't still angry with me." His gaze perused her face. "I hope you will someday forgive me for the way you were forced to marry me."

After a long moment, she answered him. "I'm resigned to my future. You're as much a pawn of my father's as I am. How can I blame you for that? You saw a chance to get Cedar Creek, and you took it."

"If you believe that about me, you must also believe that I'm weak-minded and can be manipulated. Let me assure you that I am not a pawn. If I had not wanted to marry you, no amount of coercion on your father's part would have won me over."

"You are certainly not wise to marry a woman you don't love. I'm sure you'll find our marriage a hardship before too many days have passed. That will be my one satisfaction."

He gathered his thoughts before answering her. He glanced into the distance and said, "Marrying you will be no hardship." He looked back at her. "In fact, I expect marrying you to be one of the wisest things I've done in my life. At least, I hope so."

"It always comes back to Cedar Creek." She buried her face in her hands. "Why couldn't you have just left me alone? I don't want to be married to you."

"Don't you?" he asked, his disbelief apparent in the tone of his voice. He gripped her hands and pulled them away from her face. "Say it again while you're looking into my eyes, and I'll believe you."

She met his gaze, then dipped her head. "I already agreed to marry you. That's all the reason you need."

"I'm giving you a choice, right now. If you don't want to be my wife, I'll go to your father this minute and tell him I don't want to marry you. Is that what you want me to do, Lauren?"

No, that was not what she wanted him to do, she realized for the first time. She wanted to be with him for the rest of her life. "I gave my pledge to you and I intend to honor it."

He raised her chin. "There so many things I want to tell you."

She blinked her eyes, staring at him. His dark hair was riffled by the wind, and she wanted to reach out and smooth it into place. His dark eyes seemed to burn into her, and she felt the power of his presence. "Don't you think it's too late for talk?"

He brushed a tumbled curl out of her face. "I suppose it is." He pressed his face against hers. "I'll be a good husband to you."

"There is something I need to know," she said.

She had asked him before, but he had not answered her then, and he might not answer her now. "What happened to the woman you professed to love so desperately?"

Garret raised Lauren to her feet. "I'm not sure she loves me anymore. But I believe she once did."

"Is that all you are going to tell me about her?"

"I promise you that after we have been married one year, I will answer any question you ask me about her."

"Must I wait that long?"

His mouth moved to hers, and his breath teased her lips. "Perhaps you'll learn about her sooner. A husband will tell a wife many things he won't tell the girl he's going to marry."

Gently his lips touched hers, and she felt her heart break at the same time as her body warmed to his. Garret might love another woman, but he desired her as much as she did him.

His arms tightened about her, and he held her even closer to him. She could feel the swell of his need for her as his prodding tongue entered her mouth. Lauren had never known a kiss could be so breathtaking. She pressed against him, wanting to be even closer. Confusion was replaced by hunger, and she attempted to get nearer to the hard thigh that was driving her wild.

Garret touched her breast, gently cupping it in his hand, groaning when she tossed her head back. He touched the nipple through the material of her gown and felt it swell against his fingers.

Lauren's eyes drifted shut, and she gasped. No one had ever done that to her, and the feeling was so sweet and so intense. She wanted to feel his touch on her bare flesh.

"Ohh," she said in a soft whisper.

Garret suddenly raised his head and held her away from him, knowing that someone could be watching. "Now do you understand why I want you to be my wife?"

Lauren nodded her head, as her breathing seemed to tear from her throat. Of course she knew what he was talking about. "I know about sex. I was raised on a ranch."

"Tomorrow," he said, stepping back and resisting the urge to take her in his arms once more. "You will be mine tomorrow."

He moved away from her and was soon swallowed up by the darkness. Moments later, she heard him riding away.

Her situation was as hopeless as was her love for Garret.

Estaban lay in the darkened room, his cigarette glowing each time he took a slow drag. His mind was reaching . . . his eyes burning. It was said that the beautiful Señorita McBride was going to marry the *patrón*. Hatred formed like a knot in his throat.

This was what he had been waiting for. He thought of the years that he had wandered aimlessly and without direction after his father had killed himself. He remembered the day he had hired on at the ranch that should have been his. He remembered the insult of working on the land that should be passed down to his sons. He thought of Garret Lassiter settling down with his new bride, hoping for the sons and daughters he would never have, just as Estaban would never have a family of his own.

Soon the *patrón* would be buried beneath the dirt that his family had stolen from Estaban's family.

The time was near to kill another member of Garret's family. He would kill the father, but not before the wedding. He did not want the wedding to be postponed, as it surely would be if Garret Lassiter had to mourn the death of his father.

How would he kill Barnard Lassiter? He smiled and flicked his cigarette through the open window. When San Reanido had belonged to his family, the man who had looked after the horses had been a full-blooded Apache. The Apache had taught Estaban how to use the bow and arrow, and he had practiced many hours. He could now hit a bull's-eye dead center at a hundred paces.

He would use a bow and arrow, and everyone would think that some renegade Comanche had killed Señor Barnard Lassiter.

Chapter Sixteen

Lauren was nervous and had difficulty swallowing a single bite of her breakfast. She picked up the beautiful wedding bouquet Tiny had left beside her plate and held it to her nose, taking in the wonderful aroma. Tiny had combined roses and daisies, and she wondered where he had gotten the yellow ribbon he had woven among the fragrant flowers.

"Thank you for this," she said with feeling, touching the petal of a red rose to her lips. "You are one of the kindest men I have ever known."

Tiny laid a gentle hand on Lauren's shoulder, and his face actually flushed with pleasure. Then he looked at her plate and put his hands on his

A Special Offer For Leisure Historical Romance Readers Only!

Get Four FREE* Romance Novels

A $21.96 Value!

Thrill to the most sensual, adventure-filled Historical Romances on the market today...

FROM 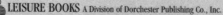 LEISURE BOOKS

As a home subscriber to the Leisure Historical Romance Book Club, you'll enjoy the best in today's BRAND-NEW Historical Romance fiction. For over twenty-five years, Leisure Books has brought you the award-winning, high-quality authors you know and love to read. Each Leisure Historical Romance will sweep you away to a world of high adventure...and intimate romance. Discover for yourself all the passion and excitement millions of readers thrill to each and every month.

SAVE AT LEAST *$5.00* EACH TIME YOU BUY!

Each month, the Leisure Historical Romance Book Club brings you four brand-new titles from Leisure Books, America's foremost publisher of Historical Romances. EACH PACKAGE WILL SAVE YOU AT LEAST $5.00 FROM THE BOOKSTORE PRICE! And you'll never miss a new title with our convenient home delivery service.

Here's how we do it. Each package will carry a 10-DAY EXAMINATION privilege. At the end of that time, if you decide to keep your books, simply pay the low invoice price of $16.96 ($17.75 US in Canada), no shipping or handling charges added*. HOME DELIVERY IS ALWAYS FREE*. With today's top Historical Romance novels selling for $5.99 and higher, our price SAVES YOU AT LEAST $5.00 with each shipment.

AND YOUR FIRST FOUR-BOOK SHIPMENT IS TOTALLY FREE!*

IT'S A BARGAIN YOU CAN'T BEAT! A Super $21.96 Value!

LEISURE BOOKS A Division of Dorchester Publishing Co., Inc.

GET YOUR 4 FREE* BOOKS NOW—
A $21.96 VALUE!

Mail the Free* Book
Certificate
Today!

4 FREE* BOOKS 🐚 A $21.96 VALUE

Free * Books Certificate

YES! I want to subscribe to the Leisure Historical Romance
Book Club. Please send me my 4 FREE* BOOKS. Then each month
I'll receive the four newest Leisure Historical Romance selections
to Preview for 10 days. If I decide to keep them, I will pay the
Special Member's Only discounted price of just $4.24 each, a total
of $16.96 ($17.75 US in Canada). This is a SAVINGS OF AT LEAST
$5.00 off the bookstore price. There are no shipping, handling, or
other charges*. There is no minimum number of books I must buy
and I may cancel the program at any time. In any case, the 4 FREE*
BOOKS are mine to keep—A BIG $21.96 Value!

*In Canada, add $5.00 shipping and handling per order for first ship-
ment. For all subsequent shipments to Canada, the cost of membership
is $17.75 US, which includes $7.75 shipping and handling per
month. [All payments must be made in US dollars]

Name _____

Address _____

City _____

State _____ *Country* _____ *Zip* _____

Telephone _____

Signature _____

If under 18, Parent or Guardian must sign. Terms, prices and conditions subject to change.
Subscription subject to acceptance. Leisure Books reserves the right to reject any order or
cancel any subscription.

(Tear Here and Mail Your FREE* Book Card Today!)

Get Four Books Totally
F R E E* —
A $21.96 Value!

(Tear Here and Mail Your FREE* Book Card Today!)

PLEASE RUSH
MY FOUR FREE*
BOOKS TO ME
RIGHT AWAY!

Leisure Historical Romance Book Club
P.O. Box 6613
Edison, NJ 08818-6613

AFFIX
STAMP
HERE

hips in disapproval. He nodded at her in jerky motions.

"I know. You're right, I should eat this morning, but I can't seem to swallow anything."

He reached for a pitcher of milk and poured some into a glass, holding it out to her.

"All right. I'll drink the milk." She took several sips, knowing she was going to need all her strength just to get through the day. She found that the milk was easier to swallow than the food had been. "How is Papa this morning?"

Tiny scribbled on paper.

Lauren read his words and raised an inquiring eyebrow. "He wants to wear a suit? Is he well enough for that? For that matter, is he strong enough to be brought downstairs?"

Tiny nodded as he scribbled on the paper, then handed it back to Lauren.

"He insists on coming downstairs, does he? Very well. We couldn't stop him anyway if he's made up his mind."

Lauren had no idea that her blue eyes took on the same challenging expression that so often lit her father's eyes, but Tiny saw it and smiled to himself. She was her father's daughter, but she had the best of Tom McBride in her—not the worst.

"I suppose my father wants to watch the ceremony so he can witness his triumph."

Tiny's eyes were filled with compassion.

Lauren finished the last of her milk and stood up. "I'm going to get dressed now. The guests should be arriving in another hour. When Callie arrives, send her up to me."

Tiny nodded.

Lauren was struggling to button the back of her gown when Callie arrived.

"Here, let me do that," Callie volunteered. "This is Faith," Callie said, nodding to the woman who had shyly entered the bedroom with her.

Lauren turned, smiling at the pretty blonde who was married to Chase. "I am happy to know you. And thank you for coming to my wedding. Is my brother with you?"

Faith smiled warmly. "Yes, he is. And we brought our son. I hope you don't mind."

Lauren looked puzzled. "I didn't know you had a son."

"Luke's eight years old; he's adopted."

"Luke McBride." Lauren laughed. "I guess that makes me an aunt."

Faith could see why Chase had taken so readily to Lauren. Lauren had not judged Chase by the circumstances of his birth or the color of his skin. Now she accepted Luke into her family as easily as she had Chase. "Thank you for being so accepting of Chase. He would never tell you this, but your visit to him meant a lot."

Lauren squeezed Faith's hand. "I grew up without a sister, and suddenly I have two." She took two roses from her bouquet and handed one to each sister-in-law. "I want both of you to stand up with me today."

A heavy knock sounded on the door, and Lauren and Callie said at the same time, "Tanner."

Tanner ambled into the room wearing a dark suit and looking too handsome for his own good. "The preacher's here, little sister, and so is the impatient bridegroom."

"Who else?" Callie asked.

"Some people from San Reanido, and Mr. Lassiter."

Lauren drew in a nervous breath and shook her gown so it cascaded behind her. "Tanner, will you give the bride away?"

Tanner looked into his sister's eyes and smiled. "I'd rather keep you."

"You will never lose me."

He drew her into his arms. "Pa's downstairs, dressed in his best and looking like he just won at a hand of cards. I can't figure him. He rarely ever changes his mind about anyone. But he's sure smiling at Garret."

Lauren glanced quickly at Callie. "It's always best if your family likes your husband. Do you like Garret?" she asked Tanner.

"Yeah," he admitted. "I always have. But I used

to think he was a bit uppity, just like Pa did, until I came to know him."

Lauren smiled. "I'm glad you like him. Because I like him, too."

When Lauren came downstairs on Tanner's arm, Garret watched her, thinking that if he lived to be a hundred he'd never see anyone more beautiful. He watched as she graciously acknowledged everyone in the room by making eye contact and nodding. It was an informal wedding—the guests were comprised mostly of family and a select few who worked on the two ranches.

Tom McBride was seated near the door, his eyes on his daughter. She stopped before him and kissed his cheek, then repeated the same ritual with Garret's father.

Then she paused before Chase. "Will you walk with me and Tanner?" she asked. "Will you stand with us as a family?"

Chase nodded, feeling a lump in his throat. He knew why she was including him and Faith—she was showing the world that he was her brother. "I'd be proud to, little sister."

Lauren bent down to the young boy who stood shyly beside Chase. "Hello, Luke. I'm your Aunt Lauren. Will you take your mother's hand and walk with us?"

Luke's dark eyes shown brilliantly, and he

glanced up at his dad. Chase nodded. "It's all right."

"Yes, ma'am . . . Aunt Lauren."

Nothing Lauren could have done would have endeared her more to Chase than that single act of kindness.

Tanner and Chase led her forward, one on each side, their wives walking behind them and Faith holding Luke's hand.

Tiny looked at Tom, who had tears in his eyes. And so did the little man.

Tanner gave Lauren's hand to Garret, and then both brothers stepped back a pace.

Garret clasped Lauren's hand in a firm grip, his gaze linked with hers all the while the minister spoke.

"Friends and family, we are gathered here today before God and this company to join this man and woman in the holy institution of marriage."

As the minister's words went on, Lauren felt as if a door had slammed and locked behind her. There would be no going back—she would soon be Garret's wife.

Garret's voice was deep and seemed to tremble a bit when he said, "I do."

Lauren soon said softly, "I do."

"By the power vested in me by the great state of Texas, I now pronounce you husband and wife."

Garret took Lauren's hands and turned her to face him. His lips were warm as they brushed hers.

"Hello, Mrs. Lassiter. You belong to me now."

Before Lauren could answer, Tanner pulled her into his arms. "Be happy, Lauren." He gave her a tight bear hug. "That's an order."

She forced a smile so her brother would not suspect the tumult going on inside her. "I shall."

Tanner glanced at Garret. There was the merest hint of a threat in his voice when he said, "You have taken the McBrides' greatest treasure—treat her like she's your greatest treasure."

"You can be sure I will," Garret replied, his eyes on Lauren's flushed face.

Lauren moved away from her husband and went directly to her father. "Papa, you should be in bed now that the ceremony is over."

Tom clasped his daughter's hands in his cold, frail ones. "You're right. I'm a bit tired." He glanced at Tiny, who was waiting nearby. "I saw her married all legal and proper. Go get my two sons to carry me upstairs."

Lauren went down on her knees beside her father. "I've done what you wanted me to do," she whispered. "Now will you keep your word about my brothers?"

"I always keep my word, gal." He surprised her when he framed her face with his cold, shaking hands. "I thought when you came down those stairs a while ago that I was seeing your ma on our wedding day. You looked like an angel, Lauren."

She wanted to be angry with him, but she could

not. She smiled and kissed his cheek. "Thank you, Papa."

Tanner and Chase positioned themselves on either side of their father and lifted him. "Everyone, eat, be merry, dance," Tom admonished the wedding guests. "This is a happy occasion, not a wake!"

Clare appeared at Lauren's side like a dark shadow, unpleasant and unwelcome, her gaze stabbing into Chase's back. "Your pa's lost his mind, claiming that half-breed for his son. I can't imagine what everyone thinks about that situation."

Lauren stepped away from Clare and watched her father being carried upstairs. "When have you ever cared about what people think?"

"I won't have that half-breed bastard in my house."

"Then I suggest you tell that to Thomas J. McBride. He has openly let it be known that Chase is his son, and Tanner and I showed everyone here today that we think of Chase as our brother. How long do you think it will take the news to spread throughout the whole county?"

Clare reached out and grabbed Lauren's arm so forcefully she ripped the sleeve of her wedding gown. "You are going to be sorry, little girl. Just you wait and see. I know this wedding was a hatched up, patched up business. I'll find out what's really going on between you and Garret."

Tiny gripped Clare's hand and pulled her away from Lauren. Although Clare struggled and tried to pry his hands away, she was no match for the little man's strength. She jerked her arm free and, much to Lauren's relief, stormed out of the room and up the stairs. There were horrified stares on the faces of the people from San Reanido. Everyone from the Circle M was accustomed to Clare's tantrums and merely shrugged.

Garret appeared at Lauren's side and took her arm. "What was that all about?"

"Just Clare being Clare." Her stepmother had managed to spoil Lauren's wedding day. Lauren was almost certain that Clare had planned it that way. Everything was wrong, and Lauren felt like crying, but being her father's daughter, she slid a smile in place and turned to her guests.

Garret's father was charming to Lauren when he embraced her. "Welcome to the family, Lauren. My boy's been mooning after you for long enough. It's time you came home and married him."

Lauren forced a smile. Mr. Lassiter did not seem to know the conditions of her marriage to his son, and she was not about to inform him.

"I'll be leaving this very day," Barnard Lassiter told Lauren. "It's time I left San Reanido to you young people. I've been wanting to go back to Virginia for some time. I would have left sooner, but I didn't want to leave Garret alone. Now that he has you, I can go without feeling guilty."

She was stunned. "You won't be coming back?"

"I'll come for visits, but the ranch belongs to you and Garret." Mr. Lassiter glanced over at his son, who was talking to the minister. "His mother would have been happy that you and Garret married."

"Mrs. Lassiter was a kind and gentle woman."

"She liked you, Lauren. She always said that Garret would end up married to you one day. Guess she was right." He raised Lauren's hand to his lips. "But this is a day to be happy, not a day for reminiscing. Go, greet your guests, and leave an old man to ponder his thoughts."

Lauren moved from one guest to another, with Garret at her side. She managed to say all the right things and engage in lively conversation, but she was glad when the last guest left and she no longer needed to wear the pasted-on smile.

Tiny was putting Tom to bed and had left the bedroom door open so air would circulate in the room. Neither of them knew that Manuelo was lurking in the hallway, listening to their conversation.

Tiny gave Tom his medicine and watched him swallow it.

Tom grimaced at the taste and gulped down water to get rid of the bitterness in his mouth. "It's done. My first plan worked just fine."

The little man nodded.

"I tell you, when the county hears that my gal landed the biggest prize stud of them all, it'll set everyone on their ear."

Tiny used sign language, and from his jerky motions it was easy to see he was angry.

"I don't care if I did use trickery to get her married. Offering Garret the Cedar Creek property was a good move on my part. The end result's all that matters. My daughter'll be set up in that grand house where she can look down on all the rest of us." Tom broke out in laughter. "My daughter—a Lassiter!"

Tiny made sign language once more.

"No. I don't want to see Tanner or Chase." He turned his face to the wall, feeling prickles of guilt for the way he'd forced Lauren into marriage. "My daughter might not have been a happy bride today, but I saw the way Garret was looking at her. He's a man who'll know how to settle her."

Tiny used his hands to signal.

"Don't go throwing accusations at me. My daughter'll come around to her husband in time." Tom's laughter ended in a hacking cough. Finally he said, "From the way Garret was looking at my gal, it won't take him long to make her forget how they were married. He'll have her in his bed before the night's over, and she'll like it."

Again Tiny motioned with his hands, this time faster and more furiously—he was angry!

"Yeah, I know," Tom agreed. "It'll take her

longer to forgive me, and I don't have that much time." He snuggled down in bed. "But I sure as hell got her married, and that's what matters."

Garret lifted Lauren into the buggy, where four high-spirited matching Arabians pulled restlessly at the reins.

Lauren settled in the soft leather seat and glanced back at the house. "It seems so strange to be leaving home so soon after coming back."

Garret climbed in beside her. "This is no longer your home. Wherever I am will be your home from now on."

As the team started off at a trot, Lauren glanced up at the window and saw Clare silhouetted there with Manuelo at her side. It seemed to Lauren that her father was not so amicable toward his wife these days. She had an unsettling thought—her father would be alone with those two now that she was leaving.

But Tiny would be there to look after her father, so there was no need to worry.

Barnard Lassiter was feeling happier than he had in a long time. His son was settled with the woman he loved, and he could leave Texas for the cooler climate of Virginia. He looked forward to spending some time with his daughter and her family.

Like his wife, Barnard had never really taken to Texas, and Texas had not taken to him. But Garret loved the state, and the ranch was the only home he remembered.

Barnard was proud of his only son. Garret had all the qualities he and his wife had instilled in him. He was honorable, trustworthy, and a damned hard worker. Garret was going to be all right.

Barnard was suddenly jerked forward as his horse went down hard. He fell and rolled down a slope and into a ditch, striking his head against a rock. Shaking off the pain, he climbed back up the embankment to discover that his horse had been shot by an arrow!

"Indians!" he cried, trying to get to his rifle.

Barnard Lassiter did not have time to think before a second arrow struck him through the heart.

He was dead before he hit the ground.

Chapter Seventeen

"Señora," Manuelo said, his dark eyes gleaming. "I listened outside the door of your husband's room like you told me to." He looked pleased with himself. "I have learned the reason for the marriage between your stepdaughter and Señor Lassiter."

Clare turned from the window. "Tell me. Tell me everything."

Garret was the first to break the strained silence between him and Lauren. "Glad it's over?"

"It was a trying day. I was sorry that your father left before I got to know him better."

"He has wanted to leave for some time."

"I know. He told me that."

In the gathering dusk, Lauren studied Garret's chiseled profile. He was handsome, but rugged and capable, too. "Tell me," she said whimsically, "what does the wife of Garret Lassiter do?"

Garret glanced at her. "Do?"

"Yes." Resentment welled inside her. "What is my function?"

He snapped the reins, and the Arabians shot forward at a run. The buggy was so well sprung that Lauren hardly felt a bump.

"That depends."

"On what?" she asked.

"The time of day."

"And at night?"

He smiled, his lips curving slightly. "I could tell you, but I'd much rather show you."

Did his voice quiver or had she imagined it?

Garret tightened his grip on the reins. Just thinking about having Lauren in his bed sent wild imaginings pounding through his head. She would never understand the tight rein he had been keeping on his feelings. Now it would be even harder because she was his wife. It scared the hell out of him that she might never forgive him for marrying her.

Lauren's voice sounded hollow, even to her. "Why would you want to be tied to a reluctant bride?"

"Like I told you before—I want you."

She lowered her gaze and studied the wilted

wedding bouquet she clutched in her hands. "I would never have married you if I hadn't been forced to."

"I know. But you could change your mind about me. I hope you will." He halted the horses and turned to her. "I want you in every way, Lauren. Do you understand what I'm saying?"

"I know what marriage is about. I'm not the same innocent girl who left Sidewinder four years ago."

"No. You're not. You are the woman who is going to occupy my bed, and I hope you'll like it." His voice became gentle, and he touched her cheek. "I don't want you to have any regrets."

"What do you mean? You could fill an ocean with my regrets."

He closed his eyes, wondering why he always said the wrong thing with her. "I like having you for my wife."

"Let's not pretend that this marriage is anything but what it is. I was forced to marry you, and I'll never forget that."

He played with a curl that rested against her breast. "It's my intention to make you forget about how our marriage started out."

"I gave a vow today that I would be your wife, and I intend to honor that vow. I always keep my word."

"That's one of the things I lo . . . like about you."

Lauren glanced sideways at him. "I'm so glad I please you."

His hand moved to her neck, and he felt the pulse racing there. "I can make you want me. You already know that."

A slow blush crept up her cheeks, and her heart thudded. "You ask a lot of me for a measly little creek."

His hand covered hers, and she did not pull away. "I will take it slow and easy with you. Do you trust me?"

"I used to, but not anymore." She slid her hand away from his. "But I'm a McBride, and I'll do what's expected of me."

"No, Lauren," Garret reminded her. "You're a Lassiter now."

"In name, Garret. But inside I'm a McBride, and we are a force to be reckoned with."

Garret's eyes dropped to her breasts, which were outlined against the tight bodice of her satin wedding gown. "Don't I know it." He snapped the reins, and the horses started off again at a trot. "Be warned, Lauren. I'm going to lay siege to you. I won't be satisfied until I win all of you."

"You be warned, Garret. This isn't a card game where you either win or lose. I'm flesh and blood, and I bleed when I'm wounded. You'll never have more from me than what you take every night."

His laugh was deep because he knew her so well. She would rear and buck, but he would gentle her in the end. "I'll settle for that for now."

Anger crawled through her mind and burst into an inferno. "I don't think you'll like me that way. You can possess my body—I gave you that right when I agreed to marry you—but that's all you'll ever have of me."

"I'll have all of you." His eyes glinted as if she had just offered him a challenge. "Before I'm through, you will beg for my kisses."

"Never!" She shook her head, and her hair swirled about her face like red-gold satin. "Never."

He glanced up at the cloud bank in the west. "We'd better get home. Jeb was right in his prediction—a storm's coming."

Lauren looked at the clouds that seemed to rumble and boil in the distance; they suited her dark mood just fine.

They reached the house just ahead of the rain. Garret helped Lauren from the buggy and took her inside.

The housekeeper came forward with a warm smile and exclaimed in her soft Irish brogue, "God love you, Garret, you got your new bride home just in time." She turned her attention to Lauren. "I'm certainly pleased to welcome you as the new mistress of San Reanido."

"Lauren, in case you don't know it, Shaughnessy came to Texas with my father and mother when they left Virginia. This is her domain, and she runs it very well. Anything you want, just tell her."

The small, white-haired woman grinned cheerfully. "I'll always defer to you, madam. I've tended two generations of Lassiters and wouldn't say no to a third generation." She took the crushed bouquet from Lauren. "But here now, I'm keeping you talking. I'll just show you upstairs." She looked back at Garret. "If you're hungry, you'll find fixings in the kitchen."

Lauren could not help but warm to Mrs. Shaughnessy, who spoke to Garret with the familiarity and authority of a beloved servant. The little Irish woman chattered all the way upstairs.

"Garret had workmen in the master suite all week, hurrying them along to get everything ready for you."

Lauren saw no reason to vent her anger on this charming housekeeper. "That was thoughtful of him."

"Pity the missus isn't here to welcome you to the family. She always said that Garret would end up married to you." She beamed. "And the missus was right. She knew better than anyone where her son's heart lay."

Mr. Lassiter had told Lauren the same thing, but they were both mistaken. She knew where Garret's heart lay; he had told her.

Mrs. Shaughnessy chattered on. "There are five servants in the house. One upstairs maids and two downstairs. Then there's Mrs. Whit, the cook, and her helper, Danny. Mrs. Whit's been with the family as long as I have. You'll meet the rest of them tomorrow."

By now they had reached wide double doors, and the housekeeper threw them open. "One of your men delivered your clothing yesterday. I had everything pressed and hung in the wardrobe. There are wardrobes with drawers in the dressing room, right through here, where I put all the delicate things." Shaughnessy opened the door to reveal an enormous dressing room with floor-to-ceiling mirrors.

Lauren stepped back into the bedroom and stared at what had to be the most beautiful room she had ever seen. A white and yellow rug was centered on the highly polished wooden floor. The bed coverings and silken curtains were lemon yellow, giving the room a feeling of airiness and light.

Mrs. Shaughnessy went to double doors that led onto a wide balcony. "I'll just close these to keep out the rain." She moved to the door. "I'll put your bouquet in water so it will stay fresh. You may want to press it in a book later on." She smiled. "Unless there's something you'll be needing, I'll just leave you alone now."

As the door closed behind the housekeeper, it was difficult for Lauren to know what to do next.

How had she ended up in this predicament?

She realized that, deep down, she was still angry, so angry it almost choked her. At first she had directed her anger at her father, but now her new husband was the object of her fury.

This was a beautiful room, with beautiful furnishings, but it was a prison nonetheless. She sat down on the bed and ran her hand over the smooth coverlet, starting to imagine what would happen to her in that bed. She felt weak with longing and surged up to her feet.

Garret expected her to be a willing partner in that bed, but she'd just show him!

Garret stood in his darkened study, watching lightning cut through the sky. He was not usually a drinking man, but he needed something tonight. He took another sip of brandy and then another.

It should be the bride who was nervous on the wedding night, he thought. Then why were his hands trembling?

He set the brandy snifter on his desk and replaced the crystal stopper in the decanter. He certainly did not want to go to his new bride drunk. He glanced down at his hands and saw that they were still trembling, and not from the brandy.

It was time to begin the seduction of his wife, and that scared the hell out of him. He had waited a long time for this night, and now that it was here, he was not so confident of his prowess.

The noble thing to do was to let Lauren nullify the marriage, but he did not feel that noble. He had married Lauren knowing she did not want to be his wife. But he was not going to let her go.

Garret sighed heavily and poured himself another drink.

Envious eyes watched the light pouring onto the balcony. When the new bride came to the window, Estaban stepped back into the shadows. This should have been his wedding night. It should have been he who took his wife into his arms and made passionate love to her.

He heard a noise and stepped further into the shadows, taking precaution not to be discovered in the garden. His lip curled sardonically; the hired help was not allowed beyond the gates.

Hatred burned anew within him. The Lassiters had destroyed the garden his grandmother had enjoyed and had spent so much time in. There was now no trace of the cactus and fountains that had been his family's delight.

Whoever had come into the garden now went away. Estaban thought it had probably been one of the gardeners making certain that the gates were locked. He struck a match and lit his cigarette, watching the red glow against the darkness. He wondered how long he should allow the *patrón* to enjoy his happiness. His father's body might not be discovered for some time.

Dammit, Estaban had not intended to kill the horse with a misguided shot. He had intended that

245

the animal should return home riderless, so everyone would know Barnard Lassiter was dead.

What did it matter? The deed was done. Someone would discover the body sooner or later.

It had begun to rain, so Estaban ground out his cigarette and moved toward the fence. He wanted to see Garret suffer, to hurt and to go on hurting. When the time was right, he would bring an end to the game—when the time was right, he would make sure that Garret knew who had deprived him of his family.

The rain was falling heavily by the time Estaban reached the fence and climbed over, dropping to the other side. The rain was good, he thought, because it would erase any footprints he might have left in the garden.

He hesitated while rain peppered the brim of his hat. Tonight, when Garret Lassiter took his beautiful wife in his arms and made love to her, he would think he was in heaven.

Soon the patrón *would find himself in hell!*

Chapter Eighteen

Garret climbed the stairs slowly, not giving in to the strong urge to rush to Lauren. She could have refused to share his bed, but she had not. She had principles, and she was deeply committed to her brothers. Garret was now paying the price for allowing Lauren's father to use him. He realized what he must look like in her eyes. If only he could tell her why he had helped trap her into marriage, but he could not—not yet.

When Garret entered the bedroom, the first thing he saw was Lauren's wedding gown draped over a couch. He turned to find Lauren standing silently at the French doors that led to the balcony, illuminated by pulsating flashes of lightning. Her white nightgown was high-necked and had long sleeves, but what she probably did not know was that it was transparent when lightning streaked behind her.

She was so beautiful. The sight of her soft curves caught and held his attention, and he found himself wishing for another lightning bolt.

Garret had removed his jacket and his white shirt was open at the neck. As he walked toward Lauren, the sight of him took her breath away. It was so intimate being in the bedroom with him, and wearing only a nightgown.

Lauren quickly turned away to watch the rain hit the glass door—the rain that had started slowly and was now pounding relentlessly.

"There is an old saying, Garret—perhaps you have heard it—that it's unlucky for the bride if it rains on her wedding day."

Garret reached out to touch her but let his hand fall to his side. "We'll make our own luck."

"Luck has nothing to do with the reason I'm here."

He glanced down at her, fascinated by her fragile profile, half visible in the shadows. "I know how difficult and confusing this must be for you."

"How could you know what I'm feeling?"

"I wish it could have been different."

He stood so close behind her that she could feel his hard thigh pressed against her. She stiffened when his hand slid around her waist, bringing her closer to his body. She became painfully aware of him and fought to keep from turning to face him so she would be in his arms. She could never resist him . . . she knew that. Even now, after all that had happened between them, she wanted to throw her nightgown off so there would be nothing between her and Garret.

"Lauren, Lauren," he groaned. "You know how easily I can overcome your resistance if I decide to. But that's not the way I want it between us."

She blinked once, twice, and swallowed with difficulty, wanting to refute his assertion, but he was telling the truth, and they both knew it. She could hardly keep from touching him, pressing tighter against him. "What more do you want from me?"

His broad shoulders stiffened, the muscles in his throat tightened. "I want all of you. But," he said, dropping his hands away from her, "I'm willing to wait. If you wish, I'll sleep in one of the other rooms tonight."

It was not her wish.

She leaned her head against the cool windowpane, emotionally exhausted and sagging in defeat. "Waiting won't change anything."

Garret's hand came down on her shoulder. He knew how to make her surrender to him. Even now she was coming alive when he touched her. "Then you want me to stay?"

"Is it a custom for the husband to leave his wife on their wedding night?"

"No. And it wouldn't be what I want. It's just, if you aren't ready . . ."

Lauren turned slowly to face him. "I don't know what you're trying to tell me. You force me to be your wife, but your pride won't let you make love to a woman who doesn't want you—is that it?"

"That's not it at all, Lauren. Hell, I have no pride where you're concerned. I'd walk to you, run or crawl to you—I would do anything to have you naked in my bed."

"You desire me," she said through trembling lips, knowing that she wanted him just as much as he wanted her. "Desire is not much of a foundation on which to build a marriage, is it? Tell me—I don't know."

"I can't think of anything better," he said, taking in a breath of air. "We would be good together. I have always known that. If you will remember, I once told you that very thing."

"I don't remember that at all. I only remember, when I was fifteen, you told me you had found the perfect woman for you. You told me how much you loved her."

He pressed his lips together and then let out his breath. "Did you ever read the letter I left with Jeb?"

Lauren frowned. "No. Jeb tried to give it to me that day I left Sidewinder. I didn't want anything to remind me of the past, so I didn't read it, and I didn't take it with me."

"If only you had read my letter, you would know all about the woman I love." His hand moved down her back to rest at her waist. "Do you want me to let you go? All you have to do is say the words, Lauren."

She wanted to tell him to leave her alone. Why had they spoken of that other woman, tonight of all nights? It was not Garret's fault—she had brought the woman into the conversation.

"Well, Lauren? You have only to say the words."

"What words would that be?"

His hand cupped her chin, lifting her face. "I want you, but not if you are frightened or uncomfortable."

"I made an agreement," she said at last. "I told you I always honor my agreements."

Garret's desperate need for her was reflected in his eyes and in the huskiness of his voice. "I can't think of anyone except you at this moment. For years you have lingered at the edge of my mind, but I was afraid to open that door and let you in until today when you really became mine."

"You're scaring me when you talk like that."

Lauren reminded him of a frightened filly about to bolt. Holding her at arm's length, he said, "Dammit, Lauren, don't be afraid of me! I'm not going to attack you."

"I know. It's . . . me I'm really afraid of."

"You're trembling," he said with concern. He

251

took her hand and led her toward the bed, wondering if she was afraid of what he might do to her. "Get under the covers, and we'll just talk for a while."

Obediently she slid under the covers, and he pulled them up to her neck.

"Are you comfortable?"

She kept her arms clamped across her chest. "How can I be?"

Garret sat down on the other side of the bed and turned the oil lamp low. "What would you like to talk about?"

"I don't know. This has been the strangest day of my life."

He removed his boots and sat back against the headboard. "Let's talk about that."

"You met Chase," she said, averting her eyes. She was willing to talk about anything that would take her mind off the way she was feeling. She raised her eyes to his. "He's my half-brother."

"Yes, I know about him. Your father told me. And then today you went to him like a mother protecting her young. That was a kindness, Lauren."

"I suppose Chase is being manipulated by my father the same as the rest of us."

"In what way?"

"I don't know. It was a shock for me to find that I had a brother I didn't know about. Today Chase seemed somehow lonely, and I wanted to let him know that he has family, and he's not alone."

"I saw something you might have missed. When you asked him to stand with you and Tanner, he was very touched. His wife, Faith, was crying."

Suddenly Lauren's expression grew stubborn. "Chase may be an object of gossip because of his heritage and because his mother was never married to my father. But be warned that I intend to stand by him. I haven't asked anything of you yet, but I ask this. Stand with me for Chase's sake."

"I'll be at your side, in this and in every difficulty throughout our life together, Lauren. I want you to know that."

She plucked at the lace that fell across her wrist, wanting to be in his arms and experience the comfort he spoke of. "Thank you."

He casually began unbuttoning his shirt. "Try not to worry about Chase. People will always need something to talk about."

She nodded. "We certainly provided grist for the mill by getting married so quickly. I imagine some of the women in town will be counting on their fingers to see if I'm going to have a child in less than nine months."

"Let them talk." He leaned back and watched her. "What else is bothering you?"

"My father and Clare." She scooted up to a sitting position and leaned back against the headboard. "I should never have come home. I almost didn't. Pity."

Garret took her hand and raised it to his lips. "I'm glad you did."

Her hand tingled where he had kissed it. "If you hadn't married me, you might have come across a woman who could bring you a river rather than a mere creek."

His amused laughter took her by surprise. "Sometimes, like now, I can still see that adorable, saucy little redhead in you."

Garret pulled her closer and slid his arm around her shoulders, pushing her hair away from her face. For a moment, he stared into the same blue eyes that had haunted him for so long. Only now she was in his bed and *almost* in his arms.

"Sweet little redhead," Garret whispered, and he pressed his cheek to hers. "You smell so good. What is that scent you're wearing?"

Her voice became choked. "It's a fragrance my aunt brought back from France." She wet her lips. "At the moment, I can't remember the name of it."

At the moment, she could not even remember her own name.

Thunder rolled and lightning flashed, and it seemed to Lauren that Garret drew strength from the storm. The ground shook while lightning restlessly unleashed its fury. In the pulsating, jagged light she could see the electricity in his eyes.

Garret gravitated toward her, catching her about the waist and bringing her fully across his body so she was sitting on his lap.

Lauren felt the hardness of his muscles and knew she should move away, but she didn't want to.

Her heart was beating—beating—beating.

Slashes of heat worked their way up her body, and she trembled with anticipation as he kissed her temple, her eyelids; then his mouth lingered near her lips.

Garret was her whole life; this moment was something she had dreamed about forever. She would give him anything he wanted, because to deny him would be to deny her own heart.

His intake of breath became a groan. "I want you. More than I've ever wanted anything in my life."

His mouth took hers, plundering it. She felt a surge of emotion as his tongue touched hers.

Garret tasted like brandy, heady and male. She was only vaguely aware that he was removing her nightgown. Suddenly she felt his hands on her bare flesh.

She cried out, twisting furiously when he dipped his head and kissed her breasts. What was he doing? *Oh, please do not stop*, she thought feverishly. An empty ache started deep inside her, a hollowness that needed to be filled by him.

A sudden gust of wind blew the door open and the lamp flickered out, but Garret and Lauren did not notice.

Lauren did not know when he had removed his

trousers, but she knew the moment his naked flesh touched hers. He took her hand and laid it against his chest. "Feel my heart beating, Lauren. Feel what you're doing to me. You are my wife and I want you, but I can still stop if you want me to."

His heartbeat was strong and steady. Without thinking about what she was doing, she moved her fingertips across his soft chest hair. She looked into his fathomless eyes, incapable of speaking.

"If I kiss you again, I can't promise to stop." He was trembling from the restraint he was keeping on himself, and he groaned when he said, "Do you want me to stop?"

For her answer, Lauren slid her body up his, touching her tongue to her lips, then dipping to kiss him.

At the touch of her lips on his, Garret turned her onto the mattress, then paused to control his passion. She was in his heart and in his brain, and soon, he would have all of her.

Lauren knew that after tonight she would be changed forever. Her wants had become deeper, the craving of her body stronger, her need for his touch unbearably sweet. Nothing else mattered.

Garret's lips brushed the outline of her collarbone while his hands made a leisurely exploration of her body. He kissed her softly, then touched, caressed, and kissed her until she had no thought beyond what he was doing to her.

To be touched by Garret, to have him desire her,

was all Lauren had ever wanted. But in the back of her mind the voice of reason, and her silly pride, told her that she would regret this when the sun came up.

He kissed her—long, drugging kisses that left her longing for more. When his hand lowered to brush against her hip, then lightly touched her inner thigh, she sighed breathlessly—just the reaction he wanted.

His mouth took an erotic journey across her breasts and down her stomach. Lauren bit her lip to keep from crying out. Her fingertips dug into his back, and she quivered with erotic delight.

Garret wedged his knee between Lauren's legs and slowly sank down to her. She felt the swell of him, and her eyes widened as she panicked. His size and the overwhelming force she felt in him took her by surprise.

He did not take her right away as she expected him to. His hand slid into the heat of her, and she bit her lip and threw her head back. Gently he caressed her, causing an ache that almost pushed her to the brink.

Lauren tossed her head from side to side as his experienced hands worked their magic. A whimper was torn from her throat. "Please, Garret." She wanted him, she needed him. "I want you to . . . please."

He lowered himself into position and slid into her moist tightness.

Lauren was startled by the sheer maleness of him. He filled the emptiness she had felt earlier.

With great care not to hurt her, he carefully slid deeper, his movements slow and sensuous, bringing pleasure in a pounding rush.

"No, sweetheart, don't move . . . not yet. I don't want to rush this."

Garret wanted her first time to be pleasurable and painless, but it was difficult for him to control his building need.

He kissed Lauren and quietly instructed her on what he was doing, since this was her first time. "I am not going to go all the way inside you, because I don't want to hurt you any more than I have to." With a quick jab, he broke through the barrier, smothering her protest with a burning kiss.

She sobbed and twisted because of the intrusion into her body; then she cried out, wanting more of him as wave after wave of pleasure rolled through her. Shock, pleasure, and strong need battled inside her. Lauren arched her hips, wanting to take more of him into her emptiness. She clawed at his back and touched her lips to his, swallowing his low groan.

Garret was on the brink of madness, wanting to give her all of him, but he knew better. He slowed his movements, and almost lost his reason when he felt her climax, not once but twice.

He had been right, he thought as his lashes

swept over his eyes. They were perfect for each other.

Lauren's body trembled and shook, and she cried from the beauty and power of what had Garret had done to her.

She buried her face in the curve of his shoulder, her fingers digging into his flesh. Beads of moisture formed on his skin, and she slid her hand up his back.

She thought their lovemaking was over, and she gloried in how alive she felt. She had never known it was possible to feel so utterly close to another person. She had become a part of him, and he was hers, at least for that moment.

But it was not over.

Now that Garret had satisfied her, he sought his own pleasure. Taking care not to let his raw passion take over his reasoning, he gentled his steady thrusts. The rush of his powerful release took him by surprise and stole his breath. His whole body exploded with a feeling so strong that he harshly called Lauren's name.

He rolled to his side and drew her into his arms, stunned by what had just happened to him. He had been with women, but nothing had prepared him for the raw, savage pleasure he had found with Lauren. His climax had left him trembling and wanting more of her. With Lauren he had found so much more than he'd ever thought possible. Lauren was his perfect mate, his other half.

Lauren was treading new ground and experiencing new and powerful emotions. Her heart was filled with love for the man who had just taken her body on a journey of passionate delight. She touched her lips to his neck and closed her eyes, loving him so much it hurt.

He pushed her hair back from her face and whispered, "Sweetheart, are you all right?"

"I . . . yes."

His arms tightened about her. He was unable to utter the love words that begged to be spoken. She would not believe him anyway—not yet. "I won't make love to you any more tonight, Lauren. You were a virgin before I took you, and I don't want you to be sore."

"I don't understand what you mean."

Garret's hand slid between her legs, and she could feel his hot breath on her cheek. "I stretched you here."

His neck muscles corded as he removed his hand, ignoring his painful erection and the strong urge to drive into that softness again, to lose himself in the same wonderment that had overtaken him moments ago. "You should try to get some rest," he whispered in a husky voice, taking several deep breaths to steady his building desire.

Lauren swallowed her disappointment and turned away from him. She wanted him to make love to her again. She wanted to spend the rest of her life in his arms. "Good night," she muttered.

Garret bent over and kissed her cheek. "Good night, Mrs. Lassiter."

Lauren did not think she could sleep, but the day had been long and tiring, and she fell asleep almost as soon as she closed her eyes.

Garret eased himself out of bed and slipped into his trousers. He moved to the chair and sat down so he could watch Lauren sleep. He buried his head in his hands, wondering how he would ever win her love and trust. He had loved her before tonight, but now she was everything to him.

Standing up, he walked out onto the balcony, leaning against the banister, staring blankly into the night. The storm had moved away, and moonlight had broken through the clouds.

He turned back to watch Lauren. Her brilliant hair fanned out on her pillow; she looked so beautiful in sleep.

He wanted to go to her, take her in his arms and make love to her again. He knew that if he woke her she would accept his kisses. But he put a leash on his own desires.

He had to take it slow with her, no matter how hard it was to deny his own needs.

Chapter Nineteen

It was barely sunup as Tanner plunged the pitchfork into the hay and tossed it over the fence to the horses. Removing his gloves, he slapped them against his thigh to remove the hay and then stepped outside to watch the sunrise.

His jaw clamped in anger when he saw Clare hurrying toward him.

"Dammit," he muttered, wondering if he could reach his horse, which was tied at the corral, before Clare reached him.

"Tanner, it's urgent!" Clare gasped pausing to catch her breath. "It's very urgent that I talk to you!"

There was irritation in his tone. "Everything's urgent with you. I don't have time for your little games today. Jeb and the others are waiting for me." He squared his hat on his head. "Good day, Clare."

Tanner untied his horse and swung into the saddle.

"Wait," Clare exclaimed, placing her hand on his thigh. "This is about Lauren and why she married Garret."

He had no time for Clare's nonsense. "We all know that my sister has always loved Garret. There's no secret about that. Why else do you think she married him?"

"Have you noticed how friendly your pa's been to Garret for the last few months?"

Tanner had thought that was strange himself, but he would not admit it to Clare. "So?"

"The marriage was all a scheme cooked up between your pa and Garret."

There was disgust in Tanner's tone when he said, "You'll stop at nothing, will you, Clare?"

"I'm telling you, your pa made a bargain with Garret to get him to marry Lauren."

Tanner was really getting impatient now. "I don't believe you."

"Then go ask your pa if you don't believe me."

"Ask him what?"

"Ask him why he offered Garret Lassiter Cedar Creek if he'd marry Lauren. Ask him why he gave away land that belonged to the Circle M." Clare's voice rose hysterically. "Just ask him!"

Tanner slowly dismounted. Clare would lie and cheat to get what she wanted, but she would not lie about something that could be so easily substantiated. "Why would Pa do that?"

"You ask him yourself. I tried to get in to see him last night, and then again this morning, but that damned Tiny wouldn't let me past the door. Me, his wife! You can't imagine the indignities I suffer with this family."

Tanner walked toward the house, his footsteps hurried. "He'll see me."

When Tanner reached his pa's bedroom, he did not bother to knock but just shoved the door open. He walked slowly toward the bed, anger curling through him. "Pa, what have you done to Lauren?"

Tom weakly raised his head and stared at his son's tightly clamped jaw and angry eyes. He had always known this moment would come—he just had not expected it to be so soon. "So Lauren told you, after she said she wouldn't."

"Lauren told me nothing, although I wish she had. Clare's the one who told me. And if you've done what Clare says, you'll regret it, Pa. Is it true?"

"Is what true?"

"Don't bait me, Pa."

"Tanner, I don't want to talk about this with you. I'm a sick man. You know I'm not supposed to get upset."

Tanner stood over his pa, determined to get the truth from him. "That just won't work with me. You seem to be well enough to run everyone's life from this bed." He pulled up a chair and sat down. "I'm not leaving this room 'til you tell me what you did to my sister."

"I'll have Tiny throw you out."

"It'll take a hell of a lot more than him to throw me out. So talk!"

Lauren awoke and stretched her arms over her head, then blinked in astonishment. It took her a moment to realize where she was. A quick glance about the room told her that Garret was not there.

She shoved the covers aside and groaned because she ached from Garret's lovemaking. When she remembered the night before, she smiled to herself.

It had been wonderful!

Lauren blushed when she remembered how wildly she had begged for and accepted everything Garret had done to her. So this was what marriage was like. She could not wait until the next time. She frowned, wondering when that would be.

There was a light knock on the door.

"Come in."

Mrs. Shaughnessy entered the room. "I just wanted you to know that your bath will be set up in the dressing room for you. Are you ready for it now?"

Lauren smiled at the housekeeper as she pulled on her heavy blue robe and belted it at the waist. "Yes, please."

Mrs. Shaughnessy directed three servants into the dressing room, where they quickly set up a copper bathtub and filled it with water.

On her way out the door, Mrs. Shaughnessy paused. "Master Garret has asked if you'd like to have breakfast on the balcony this morning."

Lauren was sure she would blush when she saw Garret. Over breakfast was as good a time as any to face him. "Yes, that would be lovely."

Garret randomly paced the floor and then sat on a chair, waiting for Lauren to come out of the dressing room. He was sure she would feel shy with him this morning, and he wanted to make it easy for her. He heard the door open and watched her emerge, her hair swept upward and knotted at the back of her head. She was wearing a pink candy-stripe gown.

"Good morning," he said, drinking in her beauty. She seemed cold and distant, not at all like the hot-blooded woman he had held in his arms the night before.

She met his eyes, determined not to blush. "You were up early." She refused to give in to her shyness.

Garret accompanied her to the balcony, pretending not to notice her blush. He pulled out a chair for her at the small round table. "I have a mare about to foal, and I'm worried about her because she's skittish. I had to calm her down a bit."

Lauren felt Garret's warm hand on her shoulder and closed her eyes. Just his touch made her wild with yearning. "What have you done for the mare?"

He moved to the other side of the table and sat. He was purposely keeping the conversation light. "I talked to her. She seems to be soothed by a gentle voice."

Lauren did not feel soothed by his voice—every move he made caused her awareness of him to increase. To distract herself, she gazed over the balcony and stood up abruptly. This view was to the rear of the house, and she was stunned by the beauty of the landscape. The land was terraced with intermingled flowers and fountains and trees. Huge cottonwood trees shaded an area where there were stone benches and cushioned chairs.

She walked to the railing. "This is so lovely! It reminds me of my aunt's garden in Savannah. Of course, this one is much larger. I never expected anything like this in Texas."

"My mother spent most of her days tending the garden. She had it designed to resemble the garden of her girlhood home, which was destroyed in the war."

"Did the Yankees burn it?"

"Yes . . . which turned out fine for me, because we moved to Texas."

Lauren dropped back into the chair. "Well, it's magnificent."

He smiled softly. "I'm glad you like it. Do you enjoy gardening?"

Lauren met his gaze. "No. You need to know this about me—I don't garden, I don't sew, and I can't do watercolors. I was taught to play the piano, which I do very well, but I sing *very* little."

He chuckled. "I see you have been instructed in everything a well-brought-up young lady should know."

"And I'm not good at most of it."

He was sure she was underestimating her talents. Garret could imagine her aunt in Savannah trying to tame the wildness in Lauren. The aunt must have used a light and loving hand, because Lauren was just as spirited as ever. "Are you hungry?"

Remembering her manners, she lifted the silver coffee urn and poured him a cup of coffee, then one for herself. "I'm starved." Her hand paused over the silver creamer. "How do you take your coffee?"

"Just the way it is."

She added cream to her own cup.

His hand dropped to hers, and she gasped as if she had been burned.

"What would you like to do today?"

Lauren knew what she wanted to do—she wanted to go back to bed with him. She was ashamed of her improper thoughts—making love in the daytime was unheard of. She quickly said, "I would like to ride."

Now Garret served her. He placed mixed fruit and a fluffy omelet on her plate. There were light scones and several kinds of melons, reminding Lauren of the wonderful breakfasts she had eaten while living with her Aunt Eugenia.

"Garret," she said, stabbing a slice of melon. "I've been meaning to ask you for some time now. How did San Reanido get its name? There is certainly nothing Spanish about the ranch."

"That was the name of the ranch when my father bought it. He and my mother decided to keep it that way. It's probably a good thing they did. You Texans would still call it San Reanido even if they had changed the name."

"Is that so?" She gave him a half smile. "If you are to be believed, we Texans are a stubborn lot."

"That's been my experience."

"So your parents kept the Spanish name to appease us Texans."

"Probably. We'll have to ask my father. My mother told me that when they first bought the land, there was a small crumbling Spanish-style house here. My father had it torn down and built the present house in its place." He studied her face for a long moment. "The Lassiters have never been accepted as true Texans, you know."

She knew her father had not accepted them, but she had not realized that others had felt the same way. "Why do you suppose that is?"

"Because you Texans guard your heritage all too well. You think of the people who came here after the war as interlopers. Although I was only three years old at the time, and have never known any other home, I'm considered an outsider."

Her eyes took on a playful gleam. "You have overcome the stigma by marrying a natural-born Texan, third generation."

"Is that so?" He smiled.

Lauren took on a serious pose, although her eyes were sparkling with humor. "There are only two ways you can become a true Texan—marry one or raise several generations on Texan soil."

He tilted his head back and laughed heartily. "I have already done the first in marrying you, my little Texan." His voice deepened. "And I'll try my damnedest to accomplish the second."

Lauren picked up her spoon and stirred her coffee, unwilling to meet Garret's eyes. To have his baby would be the most wonderful thing in the world.

Garret could feel her uneasiness, so he decided to speak of other matters. "That's a mighty pretty frock, but I fear it's not suitable for riding."

She looked into his eyes, remembering how they

had glowed with passion the night before. She unfolded her napkin and placed it on her lap. "You know I don't ride sidesaddle."

He grinned. "Yes, I know."

"What you accepted in me when I was only your neighbor, you might not accept in me as your wife."

"Lauren, I have no objections to your riding astride. I have no intention of changing you. I like you as you are."

She had expected him to object, because every time she'd seen his mother on a horse, she had been riding sidesaddle. When he gave in so easily, it left her with nothing to argue about.

Lauren thought breakfast would never end. Every time she glanced at Garret he was watching her, and she blushed. She knew that he was remembering the night before, and so was she. She stared at his long, lean fingers and remembered him touching her, and she wanted him to touch her again.

At last Garret took a final drink of his coffee and stood. "I'll be in the stable. When you're ready to ride, come on down." He paused at the door and looked back at her. "Shaughnessy wants to show you the house. But that can wait until this afternoon, or even tomorrow if you'd wish."

"I'll decide later."

Garret nodded and stepped into the hallway. He leaned against the wall, closing his eyes and taking a deep breath. It had been difficult to sit at the table making polite conversation when what he really wanted to do was strip Lauren naked and kiss every inch of her beautiful body. He wanted to unhook her gown and slide it from her body so he could feast his eyes on her. He wanted to undo her hair and let it swirl down her back.

He wanted to make love to her *now*.

Garret turned back to the door and placed his hand on the knob, thinking he would confess everything to her.

He stopped himself.

No, not yet.

Garret walked down the hallway and then downstairs, his heart heavy with guilt. He had Lauren, but she did not belong to him. Perhaps she never really would.

Lauren was surrounded by beauty. The birds were singing sweetly, and the rain had left a fresh clean smell, but she was aware of none of it.

She was miserable.

Garret had made no mention of their wedding night. He had acted as if they were just casual friends, as if the night before had meant nothing to him. They had spoken about the garden about his mare that was about to foal, about riding, but not a word had been said about the wonderful moments they had shared in bed.

272

With a heavy sigh, she stood up and went inside to change into her riding skirt.

Lauren bent low over the black stallion that reminded her so much of her father's horse, Raja. This horse had the same powerful muscles and long gait. She had been running him full-out since they had ridden away from the stable, and the magnificent animal was not even breathing hard.

She pulled back on the reins and laughed at Garret. "He's wonderful!"

Garret halted beside her. "He's yours. I tried to think of what to give you for a wedding present, and I remembered how much you love good horseflesh." He would not tell Lauren of the long hours he had spent training the horse, even before she had returned to Texas, so he would be just right for her.

"He has exceptional bloodlines and more intelligence than any horse I've ever seen. He took to you right away. He seems to know he belongs to you."

"He's mine!" Her eyes sparkled with happiness, for she was always happy when she was on a fine horse. "What's his name?"

Garret's lips curved into a grin. "Sultan."

"Sultan. I like that. I was just thinking of how much he reminds me of Raja."

"Despite his power, Sultan is very gentle, whereas Raja was a rogue and a killer."

Lauren laid her face against the long, sleek neck. "I love him. Thank you so much."

Garret envied the horse Lauren's affection. He tore his gaze away from her and stared at the sky, where high scattered clouds did little to offer shade.

"Is there any reason he's not a gelding?" she asked.

"I thought you might want to use him as a breeder sometime, because of his impressive bloodlines and his temperament."

She laughed when Sultan playfully pulled on the reins. "He still wants to run."

"Then let him run."

Lauren felt her burdens lighten and her spirits rise as she raced through the tall prairie grass that seemed to have turned green overnight, Garret's white Arabian running neck-and-neck with Sultan.

Shaughnessy was showing Lauren the house and Garret was working in his study, a ledger in front of him, when someone knocked on his door.

"Enter."

He was surprised to see Tanner and immediately assumed that Lauren's father was worse. "How is your father?"

Tanner glared at Garret. "I just had a very interesting conversation with him. You can imagine what we talked about."

Garret had not expected the truth to come out so soon, not before he explained to Lauren the reasons he'd accepted her father's offer. "And that would be?"

"I think you know."

Garret stood, bringing him eye-to-eye with Tanner. "I can guess."

"Let me save us both some time." Tanner's voice was like cold steel. "Pa told me how this marriage came about. I've come to take my sister back home. I'm damn sure not going to let her sacrifice herself for me and my brothers."

"Tanner, I—"

"I'm not through talking," Tanner said, anger burning inside him. "That damned creek isn't worth much, and it sure isn't worth one hair on my sister's head."

"I agree with you."

"Then what's this all about?"

"It's very simple. I love your sister. . . . I always have. I've never wanted anyone but her for my wife."

"Have you, dammit? Your actions sure as hell aren't those of a man in love."

"As you say, that creek isn't worth one hair on Lauren's head. Tanner, do you really think I would marry your sister to gain that damned creek property that's already cost me more than it'll ever be worth?"

Tanner had known that the Lassiters had money

but he had not realized how much until he rode onto the ranch and saw the overwhelming evidence of it. "Then why did you fall in with Pa's plans? Why did you force Lauren to marry you?"

"For all I knew, if I hadn't taken your father's offer, he might well have made the same offer to some other man. You and I both know that Lauren would do anything for you and Stone. She proved that by marrying me, and she would have done the same, no matter who your father had chosen for her husband."

"Yeah, she would have," Tanner conceded, lowering his tall frame into a chair. "And you're right about Pa. He might have offered Lauren to some other bastard if it suited his purpose. But I don't understand his thinking."

"Neither did I."

Tanner gazed hard at Garret. "I'll still take my sister home, if she wants to go."

Garret's jaw tightened. "She's my wife, and you're not taking her anywhere. If Lauren wants to leave me, that will be for her to say. But she's not leaving here with you today."

There was a light tap on the door. Garret crossed the room to open it. "Unless I'm mistaken, that will be Lauren."

Lauren moved past her husband to her brother. "I was told that you were here." Her face whitened. "It's Papa, isn't it? He's worse, isn't he?"

"No. Pa's the same," Tanner assured her. "I've come to take you home."

Lauren looked from her brother to her husband. "I don't understand. If Papa's not worse—"

"You don't have to pretend anymore, Lauren. I know why you married Garret."

"But how did you find out?"

"Clare told me, and then I made Pa admit everything."

Lauren could imagine Tanner forcing their father to tell him the truth. But his knowing the reason for her marriage did not change anything. "I didn't want you to find out."

"Like I said before," Tanner told her, taking her hand in a strong grip, "I've came to take you home."

Lauren looked at Garret and could tell by his expression that he was waiting for her to make a decision.

Garret took a step toward her. "I'm asking you to stay with me, Lauren."

She did not even have to think before she said, "I'm not going back there, Tanner. Garret is my husband."

Tanner let out an angry hiss. "You don't have to do this. I don't want you to sacrifice yourself for me. Stone and Chase wouldn't either."

Lauren slid her hand from her brother's grasp and walked to stand at Garret's side. "This isn't about you or Stone or Chase anymore, Tanner. I made a commitment before God, and I intend to honor my wedding vows."

Garret turned her to face him, his expression unreadable. "Even though I want you with me, Lauren, if you want to go, I will release you from our wedding vows."

Lauren remembered the hours he had made love to her, the time he had spent talking softly to her. Even now she could be carrying his child—it was possible. "I will not break my vow."

She went to Tanner, hoping she could make him understand. "I don't want you to be concerned about me." She took his big hand in hers. "I'm where I want to be, and I'm not leaving."

Tanner eyed Garret suspiciously, thinking Lauren might tell a different story if he got her away from Garret. "Walk me to my horse," he said.

Garret moved to his desk and sat down. Lauren looked into his eyes, wanting to reassure him. "I'll be right back," she told him.

Garret rested his elbows on the shiny surface of the desk and tapped his fingertips together. "I will be waiting for you." He turned his attention to Tanner. "You are welcome anytime. We would like to have you and Callie as our guests."

After Tanner had ushered Lauren out of the room, Garret walked to the window and leaned over, his hands braced against the molding while his stomach tightened with pain. He closed his eyes for a moment and swallowed hard. He had been so afraid that Lauren was going to leave him, but he thanked God that she had agreed to stay.

Once outside, Tanner's hand dropped heavily on Lauren's shoulder. "You can speak freely now. Just say the word, and I'll take you away from here."

Lauren turned to her brother, wishing he had not discovered the details of her marriage. "You don't understand. I love Garret, and I want to be with him. This is my home now."

"You can still love him after he plotted with Pa to marry you?"

"You, of all people, know that I have always loved him. That hasn't changed."

"Then you are happy?"

"I hope to be. I said I loved him—I didn't say he loved me."

Tanner opened his mouth to speak, then clamped it in a hard line, shaking his head in confusion. Something was not right here. Garret had said much the same thing to him moments ago. Tanner had a sudden realization: Lauren was going to be all right with Garret. Even if Lauren was his sister, it was not his place to tell her how her husband felt about her. "I'll leave the two of you to straighten this out between you." He mounted his horse and looked down at her. "If I were you, I'd have a serious talk with Garret. Maybe ask him how he feels about you."

Lauren merely nodded and watched her brother ride away, wishing Clare had not found out about the conditions of her marriage.

Slowly Lauren moved up the steps and entered the house. It was a lovely home, artfully decorated and large enough for children to live, grow, and flourish in. Her eyes softened when she thought of having Garret's baby. Any children she had would never have to endure what she and her brothers had gone through with their father—she would see to that.

Garret was waiting for her when she came through the door of his study.

"Are you all right?" he asked with concern.

"Yes." She dropped into a chair and leaned her head back. "I should have known this would happen. Clare will always be my torment. She's always sneaking around making trouble whenever and wherever she can. I just hope Tanner hasn't been hurt by this."

"What about you, Lauren? Are you hurt by this?"

"Only inasmuch as it involves the people I love."

"Yes," he said hoarsely. "The people you love."

He stared at her, remembering the way she had felt in his arms, how eagerly she had welcomed his lovemaking. He glanced at the tight bodice of her gown and remembered the silkiness of her breasts. He was glad he was sitting behind the desk so she would not see how his body was reacting to her.

Lauren met Garret's gaze, and she knew that he was remembering their night of lovemaking. She lowered her head and blushed, feeling her insides twist.

Garret's dark eyes clouded, and Lauren watched him stand, as if dismissing her.

"Thank you for choosing to stay with me. You didn't have to."

She sighed and swallowed. "You're my husband. I made a vow to honor you."

He looked straight into her eyes. "And to love me."

"Some vows are only words."

Garret dropped back into his chair and started thumbing through the papers on his desk. "Yes . . . they are."

Chapter Twenty

Lauren was propped up in bed, writing letters to her aunt and cousins. Signing her name, she placed the last letter on the bedside table and turned down the oil lamp. Sliding down on the pillow, she watched silver moonlight pour through the open French doors that led to the balcony.

It was useless for her to try not to think about Garret, because he was all she thought about. He had been so reserved during dinner and had excused himself shortly afterwards to see to the mare that was about to foal.

Lauren turned from her back to her stomach, wishing she could fall asleep, but just thinking about Garret touching her, holding her, making love to her brought all her senses alive; the blood pumping through her body made her feel more awake than ever. She reached out and touched his pillow, wishing he were there.

Restlessly she turned on her side and closed her eyes, not wanting to seem as if she were waiting for Garret when he finally came in—even though she was.

The door opened, and Lauren squeezed her eyes tighter. She heard Garret move about the room, undressing. She felt the mattress shift when he lay down, and her breath became trapped in her throat.

He laid his face against her silken cheek. "Are you asleep, Lauren?"

He had only touched her, and she was falling apart inside. She turned to him. "I'm awake. How is the mare?"

"For a while it looked like she was going to foal tonight, but she finally settled down. It would be better if she were to wait another week or two. Charley is going to sleep in the stable tonight to make sure she's all right."

"Nothing can be done if the foal is ready to be born."

"Unfortunately, you're right. I've decided that if there's no progress by tomorrow, I'll ride to Sidewinder to fetch the veterinarian." He drew in a worried breath. "It's just that this particular mare is so skittish. The only way to settle her down is to talk to her."

Lauren knew how the mare felt—she was a little skittish herself, especially when Garret looked at her the way he was looking at her now.

Garret slid his hand up and down her arm, then applied just the slightest pressure, bringing her closer to him. "I could hardly think about what I was doing, knowing that you were here in my bed." His voice quivered. "I could have lost you today. I thought I had when Tanner came."

She swallowed a lump but could think of nothing to say, because pure lust was surging through her like quicksilver.

Garret was massaging her shoulder as his gaze went to her bedside table. "I see you have been writing letters."

His wonderful hands were working magic on her body just as they had the night before. "Yes. I wrote three."

He brushed her hair back. "I want to thank you again for standing with me when Tanner was here today."

"I already told you why I stayed." Of course, she had not told him she could not bear the thought of being away from him, that she ached for him to touch her, to kiss her.

"Did you know I wanted to kiss you today when you were on that damned horse with your hair flying out around you? I wanted to kiss you when you sat across from me at dinner tonight?"

Garret watched her eyes flame, and desire

ripped through him. He could read surrender in those blue eyes, and his mouth sought hers. He held her so tenderly and kissed her so sweetly at first. Then his mouth became hard, seeking, demanding.

In a swift movement that took Lauren by surprise, Garret pulled her nightgown up past her hips, lifting it over her head. His gaze moved over her beautiful body, the long, shapely legs, the flat stomach, the soft curves.

As he appraised her body, Lauren felt the empty ache start deep inside her. "Do I please you?" She had not meant to ask him such a question—it just slipped out.

"Please me? I can't stop thinking about how much I want to be with you." His hand moved to her softness, and he slowly massaged her, making her stiffen at first. But before long her head fell weakly against his chest. He removed his hand and clasped her chin, looking deep into her eyes. "You are exciting and unpredictable. Do you please me? I've never been so pleased in all my life."

Garret brought her closer to him so he would have unhampered access to her breast . . . she gave him free rein.

Lauren melted inside when Garret dipped his head and took a nipple in his mouth. A gasp escaped her lips when he brought her against him and she found that he was naked, too. His hair was damp, and she realized he must have bathed before he came upstairs.

"Say you missed me," he urged.

She had been afraid that he would be tired of her after only one night. But she could definitely feel the swell of him. He had not tired of her yet. "I . . . did not . . ."

"I know, I know how you feel." He pressed his face against her breasts. He trailed his hand down her stomach and rested it against her thigh. "For now, I'll settle for the knowledge that you want me as much as I want you."

He kissed her as if he were branding her his own. "Little redhead, I love the way you come alive in my arms."

"Yes," she whimpered.

His hand moved back to her thighs, and he slowly opened them. "Are you sore there, sweetheart?"

"No."

"You would have been if I hadn't stopped myself last night. You set me on fire." His voice deepened and trembled. "I want to be inside you, Lauren."

She took a quivering breath. "Is marriage supposed to be like this?"

He pulled back and frowned. "Like what?"

"The feelings—the . . . pleasure."

Garret grinned. "How can I know? I've never been married before." His hand was spread across her stomach. "I believe that my father had a similar feeling for my mother. I often observed a look or a touch that passed between them. I believe they were passionate about each other."

"It must have been comforting growing up and knowing that your parents loved each other. My aunt and uncle have that kind of marriage."

"And you want that for yourself?"

She shook her head. "It's not a question of love. What we have is something else."

Her words caused him pain, and he struck back. "Let's give it a name, Lauren. Let's call it lust. I lust after you so damned bad, I want to stay in you all the time."

"Yes, that's what it is." She turned her gaze away from him. "But it's a powerful emotion. I've never felt it with anyone except you."

He grabbed her chin and forced her to look at him. "Are you sure? Do you mean it?"

"Yes. And you want me that way, too."

He rubbed his chin against her cheek. "Want you—I want you so much. It's tearing me apart inside." His arms went around her, and he held her close. "There's so much more to lovemaking than what we did last night."

"There is?" Her voice held a note of excitement. "Will you show me?"

In that moment, Garret's heart was full. Lauren was honest and open about her reaction to his lovemaking, and desire slammed into his gut like a clenched fist. His mouth settled on hers, and he groaned. Her legs opened for him, and he slid between them, burrowing into her softness.

Lauren raised her hips to meet his thrusts and found even more pleasure. The night was velvet, magic, as he made her body sing to his tune, over and over again.

How could she not love this man who had taken her heart and body?

She wanted to shout to the world that she loved him, but she could not even utter the words to him. Garret had admitted to lust, but he never spoke of love. He mentioned need, want, but his heart was still with the woman he loved, and it probably always would be.

The night shadows grew deeper as Garret held Lauren in his arms. Her back was to him, and his mouth rested against her temple. She felt his breath stirring her hair, and she closed her eyes, never wanting to leave the sanctuary of his arms.

Garret was love to her . . . he was safety . . . he was her life.

"Are you sleepy?" he asked, his hand moving to caress her breast.

Lauren turned to him. "No."

She saw his smile.

Garret was dazzled by her. When his gaze settled on her breasts, he watched the nipples harden and press against her thin nightgown. "Have I told you how much you delight me?" His voice was raspy and edged with leashed passion.

She nodded. "You did mention it in a moment of intimacy."

He moved to her, fitting her perfectly against him. "I would like to stay in bed with you for the rest of my life."

"Highly impractical," she said, smiling.

He touched his mouth to hers and then pulled back to study her eyes. "Lauren, what have you done to me?"

Suddenly she felt playful and bold. She raised her head and gave him a seductive smile as she stretched catlike against him, snuggling closer to his warmth. "I've merely fulfilled my wifely duties. Isn't that what I'm supposed to do?"

His body responded violently to her playfulness. "Kiss me, Lauren," he said with urgency. "Kiss me like you would if you loved me."

She did not understand what he was asking of her, but her mouth found his, and she put all the tenderness and love she felt for him in her kiss.

"I want so much more," he said, his hands clasping her hips and drawing her tighter. "I want all of you." His insides tightened. If she only knew how long he had waited for her. If only he could make her believe how true his heart had been to her.

"I don't know what you want of me."

He took her lips at the same time as he drove

his swollen erection into her. He filled her, and her satin essence sheathed him.

Lauren turned her head as tears seeped out of the corners of her eyes. Love was such torture. It had been easier to endure heartbreak before Garret had awakened her body.

Lauren's body quaked with his, and she collapsed against him, burying her face in his shoulder. He had magnificently taken her to the heights of passion.

She was surprised when he scooped her up in his arms and carried her into the dressing room, immersing her in the copper bathtub. She laughed when he climbed in with her, but stopped giggling when he lathered his hands with soap and began washing her in the most intimate places.

Water swirled around them, and Lauren did not know how she ended up sitting on Garret's lap. He positioned her above him and slowly lowered her while her eyes widened with puzzlement and then closed in pure ecstasy when he buried himself deep inside her.

Lauren grabbed his shoulders while he pounded upward into her. Her head went back because she felt too weak to hold it up.

"Garret," she sobbed. "Don't stop."

"I may not last past the first week," he whispered softly and groaned as he emptied himself into her, then held her as she trembled against him. She had wiggled to move off him, and he was surprised when he swelled again. "I may not last through this night."

When the storm of their passion had passed, Lauren raised her head and caught the soft expression on Garret's face. His dark eyes were so luminous they almost seemed filled with tears. She touched his cheek and found it wet, no doubt from the bath water. She touched her tongue to the wetness and found that it was salty like tears.

Garret scooped her into his arms and wrapped her in a large towel, carrying her to the bed. Neither of them spoke—their bodies did the talking for them.

Lauren lay awake watching Garret sleep. He was beautiful of face and soul. She wondered what he would be like when they had children. She knew that he would be a strong and loving father.

She prayed that Garret had already planted his child in her. She wanted to have his son. Then, perhaps, he would love her a little.

She closed her eyes and sighed. A baby would not make him love her more. Her father had given her mother three babies, and he had never loved her.

Garret rode out early the next morning for Sidewinder. He was still worried about the little mare and had gone for the veterinarian. Lauren was talking to Shaughnessy about rearranging the morning room so that when she sat at the desk the sunlight would be behind her.

A frantic pounding on the door startled both women. The housekeeper rushed forward and opened the door. "Charley, whatever's wrong with you?"

The short, lean man stepped into the entry and removed his hat. "It's the mare. She's delivering her foal, and it's going bad. It's too late to wait for the doctor from town."

Lauren stepped toward Charley, and Mrs. Shaughnessy quickly introduced them. "This is Charley Haskel. He's the foreman."

"Yes, we've met." Lauren recalled that Garret had told her about Charley. Like Shaughnessy, he had worked for the Lassiters back in Virginia and had come to Texas with them.

"How can I be of help, Charley?" Lauren asked quickly.

"The mare—the Arabian that Mr. Lassiter bought last spring—she's about to drop her foal, ma'am. Something's wrong, and the birth ain't going right."

Lauren was already running for the stairs. "Stay with her, and I'll be out as soon as I change."

Moments later, Lauren emerged from the house, wearing her leather riding skirt, the most sensible thing she could think of to put on.

Charley looked at the boss's wife, concern etched in the heavy creases of his face. "I've sent a rider for Mr. Lassiter. But he won't reach him in time, ma'am."

"Where is the mare?"

Charley did not think it would be proper for Mrs. Lassiter to be present at the birth, especially if it went wrong as he was sure it would. But he was certainly not going to tell the boss's wife what to do. He led her to the last stall. "I think her foal's breech. I can turn it, but it'll probably kill the mare. I didn't want to do anything without talking to Mr. Lassiter first."

Lauren bent down and laid her hand against the mare's stomach. She could feel a contraction. "She's certainly in labor. You don't think it's false like yesterday?"

"No, ma'am. It's real, all right."

"It seems she's pretty far into it."

"Yes, ma'am," Charley answered, hunkering down beside her. "In the later stages would be my guess."

"Then she and the foal will die if we don't help her."

Charley nodded. "That's the right of it, ma'am."

She looked into his troubled gray eyes. "Then let's do something!"

Charley hesitated for only a moment, taken aback, and then he nodded. After all, she was a rancher's daughter and knew about such things. "If you'll try and keep her calm, I'll do the rest, Mrs. Lassiter."

Lauren sat down and took the mare's head on her lap. But the frightened animal was in pain and she tried to get to her feet. "What's her name, Charley?"

"Aqaba."

Garret had told her that the mare seemed to calm when he spoke to her in a soft voice. The horse was straining now and giving loud grunts of pain. "Aqaba," Lauren said softly. "It's going to be all right." She eased the horse's head down on her lap and continued to speak. "I know it hurts, but there's life inside you wanting to be born."

The mare reared her head when pain ripped through her, but Lauren managed to calm her enough for Charley to avoid flying hooves and get into position to help. Tears gathered in Lauren's eyes as she watched the beautiful mare struggle with pain. It was a life-and-death fight, and it became important to her that this mare live.

"Save her, Charley. Don't let her die."

He looked doubtful. "I'll try, ma'am." He felt admiration for Mr. Lassiter's wife. He had seen her through the years, of course, on his trips to Sidewinder. And he had often observed Mr. Lassiter's reaction to her. He was not surprised that the two of them should marry so soon after her return to Texas. He had known all along that the boss liked that little gal.

"What in the hell's happening here?" Will Phelps asked, ambling to the back of the stable.

The Agreement

He stopped in his tracks when he saw the boss's wife. "Excuse me, ma'am," he said, snatching his hat off. "I didn't see you there or I wouldn't have said what I did."

"What's your name?" Lauren asked quickly.

"Will, ma'am—I'm Will Phelps."

Lauren softly rubbed the mare's face. "Will, Charley and I need your help."

The wrangler bent down beside the foreman. "Oh, no! The boss ain't gonna like this. It's breech, ain't it?"

Soon several other men joined them, and Lauren enlisted their help as she had Will's.

Estaban stood at the front of the stable, but he did not join the others. He viewed the camaraderie between the *patrón*'s wife and the workers with malicious eyes. Even dressed as she was, Señora Lassiter was a beauty. The *patrón* must love her very much. He listened to her voice as she spoke to the frightened mare. Garret Lassiter would be angry with her for being so familiar with the men. Certainly no respectable Spanish woman would do such a disgraceful thing.

Estaban smiled to himself. It was too soon to strike again at Garret Lassiter, because his father's body had not yet been found. He waited for the day when the *patrón* would grieve for his father, just as he had grieved for his mother.

Then he would strike again.

295

Estaban heard a rider coming and sought the shadows. His time would come, but not yet.

When Garret rode up, he found the stable brightly lit and feared the mare was having trouble. Dismounting, he walked inside, to discover that every lantern in the place had been hung near Aqaba's stall. Unfortunately, the veterinarian had been called away to another ranch, and Garret had come back without him.

Struck by amazement, Garret stared at his wife, sitting on the ground with straw in her hair, rubbing dry a newborn foal. She was surrounded by twelve of his ranch hands, all conversing and laughing as if they had known each other for years.

Will, who was mostly a solitary man, beamed at Lauren. "You surely do have a way with horses, Mrs. Lassiter. You quieted Aqaba down enough so that we could turn the foal and save both of them."

"This little filly's lucky to be alive, Will." She laughed delightedly when the foal tried to stand and fell back on wobbly legs. "Charley, will you hand me another towel? This one's soaked."

Garret stood back and watched his wife charm his men. She had them at her mercy, and he could tell by the looks on their faces that they would do anything for a smile from her.

"What happened here?" he asked, stepping forward.

The men moved away from Lauren and looked at their boss with uncertainty—all except Charley, who did not seem to be intimidated by him.

"Aqaba had her foal," Charley said with the assurance of long acquaintance. "It was breech, but they'll both be fine now."

The other men relaxed when they saw Garret smile and kneel down beside his wife. "Now, is that a fact?" He looked into Lauren's sparkling eyes and pulled a straw from her hair. "A little filly, hmm?"

Lauren stood up and stretched her cramped muscles. "Charley, Will, the rest of you, let's go to the house and see if Mrs. Whit has anything good to eat. I'm starved after this, and I know you all are, too."

The men looked at Garret for confirmation. They had never been invited to the big house to eat.

"What are you waiting for?" Garret asked, grinning. "After you've washed, come on up."

It was a joyous group that sat around the big round kitchen table eating and recounting their experiences with the birth.

"I ain't never seen anything like Mrs. Lassiter calming that mare down!" Will exclaimed, shaking his head. "It was like the mare knew you was a female just like her."

Charley laughed. "Are you calling Mrs. Lassiter a horse?"

Will's face reddened, and he glanced at Lauren to see if she had been offended. "Ma'am, that wasn't my intention."

Lauren laughed delightedly at Will's embarrassment. "You're right, Will. I think Aqaba did sense that we were both female."

Garret sat back and watched the men adore Lauren. Not many women could have won over these hardened cowhands, and even fewer would have got down on the floor and helped a mare foaling.

Lauren was waving her fork in the air. "Did you see the way that filly shot out when Charley turned her?"

"Yeah," George, a confirmed bachelor, joined in. "You should have seen the look on your face, Mrs. Lassiter, when the mare tried to get up and you was trying to hold her down. If me and Manny hadn't leaped for her head, she'd-a dragged you up with her."

They all laughed at that.

Garret's arm rested over the back of Lauren's chair, and he could not resist touching a red-gold curl that rested on her shoulder.

Lauren turned to look into her husband's eyes and gave him an inquiring glance. He had hardly spoken a word since returning home.

He smiled at her, and she saw desire burning in those dark eyes—a promise of the night to come when she would be in his arms.

Chapter Twenty-one

Lauren came out of the dressing room to find Garret standing on the balcony. She went to him with hope in her heart. Everything would be perfect if only—

"What will you name the little filly?" Garret asked without looking at her—he was staring out at the night sky.

"Do you mean I can name her?"

"Of course. You helped save her life and that of her mother, a very rare and high-priced Arabian."

"I'd like to take the credit for saving them, but the credit must go to Charley. With Will's help, he managed to turn the filly and saved them both."

Garret's attention was still on the sky, but she could see his pulse throbbing in his throat. "You won them all over. From this day forward, they will be your willing slaves."

"I liked them very much. Charley doesn't look anything like Jeb, but he reminds me of him in a lot of ways. They have the same gentleness."

"I don't think anyone has ever described Charley as gentle. Most of the hands live in terror of him. He rules this ranch like a king." Garret dropped his gaze to her, and his voice became lower. "I was jealous of every smile you gave them tonight."

Lauren noticed that Garret's mouth curved in a smile, so she did not believe he was really jealous. "I want to name the foal Milagro."

"Hmm—Spanish for miracle."

"She is a miracle." Lauren allowed her gaze to follow Garret's into the heavens. "Did you see Chase when you were in Sidewinder today?"

"No. But I had a meeting with Mr. Hanes."

"The solicitor?"

"Yes."

She did not ask him what the meeting was about, and he did not tell her. "I'm going to ride over to see my father tomorrow. I'll probably be gone most of the day. I want to see Tanner and Callie, too."

"I'll have Charley ride over with you."

"There is no need—"

"Humor me in this. I don't want you to ride about the country alone. It's too dangerous."

"I always have."

"I know that. It's because of your impulsiveness that you need protecting. Next time, I may not be there to shoot a rogue stallion if you get in trouble."

She smiled. "I never should have ridden Raja. I know that now."

He remembered being afraid that the stallion was going to trample Lauren to death. "No, you shouldn't have."

He took her hand and turned her to face him. "You've had a busy day."

"I'm not tired. I could stay awake for hours." She lowered her head so her hair would hide her blush. What must he think of her? She had practically invited him to make love to her.

He raised her chin and laughed warmly. "You are the most extraordinary woman I've ever known."

"In what way?"

"You're not ashamed to show your feelings."

"I'm usually sorry the moment the words have left my mouth," she mumbled, leaning against the railing and propping her chin on her hand. "I just don't think before I speak. It's a great failing of mine."

"Don't ever change, Lauren. Your kind of honesty is rare in a woman. Many women I've known—" Garret knew he had made a mistake the minute her eyes narrowed.

Lauren felt a prickle of jealousy just thinking about all the women he must have known. "So you are telling me you're an authority on women. Well, aren't you a prince!"

He could hardly keep from smiling. "Come here," he said, pulling her into his arms and holding her close. "You are the only woman I care about, and I'm certainly no authority on you. Most of the time you have me completely baffled."

"I don't want you to know all about me."

"Hmm," he said, concentrating more on her mouth than on what she said. He dipped his head and touched his lips to hers. "Today, riding home, I thought about doing this to you." He traced the outline of her nipple through the thin material of her gown. "And this." He lifted her into his arms, carried her inside, and laid her on the bed, going down beside her. He removed her gown and stared at her beautiful body, then pulled her against him. His hand slid down her thigh. "And this."

To Lauren, it had been a magical night. Garret had made love to her twice, and they had both fallen asleep exhausted. In those times when he was holding her and needing her, she could almost imagine that he loved her as much as she loved him. But at times like now, as she watched him sleeping, she knew it was not so.

Garret was holding something back—she could feel it. Oh, who was the woman who held his heart prisoner? She wished she knew, and yet she was afraid to find out.

The soft moonlight touched his naked body, and he was magnificent! He was tall and muscled, with dark hair on his chest that trailed down his stomach. His shoulders were wide, and his face chiseled and handsome. She could not resist the impulse to touch him, so she lightly brushed his ebony hair.

Garret's eyes opened, and he stared at her for a moment. He smiled, taking her hand and raising it to his lips. "You can touch me, Lauren. I'm your husband."

She averted her eyes. "I woke up."

"Sweetheart, don't be embarrassed with me. You have a beautiful body, and I like to touch you and look at you. You can do the same with me."

She said nothing. It hurt too much even to breathe.

He took her hand and placed it on his chest. "Can you feel my heart beating?"

She did.

"It always beats faster when I'm near you. At the moment, it's about to burst out of my chest."

Her hand moved over the curly hair on his chest and down to his stomach. She felt him go taut, and her eyes widened when she saw his erection.

Garret pulled her on top of him and adjusted her in just the right position. She gasped and closed her eyes as he filled her ache.

"Garret, oh, Garret."

It was some time before they both went back to sleep.

Lauren left Charley talking to Jeb and went into the house. She removed her hat and gloves and dropped them on a chair, hoping she would not have to see Clare. No one was about as she climbed the stairs and found Tiny just outside her father's bedroom.

"How is he?"

Tiny nodded and opened the door so she could see for herself. But before Lauren could set one foot in her father's room, Clare came out of her bedroom and walked toward her with a sneer on her lips.

"Well, well, if it isn't the little bride. What's the matter, is married bliss not what you expected? Have you come running home to your pa?"

With dread in her heart, Lauren turned to her stepmother. "Clare, don't you get tired of stirring the pot? I know you tried to start trouble by telling Tanner about the reason for my marriage to Garret. Well, it didn't have the effect you hoped it would."

Clare wore a light green gown, and she looked beautiful, almost angelic if it had not been for the angry twist to her mouth. "I don't know what you're talking about."

"I didn't come here to fight with you."

Clare glared at Lauren with so much hatred that Lauren had to look away.

"Are you satisfied with the property your pa settled on you, or have you come back for more? Do you want to see the Circle M carved up in small portions?"

Lauren met Tiny's eyes, and he nodded toward her father's room. "Clare, I refuse to bandy words with you. I want to see my father."

"Why not? Everyone gets to see him but me. He's even taken to talking in the evenings with Tanner and that milk-face wife of his. But does he want to spend time with his own wife? No!"

Lauren was weary of the conversation. Clare had always been irrational, but she was acting stranger than usual. Lauren moved into her father's bedroom and closed the door in Clare's face. Tiny had remained outside the door, and Lauren could imagine him standing guard.

"I thought I heard your voice, gal."

Tom McBride was propped against his pillow with a stack of papers on his lap. Lauren bent to kiss his cheek. "Are you still running the ranch from your bed?"

He slid the papers into a black leather satchel and quickly shut it, as if he did not want her to see what he had been doing. "Yeah. I'll see to the running of the Circle M as long as I'm able."

"And so you should."

He looked at her carefully. "You aren't still mad at me, are you?"

The fact that he would even ask what her feelings were was new to Lauren. "I'm not happy about what you did, Papa. But I still love you."

He gave her a self-satisfied grin. "I knew you couldn't stay mad at me for long." He ran his hand over the satchel and opened it, withdrawing an official-looking document. "You might as well give this to your husband. It's the deed to Cedar Creek."

Her hand trembled as she took the deed. What she wanted to do was tear it to shreds. She clutched it, shaking her head. "You may have thought you were doing what was best for me, Papa—but that's not the way it is."

"As time passes, you'll see I did right by you."

"Did it ever occur to you to just ask me if I wanted to marry Garret?"

"No," he said with conviction. "It never did. Because I know your nature, and you wouldn't have done it. I didn't have the luxury of time on my side."

She laid her hand on his frail one, noticing that the blue veins seemed more prominent than usual. "I have a reason for being here today." She folded the deed and pushed it into her pocket. "I want to talk to you about my brothers."

"I figured you'd get around to that."

"You promised that if I married Garret they

306

would get their inheritance. And after the wedding, when I asked you, you said you would keep your word. Is that still the way you feel?"

"I only have to give my word once, gal—you know that about me."

"I just needed to hear you say it again."

Tom McBride looked into his daughter's eyes and noticed the sorrow reflected there. "The inheritance I leave to each of you may not be what you expect, but it will be the greatest thing I can give you."

"What is that supposed to mean?"

"I'm tired now. Leave me in peace and go pester someone else." The smile he gave her took the edge off his words.

She stood and kissed his cheek. "I'll be back tomorrow."

"Gal," he said in irritation. "I don't want you running over here every day. You're a wife now—bedevil your husband and leave me be."

Lauren crossed the room. "Rest well, Papa."

When Lauren went downstairs, she was delighted to find Tanner and Callie waiting for her. Lauren had lunch with them, and they chatted for a while. Then Tanner had to ride out to help Jeb.

Lauren stacked the dirty dishes and submerged them in soapy water while Callie picked up the dishtowel.

"Did Tanner tell you about Clare's latest escapade?" Lauren asked, holding up a plate for inspection and then handing it to her sister-in-law.

"No, he didn't. But I know he was upset about something. Do you want to tell me what happened?"

They heard footsteps on the stairs, and Lauren raised her eyebrows at Callie. "That'll be Clare. I'll tell you later."

"Well, well, all the McBride women together," Clare said, moving to the coffee pot on the back of the stove and pouring herself a cup. "How charming to meet this way."

"I'm not a McBride anymore—I'm a Lassiter."

"Oh, that's right," Clare said scathingly. "The bride who was married off for the price of a creek, and cheap at that."

Lauren's face whitened, and she began to tremble. Clare still knew how to drive home a point.

Callie saw the tears that gathered in Lauren's eyes, and she went on the attack. "That's enough, Clare."

But Clare had only begun. "Did sweet little Lauren tell you that she sold her brothers out? Because of her, Cedar Creek is no longer a part of the Circle M."

Callie stepped between Lauren and Clare, her body rigid with anger. "I said that's enough!"

Clare turned her anger on the woman who had married Tanner. "There is already a mistress of this house, and the last time I looked it wasn't you.

No one orders me about in my own house, especially not you!"

Lauren took the dishtowel from Callie and handed it to Clare. "Then you can finish here since you're the mistress. Callie and I are leaving."

"Not so fast," Clare said, throwing the dishtowel down and stomping on it. "Mrs. Tanner McBride, get Lauren to tell you what hooks she used to catch herself a husband."

Callie had to restrain herself from punching Clare in the face. "Anyone who looks like Lauren doesn't have to use anything to get a husband."

"Well, that's not how it happened—ask her. Our little Lauren here got the biggest prize stud in the whole county—a Lassiter. And, she got him by selling out her brothers' birthrights."

Lauren sucked in her breath, hoping Clare would never know just how deeply her accusations were hurting her. She did not even have the heart to meet Clare's probing gaze.

Callie took Lauren's hand and led her to the back door. "We're getting out of here."

Lauren barely made it out the door before tears began to fall. She wanted to bury her face against Garret's shoulder and feel his arms around her. "I'm going home."

"Clare'll be looking out the window," Callie cautioned. "Don't let her see you this way. Laugh, do anything to make her believe her prodding didn't hurt you."

"I don't feel like laughing." Lauren raised her head and walked with Callie toward the barn. "I hope you know it isn't like Clare said."

"Of course I know it. You told me about the agreement between your pa and Garret. From your conversation with Clare, I gather she told Tanner about it, too."

"Yes, and Tanner was angry, but not for the reasons Clare thinks. He's not like that."

"Of course he's not. I knew he'd paid a visit to San Reanido yesterday because he was worried about you. What did Tanner say?"

"He was very angry with Pa and Garret. He wanted to bring me back home."

"That *sounds* like something my husband would do. But why do you stay with Garret now that Tanner knows the truth?"

Lauren led Sultan out of a stall, stopping him outside the barn. "Because I love him, and he's my husband." She dropped her eyes, feeling miserable. "I told you about the other woman Garret loves."

"Lauren, I don't think Garret loves anyone but you. If there was another woman he cared about, he's surely forgotten her by now."

"No. He hasn't forgotten her."

"How can you be so sure?"

Lauren shoved her foot into the stirrup and mounted. "Because he implies things about her."

"What!"

Lauren heard riders approaching and assumed it was Circle M hands returning to the ranch. "Garret didn't say anything outright. But when I ask him about her, he's vague and changes the subject. I think it hurts him to talk about her, especially with me."

Bootsteps crunched on the gravel at the front of the barn, and Lauren looked up to see Garret striding toward her, his steps confident . . . his manner unreadable.

Lauren swung her leg over the horse and dismounted, fighting the urge to run into his arms. She purposely slowed her steps as she approached him. "I didn't expect to see you here."

Callie stepped back into the shadows and watched.

"I had business in Sidewinder, and since I was close by, I thought I'd ride over and we could go home together."

Lauren knew that it was an hour out of Garret's way to come by the Circle M. But she was glad he was there.

Callie carefully watched the exchange between Lauren and Garret, feeling no guilt. She had a very strong suspicion that Garret loved Lauren, and she wanted to see for herself. She watched Garret draw Lauren into his arms. Although Lauren could not see it, Callie watched Garret's eyes close; he swallowed hard, his arms tightening as if he were holding someone very precious to him.

311

There was no doubt in Callie's mind about Garret's feelings for Lauren—they were powerful and deep, and he was definitely in love with her. If there had been another woman in his life, she was nothing to him now, not even a lingering memory.

When Callie stepped forward, Garret loosened his hold on his wife, and it took him a moment to speak. "I'm sorry, I didn't see you there. What are you two lovely ladies doing?"

"Hiding from Clare," Callie answered as her new brother-in-law slid his arm around her shoulder.

"Oh, her."

Callie moved toward her mount. "I have to get home so I can have Tanner's supper ready when he gets there. You can't imagine that man's appetite."

Garret looked down at Lauren and whispered so only she could hear. "Yes, I can, if it's anything like mine."

Neither of them watched Callie ride away, because they were gazing into each other's eyes.

Garret's hand slid around Lauren's waist. "I was lonesome without you."

"I'm ready to go home now."

"You called San Reanido home. It's important to me that you feel that way."

Lauren could not meet his eyes. She loved this man. Wherever he was would be home to her.

"I'll be glad when we fill the house with children," he said, touching the back of her neck and smiling when she sighed.

"I want many children," she agreed.

"How many?"

"I don't know—six—ten." She placed her hand on her abdomen, hoping she had already conceived his child.

Garret let out a teasing breath. "I hope I have the strength to hold out until the deed is done. You are a very passionate woman, Lauren."

She ducked her head, but he was not going to let her off so easily. Placing his hands on both sides of her face, he forced her to meet his gaze while he laughingly kissed her. "I love it when you blush."

"I loathe it when I blush."

His hand moved to her arm and rested there, just touching the side of her breast. "I can't wait to see your belly swell with my seed growing in it."

Lauren hid her face against his neck. Oh, she did love him so!

"I think we'd better leave," he said, walking Lauren to her horse and lifting her onto the saddle. "Or, I'll take you into one of those stalls."

"What about Charley?"

Garret grinned. "Let him get his own woman; he can't have mine."

She let out an impatient breath, not finding anything funny in his humor. "Garret, Charley rode over with me. Shouldn't he ride back with us?"

"No. He can find his own way home."

Lauren suddenly remembered the deed she had placed in her pocket, and it tempered her happy mood. "Papa said to give you this," she said, shoving the deed at Garret and digging her heels into Sultan's flanks.

Garret stared down at the deed to Cedar Creek. "Dammit," he muttered.

After Clare watched Lauren and Garret ride away, she dropped the curtains back in place, her fingers gripping the delicate lace. She had witnessed the scene between the newlyweds. She could feel their need for each other even from a distance, and it tore at her insides. Why should Lauren be happy? What right did she have to inspire desire in someone like Garret Lassiter? He was all male, and Clare could imagine what it would feel like to be the object of his powerful lust.

She wet her lips, wondering what it would feel like to have his mouth on hers. It would not be like Tanner, but it would be good. She turned around, staring at her face in the mirror. She was still young and beautiful and had to suffer the touch of an aged and decaying man. Garret was young and virile and probably kept inside Lauren most of the time. Her body shook and burned with the hunger of desire. It had been so long since she had felt a real man's hands on her body.

Manuelo appeared at her side. He did not like to see Clare unhappy. "Do you want me to do anything about Señora Lauren?" he asked pointedly, his dark eyes questioning.

"She has everything, and I have nothing."

"But, señora—"

She turned to him, feeling completely defeated. "Lauren should thank me. If I hadn't insisted on her going to Savannah, she would never have come home a lady."

Manuelo felt the frustration in his sweet señora. But this time he could not help her.

Chapter Twenty-two

The two high-spirited horses raced abreast through tall buffalo grass that muted their hoof falls. Lauren's stallion did not even break his stride when a covey of quail crossed their path in search of insects. Lauren and Garret galloped through a deep canyon where the pounding of the horses' hooves echoed against the gray flint walls. They rode out of the canyon and along a ridge where the wind kissed their cheeks.

Lauren glanced at her husband. It filled her with joy to be riding beside him; at the moment she had forgotten all about Clare's hateful words and the Cedar Creek deed.

She smiled at Garret and nudged the heels of her boots into her horse's flanks, sending Garret a challenge. "The first one to that cottonwood tree," she called out.

He accepted the challenge and urged his horse forward. "What does the winner get?"

She leaned low over Sultan's neck. "To be winner!"

Lauren reached the cottonwood a mere head before Garret. "I won," she laughed.

Garret reined in his horse. "So you did."

She looked at him suspiciously. "Did you let me win?"

He drew even with her and pulled her off her horse and into his arms. "I'll always want you to win."

His mouth was soft on hers, and she fit on his lap as if she had always belonged there.

"Sweet Lauren. Today was the first time you left me, and I went running after you like a lost calf."

She tossed back her head and laughed. "Somehow you just don't fit that description. I have my doubts that the great Garret Lassiter would run after any woman."

"Not just any woman," he answered, feigning a serious expression. "My wife wouldn't like it if I trailed after other women."

"No, she wouldn't," she said, watching the wind ripple through his ebony hair. To be in his arms and have him lightly tease her was new to her. She met his gaze and wanted to hold on to the moment forever.

Lauren did not object when he eased her to the ground and dismounted. "My horse is tired after the trip to town, but your Sultan can carry us both without missing a step." He mounted Sultan, pulled Lauren up in front of him, and kicked his heels into Sultan's flanks. But Lauren's horse did not move. In fact, the beast tossed his mane and just stood there.

This time Garret used more pressure against the horse's flanks, but once again Sultan did not move.

Lauren leaned forward, patted Sultan's neck, and spoke softly. "I'm here. Take us home."

To Garret's shock, Sultan moved forward. "I'll be damned. He is one of those rare animals who will respond to only one person, and in this case, you are that person, Lauren."

Lauren leaned back against Garret, feeling his muscles flex, and nestled closer to him. He glanced down at her, and his hand moved between her legs. Even through her riding skirt she could feel the heat of his hand. Desire spiraled though her as he massaged her between the thighs, bringing a whimper to her lips.

She totally surrendered and was soon mindless beneath his stroking caresses.

Lauren was disappointed and trembling when Garret suddenly withdrew his hand, his gruff voice sounding in her ear. "Forgive me. It seems I can't even keep my hands off you out here where anyone could come upon us."

"I—"

He smiled as he looked into her feverish eyes, knowing what he had done to her. "Later," he promised, brushing his mouth against hers. "I'll have all of you tonight."

Lauren closed her eyes, sighed and rested against his shoulder. Tonight, she thought, Oh, tonight.

The folks of Sidewinder paused as they went about their daily bustle to stare at the fashionably dressed man and woman who disembarked from the stage. They were still curious when, moments later, the couple came out of the stage office and crossed the dusty street toward the sheriff's office.

Chase McBride was standing outside his office and was also watching the couple advance toward him. He did not know who they were, but they certainly had never been to West Texas or they would not be wearing such finery in all this heat.

As the couple climbed the steps, they both looked at Chase inquiringly. "Would you be the sheriff, sir?" the man asked in a Southern accent.

"Yes, I am."

The man offered Chase his hand. "I'm Morgan Colfax, and this is my wife."

Chase shook hands with the man and removed his hat, nodding to the lady. "What can I do for you folks?"

"We were told that your name is McBride, and

that you have a connection with our niece."

"That depends on who your niece is," Chase replied, already guessing their identities. He looked at the woman—her hair was the same color as Lauren's.

"Lauren McBride," Morgan Colfax replied.

"Then you must be Lauren's aunt and uncle from Georgia."

"Yes, that's right," Colfax confirmed.

"I suggest we step inside out of the heat and dust, ma'am," Chase offered, holding the door for Mrs. Colfax. When they were inside, Chase left the door open to catch what slight breeze was stirring.

Mrs. Colfax's eyes widened with curious horror when she glanced at the Wanted posters attached to the walls. She dusted the chair with her handkerchief before she sat down. "Are you an acquaintance or perhaps a relative of Lauren's?" she asked worriedly.

Chase slowly sat down, wondering how much to tell Mr. and Mrs. Colfax. He decided on the truth, since it was already common knowledge in Sidewinder, and they would find out soon enough anyway. "Lauren is my half-sister."

Eugenia leaned back, looking relieved. "I'm so glad to meet someone who knows her. I have been half out of my mind with worry. You can imagine my distress when I received a letter saying she was going to be married."

"Yes, ma'am, she's married, but why would that cause you any distress?"

"Then we're too late to stop the wedding."

"I'm afraid so. But why would you want to?" Chase asked.

"Our biggest worry is why Lauren would marry so soon after returning to Texas. We can't understand that," Eugenia said.

"Then you should go to San Reanido and speak directly to her about it."

"Is that where she's living?" Eugenia asked.

"Yes, ma'am. It's her husband's ranch."

"Then if you could direct us to where we might hire a horse and buggy and give us directions to the ranch, we'll be off," Morgan said, helping his wife to stand.

Chase shook his head. "You would probably be lost after the first mile. I'll take you to the livery stable and then accompany you to the ranch myself."

Mrs. Colfax smiled warmly at the handsome young sheriff. "That is most kind of you, sir."

"Not at all, ma'am. I'm always glad for any excuse to see my sister."

Garret had left two days before for Dallas where he would be shipping an Arabian stallion to its new owner in Boston. Lauren felt restless and uneasy without him. She had not slept well the night before because she kept reaching out for him.

There was an emptiness inside her—she had not known that she would miss him so much.

She went downstairs to the kitchen to speak to the cook, who was slicing onions into a pot of bubbling stew. Lauren wanted to send some stew to her father because Mrs. Whit was a very good cook, and her father loved beef stew.

"That smells delicious!"

The sweet-faced woman beamed at the compliment. "It's an old Southern recipe that's been in my family for years, Mrs. Lassiter. It's the fresh herbs and spices that make the difference."

"Well, whatever you did to it, I can't wait to taste it, and I know my father will love it."

"Excuse me, ma'am," Shaughnessy said from the doorway. "You have guests—a Mr. and Mrs. Colfax—and the sheriff's with them."

Eugenia glanced about her with a frown. "This is an extraordinary home. I somehow didn't expect to find a house like this in Texas." She looked at the sheriff. "Has your sister known Mr. Lassiter long?"

"I'm told they've known each other all her life."

"Mr. Lassiter is a cattle rancher?" Morgan asked.

"No. He raises horses," Chase replied.

Morgan pulled the blue brocade curtain aside and stared out at what was obviously a well-run and profitable ranch. "This Lassiter seems to be good at it."

Chase glanced over Mr. Colfax's shoulder. "This is my first time here. I'm told San Reanido is very successful."

Eugenia stared at the tasteful and expensive French furnishings. "I just want to know that my niece is happy."

Lauren appeared at the door and ran across the room into her aunt's arms. "You're here! I never expected you would come all the way to Texas!"

Eugenia hugged Lauren and then held her away from her. "We had to come after we got your letter."

"I'm glad you did." She moved across the room and hugged her uncle. "I'm so happy to see you." Then her eyes went to Chase, and she smiled, going to him and putting her arm around his waist. "I see you have met my brother."

"Yes. Sheriff McBride was kind enough to escort us here," her aunt said, a little confused as to how the sheriff was connected to her niece. He was very dark, but he did have the McBride blue eyes. However, Eugenia was much too polite to ask about the connection. Of course, she intended to quiz Lauren about it later on.

Chase looked down at Lauren. "I'd best be going."

"Can't you stay for dinner?" Lauren asked in

disappointment. "I'd like you to get to know my aunt and uncle."

"I can't today. Faith is putting on a big spread for Tanner and Callie at supper tonight." He smiled. "They'll be our first guests."

"Then bring Faith and Luke out this weekend, and I'll invite Tanner and Callie. That should be fun." She beamed at her aunt and uncle. "I have real cause to celebrate."

"Walk with me to the door," Chase said in a tone of authority. He nodded toward her aunt and uncle. "Ma'am; sir."

Morgan Colfax shook Chase's hand. "Thank you for all your trouble. We appreciate your bringing us out here." Morgan smiled. "And you were right, we would have been lost after the first mile."

"I'll return the rig to the livery stable for you."

Lauren excused herself and accompanied her brother to the door.

"Lauren," he said, turning to her, "I won't be accepting your invitation for the weekend. I don't belong with them, and you know it." He nodded down the hall toward the morning room.

"You're wrong. You belong with your family, and that means me and Tanner. You're our brother. If I want you to be here, that should be enough reason for you."

"Have you thought that Mr. and Mrs. Colfax might feel uncomfortable if they learn the details of my birth?"

"I know my aunt and uncle, and they will accept you for what you are—my brother."

"If you're sure."

She slid her arms around him and pressed her cheek to his hard chest. "I love you. I want you to know that."

He cleared his throat as feelings of family and belonging washed over him. "I have to leave now if I'm going to make it home before dark."

Over Chase's shoulder, Lauren watched Mrs. Shaughnessy directing the unloading of trunks. "We'll expect you on Saturday, Chase."

"I'll ask Faith."

"Tell her how much I want her to be here."

Lauren watched Chase walk away, wishing she could make him understand how much he meant to her. She was sad that he had to consider whether or not people would accept him. She waved to him as he drove the buggy away and watched him until he was out of sight.

She then hurried back to her aunt and uncle.

"I can't tell you how happy I am to see you! I know Barbara couldn't make the trip so soon after the baby's birth, but I wish Carolyn had come with you. Is the baby a boy or a girl?"

"I have the most beautiful granddaughter in the world," Morgan Colfax bragged.

"How wonderful! Why didn't Carolyn come with you?"

Eugenia shook her head. "Carolyn is in love and

didn't want to leave Savannah. Do you recall Price Danner?"

"Wasn't his father the owner of the bank in Alexandria?"

"Yes, that's him," Eugenia told her. "Carolyn and Price are unofficially engaged. We've already decided to make the announcement when we get back home."

Lauren kissed her aunt's cheek. "You've come to Texas to find out what kind of trouble I've gotten myself into, haven't you?"

Eugenia tilted Lauren's chin and looked into her eyes. "Do you love this man you married?"

"Desperately."

Her uncle nodded with a satisfied expression. "I told you, Eugenia. I said Lauren was too stubborn to marry anyone unless she loved him." His gaze met Lauren's. "However, we had to know for sure. Your aunt insisted that we get here with all haste. And so we did."

Lauren laughed. "You know me, don't you, Uncle Morgan?"

"That I do," he admitted. "When you meet a person across a chessboard as often as I've met you, you get to know them very well."

Eugenia gestured around the room. "It looks like your Mr. Lassiter has done well by you." She laughed. "Unless I discover that he has a wart on his nose, or is a man in his dotage, I'm inclined to believe you have made a good match."

"Unfortunately, Garret's away just now. But I expect him back in two or three days."

"Garret?" her aunt questioned. Her eyes brightened as she remembered Lauren speaking about him. "That's the young man you pined for when you first came to live with us. Yes, that was his name—Garret!" There was real relief in her aunt's eyes. "I do feel better now."

Lauren would never tell her aunt or uncle the circumstances of her marriage because it would upset them and they would not understand. "When you meet him, you'll like him." She hugged her aunt. "And he'll love you both."

"I admit I'm anxious to take a look at this place," Morgan remarked. "I saw stables and paddocks and spotted some mighty fine horseflesh. I noticed some of the stock is Appaloosa."

"Garret prefers Appaloosa and Arabian horses. He can explain his breeding policy to you—it's fascinating. And," Lauren added, "there's something else you'll like about him. His family comes from Virginia. In fact, his father has moved back there."

"Ah," her aunt said with a teasing note in her voice. "A gentleman from the South. If you had written me all this, I wouldn't have been so worried."

"I did. The letter must have missed you."

"When I came in, I could have sworn I smelled beef stew, and it smelled the same as my mother used to make," Morgan said.

Lauren linked her arms through both of theirs. "You are in for a real treat. Mrs. Whit is the cook, and she's from the South as well."

Lauren tossed and turned on the bed, fighting with the covers, then taking turns flattening and fluffing her pillow. She felt so empty inside when Garret was not with her. She wondered how she had become attached to him so quickly.

What if he got hurt while he was away and she could not get to him in time?

Lauren sat up in bed, her heart pounding. Love was so painful. Why did it have to hurt so much? Garret knew how to take care of himself. And besides, he had Charley with him.

At last, in the early hours before dawn, Lauren fell asleep.

Garret quickly climbed the stairs, urgency burning inside him. Even without light he had no trouble finding his way to the bedroom. He went inside and softly closed the door behind him. He had been so anxious to get home to Lauren that he had left Charley to finish the business in Dallas.

He knelt down beside his wife, not wanting to startle her. The soft moonlight fell across her hair, and he watched the rise and fall of her breasts with each breath she took. He wanted to hold her, to have her awaken in his arms.

"Lauren," he whispered, touching his lips to

hers and sliding his arms around her. "Wake up, sweetheart."

Lauren's arms came around him, and she hugged him tightly. "You're home!"

He chuckled with delight because she was glad to see him. "It seems I couldn't stay away from you."

"The horse has already been shipped out of Dallas?"

"Charley stayed behind to make sure the horse was properly loaded on the train."

"You must have ridden all night to get here," she said in amazement.

He touched her lips. "You were so much on my mind that Charley claimed I was useless, and he sent me home." He stood up and began to unbutton his shirt. "I'm covered with trail dust. I'll just bathe quickly, and then I'll be back."

Lauren got on her knees and reached out to him. His arms encircled her, and the bath was forgotten as her soft body pressed against his.

"Sweetheart," he murmured.

Lauren pushed his shirt aside so she could feel his hard chest. She raised her face to his, inviting a kiss.

Garret did not remember going down to the bed. He only knew that Lauren was warm and desirable, and she wanted him as much as he wanted her.

Garret's mouth found a swollen nipple, and

Lauren dug her fingers into his shoulders.

"I don't think I'll ever be able to leave you again." He kissed her long and hard, then raised his head. "Say you missed me."

"I missed you."

There was an urgency about him as he shoved her gown up. He had to get inside her or he was going to explode. Roughly he removed her gown, tossing it on the floor. He fumbled with his trousers and was finally naked and between her legs. With a powerful thrust he drove deep, and she groaned, arching her hips upward to receive his full length. "What a sweet, sweet homecoming," he said, breathing heavily in her ear.

Chapter Twenty-three

In spite of having very little sleep, Garret awoke with the first rays of sunlight. He tried not to make any noise that would disturb Lauren. He left the dressing room, having just shaved, and walked out on the balcony. It was already hot, and as the day progressed, it would get even hotter.

Garret was about to go back inside when he caught a glimpse of a stranger walking in the garden. He frowned, pausing to get a better look. No one ever went into the garden except for the two men who were responsible for its upkeep. This man had the appearance of a gentleman, but he was a stranger to Garret.

Lauren awoke and stretched. "Is it morning already?"

"Lauren, there's a man in our garden."

She sat up and clamped her hand over her mouth. "How could I have forgotten to tell you? My Aunt Eugenia and Uncle Morgan are here."

His eyelids hooded his eyes. "I can think of one very good reason you forgot." He slid in bed beside her and drew her to him. "So your aunt and uncle came to look me over to see if I'm a proper husband for their niece, hmm?"

"Something like that."

He groaned. "I hope they aren't as difficult to convince as your father was."

"Don't worry, they'll love you."

"Do *you* love me?" His gaze was seeking.

Lauren wiggled out of his embrace and swung her feet to the floor. "Go on out and introduce yourself to Uncle Morgan. As soon as I've bathed, I'll join you."

By the time Garret reached the garden, Lauren's aunt had joined her husband. He approached them with a smile on his face. "Hello. Welcome to San Reanido."

Morgan shook Garret's hand. "I'm assuming you're Lauren's husband, Garret." Morgan took his wife's hand and pulled her forward. "This is Lauren's Aunt Eugenia."

Garret smiled at the elegant woman with hair almost the same color as Lauren's. "I can see where Lauren gets her good looks."

Eugenia kissed Garret's cheek. "Lauren was right—you are a Southerner."

"Don't let it get around. I'm trying to pass as a Texan."

Eugenia was delighted with Lauren's handsome and charming husband. "I know why you chose my niece as your wife, and now that I've met you, I know why Lauren chose you. You are quite the handsome one, aren't you?"

"I am humbled by your praise," Garret said, laughing. He liked Lauren's aunt immediately. "I can see where your niece gets her sauciness and straightforward manners."

"You have no idea what they're like when they are together," Morgan declared. "A man doesn't stand a chance. But it's as close to Paradise as mortal man can get in this lifetime."

Garret laughed. "So this is what I have to look forward to with the two of them under my roof."

"I'm afraid so," Morgan said, smiling and winking at his wife.

Eugenia Colfax observed Garret as the three of them strolled through the garden. If first impressions counted, Garret Lassiter was everything she could have hoped for in Lauren's husband and even more. Yet there was something about him she could not quite grasp—it was the expression in those dark eyes. What was it? Uncertainty? Guilt? She did not know him well enough to discern which.

Morgan's voice held a hint of excitement. "I can't wait to see your horses. I saw some mighty fine specimens running in the paddock this morning. Can't say I've ever ridden an Arabian. Those I saw must be over fifteen hands."

"More like over sixteen hands," Garret told him. "If you would like, I'll arrange for you to ride one this very day. You only have to decide if you want one with speed or spirit."

"Both, I should think," Morgan stated excitedly.

"I can arrange that, too."

Eugenia heard Lauren coming down the path and stopped to wait for her. Lauren wore a spring-yellow gown, her hair loose about her shoulders, and she was breathtaking, her aunt thought. Eugenia glanced at Garret and sensed the turmoil in him. He was like a caged lion on the prowl when he looked at her niece, and Eugenia wondered why.

Lauren caught up with them and linked her arm through her uncle's. "Isn't it a glorious day?"

"That it is, my dear. Your husband is going to put me on my first Arabian."

Lauren smiled at Garret. "He has many to choose from. Wait until you see my Sultan."

"You can see him," Garret told Morgan, "but that stallion won't allow anyone but Lauren to ride him." He smiled. "Sultan did make an exception in my case once. But only, I suspect, because Lauren was on him with me."

Lauren felt the blush on her face and turned to glance at a brightly colored butterfly so her aunt would not notice. When she turned back to Garret, he raised his brow and grinned.

"I was hoping Tanner would be here this morning," Eugenia said in a disappointed tone. "I wish Stone weren't away. I want to see my sister's sons."

"Did I hear someone mention my name?" Eugenia turned into the arms of Tanner. He laughed down at her. "You're a long way from home, Aunt."

Lauren whispered to Garret, "It's a good day."

The weekend had been filled with good food, laughter, and the joy of a family coming together. After one of Mrs. Whit's superb meals, everyone had gathered on the veranda while a gentle breeze stirred the fireflies. Night sounds surrounded the gathering: a hooting barn owl, the far-off cry of a wolf, the answer of its mate.

Eugenia thought that the only thing missing from this perfect place was the sound of children's laughter. She could imagine Lauren's children running and playing in this wonderful garden.

At first, Chase hung back and rarely joined in the conversation. But Lauren would not have that. Before the end of the first hour, Chase knew he belonged to a real family for the first time in his life.

Chase was chatting easily with Morgan as the older man told him about spending the morning on the finest horse he'd ever ridden. Faith was laughing at some antic Callie was pulling on Tanner. Lauren was sitting with Chase's son, Luke, telling him about the new foal and promising to take him to see it in the morning.

Eugenia noticed that only one person seemed detached from the rest of them. Garret was sitting on the top step, listening to Tanner tell Chase how their sister could outride most men he knew. Eugenia settled on the step beside Garret, who could not seem to keep his gaze from wandering to Lauren. "I like it here, Garret."

"I'm glad you do. I hope you and Morgan will visit often. I have never seen Lauren happier."

"Her happiness is important to you, isn't it?"

He turned in Eugenia's direction. "Of course. It's the most important thing to me."

"You should have seen her in Savannah. Many of the young men were in love with her. She's so vibrant and full of life. When she walks into a room, she draws every eye."

"So you are telling me that Lauren could have had her pick of any gentleman she wanted in Savannah?"

"Yes, she could have. But what I am really telling you is she never gave any of those young men a second glance." Eugenia paused. "Come to think of it, her elusiveness was probably part of her attraction for the gentlemen."

"What are you trying to say?" Garret asked, his eyes going to his wife, who was tapping Chase on the chest to make a point about something.

"I'm saying that Lauren was already in love. None of the others mattered to her."

Garret lowered his head. "I suspected that might be the case. I suppose you think she would have eventually gone back to Savannah and married that man if she hadn't married me."

"Garret, you fool. You are that man!"

He raised troubled eyes to Eugenia. "There was a time when I might have been, but you don't know what I've done."

Eugenia took a deep breath of the honeysuckle-scented air. "And I don't want to know. It's not my business." She placed her hand on Garret's. "I'm not blind. You think Lauren doesn't love you," she said in amazement. "I've been trying to think what's bothering you, and now I know."

Garret stood up. "I need to check on a horse that picked up a bad stone bruise." He glanced at Lauren. "Tell her not to wait up for me."

Eugenia watched Garret walk away. Then she turned to Lauren, who was speaking animatedly to Faith about her disgust with feathers on ladies' hats. What guilt was Garret carrying on his shoulders? Lauren had said nothing to her about any trouble. Eugenia would not interfere, but if Lauren

came to her for advice, she would counsel her to
see to her husband's happiness. She knew for a
certainty that Garret and Lauren loved each other,
and their love could easily overcome any obsta-
cles. They had only to reach out to each other.

Lauren lay in the bed wondering if Garret had
fallen asleep. He had come to bed after everyone
else had gone to their bedrooms. But he had not
touched her or made any move to do so. He had
not touched her in over a week, and she did not
know why.

What had she done to make him turn away from
her? This was probably what happened to people
when they married for the wrong reasons.

She knew what was wrong—Garret was tired
of her.

Lauren rolled onto her side, wishing she could
cry, but she did not dare. Garret would hear her
if he was awake.

Her aunt and uncle would be leaving tomorrow.
After she accompanied them to the stage, she
would ride to the Circle M; the answer she was
looking for was there. She was weary of people
trying to convince her that Garret loved her when
she knew it was not so. Garret had told her that
he had written her about the woman he loved in
the letter he had given Jeb. Although it would be
painful, Lauren was ready to find out who the
woman was.

"Lauren."

"I didn't know if you were awake."

"Would you like me to go into Sidewinder with you tomorrow?"

"No. There is no reason for you to do that. I'm going over to my father's afterwards."

"I see. Then take Charley with you."

"I intend to tie Sultan to the buggy; then Charley can bring the buggy home, and I can ride on to the Circle M."

Lauren ached for Garret to reach out to her or to argue with her and insist that Charley stay with her tomorrow. When she felt him move, she closed her eyes, waiting for his touch, but he had merely turned his face away from her.

"It's not a good idea for you to ride about the countryside unescorted, Lauren."

"I can take care of myself. I don't need anyone."

She watched the moonlight play across his features. His voice was hard. His jaw tensed. "You need me, Lauren, because we've got one thing going for us."

"What?"

"We're good in bed together—damned good, don't you think?"

She did not answer. Her hand was clamped over her mouth to keep from crying out her misery.

"Good night, Lauren."

*   *   *

Lauren said a tearful good-bye to her aunt and uncle, then sent Charley back to San Reanido with the buggy. When she rode up to the Circle M, she dismounted and went in search of Jeb.

He was in the barn with the forge going, so it was uncomfortably hot inside. He gripped the hoof of a horse and was hammering on a new shoe while Tiny stood nearby, watching. They both glanced up and greeted Lauren.

"How's Papa?"

Jeb had placed a horseshoe nail in his mouth and did not speak until he had driven it into the hoof. "He's about the same."

She smiled at Tiny. "I just saw my aunt and uncle off on the stage."

"Tanner says your aunt looks like your ma," Jeb said.

"I'm told that, too. Jeb, do you remember that letter Garret wrote me when I left Texas? Do you still have it?"

"You know," he said, releasing the horse's foreleg. "It's a funny thing. I searched through my trunk just the other day lookin' for that letter so I could give it to you, but it's gone. It had been in that old trunk for years. I just don't know where it got off to."

"How strange." She sighed, feeling crushing disappointment. She had been ready to learn the truth about Garret's feelings. "Now I suppose I'll never know what was in that letter."

Jeb looked at her searchingly. With a strange expression on his face, he said, "You could ask Garret."

"Yes. Yes, I could." But Lauren knew she would never do that.

Tiny moved away, leaving Lauren and Jeb in the barn. He did not know what letter Lauren was talking about, but if anything was missing, it was an easy bet that Manuelo had something to do with it. And if Manuelo was the culprit, then chances were that Clare was involved.

Tiny intended to find out.

Chapter Twenty-four

The house at San Reanido was very well ordered. Since Mrs. Shaughnessy was so efficient, Lauren was left with very little to do. She was not a person who took well to idleness, and she certainly did not allow others to take care of her. She had to be active and busy.

She was on her way to the stable to check on Aqaba's foal and to give Sultan a good rubdown when Chase rode up.

"Good morning," she said, striding forward. "It's good to see you. Why didn't you bring Faith and Luke with you? I want to talk to Garret about finding a gentle horse for Luke. He's old enough to take care of his own horse—what do you think?"

"This isn't a social call, Lauren. Is Garret home?"

"Yes. He's in the study." She frowned. "It isn't Papa, is it?"

Chase's dark eyes were sad. "No. I don't know how to tell you this. It's Garret's pa."

"What?" Her hand shook as she clutched his shirtfront. "Oh, no, please! What happened?"

Chase hugged her to him for a moment, trying to give her a measure of comfort. "Take me to Garret, and I'll tell you both at the same time."

Lauren fought against tears, knowing she needed to be strong for her husband. She watched her brother hoist a saddlebag over his shoulder; it had the San Reanido brand seared into the leather. She hurriedly led him into the house, feeling devastating pain for the loss of that dear man and for what his death would mean to Garret.

Without knocking on the study door, she entered, her gaze on Garret, who looked up in surprise.

"Chase, what a pleasure to see you." Garret closed his ledger and stood, walking toward his brother-in-law and shaking his hand. Garret did not yet realize that something was wrong. But when he looked into Lauren's tear-filled eyes, he thought that her father had died.

"Garret," Chase began, wishing to hell he did not have to be the one to bring such sad news.

"It's your pa. He never made it to Virginia. He never even made it into Sidewinder."

Garret reeled under the impact of overwhelming grief and stumbled back a step. "Dead? My father's dead?"

"I'm sorry," Chase said, squeezing Garret's hand. He placed the saddlebag on the floor in front of Garret. "This belonged to your father, didn't it?"

Garret did not flinch, but Lauren saw his mouth tremble as he recognized the saddlebag. "Yes, this is . . . was . . . my father's."

Chase nodded grimly. "Jeb found it with the body. That's how we identified him."

Garret was having difficulty accepting the terrible news about his father. Lauren watched his body shudder as he attempted to regain control of his emotions.

"I want to know everything you know, Chase," Garret said at last.

Chase placed a hand on Garret's arm to steady him. "It must have happened right after the wedding, when your father was on his way into Sidewinder."

"Oh, God," Garret whispered. "All the time I was thinking life was so good—my father lay dead." He raised his gaze to Chase. "He didn't suffer, did he?"

Chase led Garret forward and pressed his resisting body down into a chair. "I don't know, but I don't think so."

"I hadn't heard from him, but I wasn't worried, because he never has been one for writing letters." He buried his face in his hands. "My father dead— how is it possible?"

"Jeb saw buzzards circling and went to investigate, thinking a calf was down. He came upon your father's body."

"Was it an accident?"

"No. He was killed by someone."

Garret shook his head. "My father's horse had been trained to come home. Did my father's murderer steal his horse?" Garret was rambling, saying the first thing that came to his mind. "We can find the killer if we find that horse."

"I'm afraid that won't be possible," Chase told him. "The horse was killed at the same time. That's why it didn't come home, and that's why we didn't know your father never made it to his destination."

"Father loved that horse. He was going to have it shipped to Virginia."

Garret buried his face in his hands once more, and Lauren went down on the floor beside him, her arms sliding around him. "I'm so sorry," she said as grief overcame her. "So very sorry."

Garret held himself rigid and raised his head. "How did it happen?"

"This is the part that's got me puzzled, Garret.

Your pa and his horse were both shot with arrows. It wasn't robbery, because whoever killed him left his saddlebag. I examined it, and it contains a great deal of money."

"Comanche?" Garret asked. "There hasn't been any trouble with them around here in years—not in this part of Texas."

This was the part Chase had been dreading. "I went to the site to see what I could find out, but it was impossible to read the signs. So much time has passed. The body had decomposed. Still I'm sure it wasn't Comanche. In fact, I'm sure it wasn't an Indian at all."

Garret looked dazed. "If not an Indian, then who?"

Chase settled into a chair nearby, his gaze on his sister. "I don't know, but I sure as hell intend to find out."

Garret stood and walked to the window. "What has been done with my father's body?"

"Jeb brought him in to Doc Pierce, who is taking care of all the details. He'll be accompanying your father's body here later today. Before I left town, I notified the minister and sent my deputy to tell the rest of the family. I suspect they'll all be here soon. I didn't know what to do about letting your sister in Virginia know. If you'll give me her address, I'll send a wire off to her."

Garret's shoulders slumped. "Thank you. I'll

want my father to be buried beside my mother here at the ranch."

Lauren stood, knowing she needed to be strong for her husband. He was being so stoic, keeping such a tight rein on his emotions.

"Chase, I hear riders. It'll probably be the family. Will you take care of them?" Lauren asked.

Chase nodded, clutching his hat and moving to the door. "Don't worry about anything. You two stay in here as long as you need to. Come out when you're ready."

In that moment, Lauren loved Chase more than ever for handling such a heartbreaking situation with such kindness and consideration. "Thank you."

When the door closed behind Chase, Lauren walked to her husband. He glanced up at her with incredibly sad eyes. She held her arms out to him, and he leaned heavily against her, his whole body shaking.

"It's all right to cry, Garret. Your father was worthy of our tears."

And he did cry.

And so did she.

The service was held late in the afternoon, just as the sun was painting the sky with splashes of red. Lauren stood beside Garret as the minister spoke glowing words about Barnard Lassiter's good character and how he had been a loving husband and father.

Garret stood ramrod straight, his gaze touching on nothing in particular. He did not see the glorious blast of color as the last dying rays of the sun seemed to cling to the now deep gray sky.

Later, Garret moved among family and friends with seeming ease. But Lauren knew he was holding on by sheer force of will. He had loved his father, and Barnard Lassiter's death had been a terrible blow to him.

Tanner took Lauren's arm and led her out of the room. "I'm going to get all the neighbors out of here, and then we'll be leaving, too, unless you want us to stay. Garret has had enough of all of us at the moment."

She leaned her head against her brother's shoulder. "He's hurting so badly, and there's nothing I can do to help him."

"Just stay near him. You know what he's feeling because you lost Ma."

Tears brimmed in her eyes and ran down her cheeks. "I don't know what to do."

"Have you told him you love him yet?"

She dabbed at her eyes with a handkerchief. "No. I can't."

"Dammit it, Lauren, tell him! He needs to know."

"He has enough on his mind for now. He certainly doesn't need a declaration of love from me."

It was on the tip of Tanner's tongue to tell Lauren that her husband was just as stubborn as she.

"I've never seen two such unreasonable people." Tanner glanced over Lauren's shoulder at Callie as she comforted Mrs. Shaughnessy, who was almost inconsolable. "Well, maybe Callie and I were every bit as foolish, but it doesn't have to be this way."

Lauren straightened away from him. "I need to speak to Garret's men. They're ready to leave."

Tanner let out his breath in irritation. "You haven't heard one word I've been saying, have you?"

"I heard you, Tanner. I just don't want to do anything that will put another burden on my husband at this time."

"Dammit, Lauren—"

"Tanner!" Callie appeared beside him. "Will you keep your voice down."

Tanner bit back his retort. "I can't fight you both." He took Callie's arm. "Come on, let's herd everyone out of here."

That night, Lauren lay beside Garret as he slept fitfully. Once, he reached out to her, and she held him in her arms. He laid his head against her breasts, and she found her nightgown wet with tears.

She kissed him softly, and he pulled her to him. "I need you."

"I'm here for you."

He yanked her gown up and plunged into her without kissing her or saying anything. His powerful thrusts slammed into her, and her body came alive as it always did when he made love to her. But she knew he wasn't really making love . . . he was trying to escape his sorrow.

Afterward, he moved to his side of the bed, and Lauren cried quietly. He needed to be with the woman he loved at this time. She almost wished that woman could be here if it would bring Garret any measure of peace.

Lauren had not seen much of Garret since his father had been laid to rest. He kept busy in the daylight hours and sometimes even late into the night. He usually had dinner with her, but he always went to his study afterward and would come to bed much later.

At first, Lauren thought it was Garret's way of grieving for his father, but she had come to believe that he was trying to avoid her. What had she done?

The tension between them was building, and she did not know how much longer she could stand it.

Garret had not attempted to make love to her, or even touch her, since the night he had taken her to escape his grief. Lauren was convinced that he was regretting their marriage.

Last night Garret had not come to bed at all, and she had slept uneasily without him beside her.

Would he come to her tonight?

Lauren was walking past Garret's study when she discovered that the door was open a crack. She could hear the rustle of paper inside. She knocked lightly.

"Come in," Garret said.

He was drumming his fingers on the desk in thoughtfulness or irritation. She didn't know which.

"Hello, Lauren."

She stood in the doorway, reluctant to enter the room. Her glance fell on the leather couch, and she saw the quilt and pillow there. Her heart was suddenly heavy. Garret would rather sleep in his study than share a bed with her.

"I have just been wondering how you're doing."

"Have you now?" he replied grimly.

Lauren could feel leashed anger in him. His eyes were keen and focused like a predatory bird. Something was definitely wrong. "Garret, is something bothering you? Have I done something to displease you?"

"Why would you imagine that?" he asked dryly.

"I presumed that—"

"You presumed," he interrupted, "since I no longer seek your bed that I'm angry with you." He stared down at his hands. "No, Lauren, you have done nothing wrong." Anger gathered in his eyes like an impending storm. "The fault lies with me."

She tilted her chin and looked into his eyes. "You're busy. I'll just leave you to your work."

"Lauren." His eyes glinted, and the line of his mouth thinned. "It really isn't you that I'm angry with."

The expression in his eyes belied his words.

"It doesn't matter, Garret." She moved backwards. "If you will excuse me."

"Lauren, wait—"

She stepped out and closed the door soundly behind her.

Garret buried his face in his hands. Their life together had not gone as he had hoped it would. Lauren had played her part as his wife, never complaining, never turning him away when he claimed his husbandly rights. Her Aunt Eugenia had made him realize how unfair he had been to Lauren when she told him how many men had loved Lauren in Savannah. He was the only one who had taken advantage of her. He felt that he was unworthy to be her husband.

Lauren had been forced to marry him because she had had no other choice. He was disgusted with his own mendacity.

Lauren's aunt was convinced that her niece loved him, and perhaps she had loved him in a pure way when she had been a young girl. But she had been an innocent then. Now Lauren was a woman who deserved so much more than life had handed her—she deserved to be happy.

The most difficult part had been to distance himself from Lauren. Last night he had wanted her so damned bad that it had hurt. He could not sleep in the same bed with her without wanting to make love to her.

Garret rubbed his forehead to relieve the dull ache. He had drunk too much last night. It was a mistake he would not make again.

Standing up, he went to the window and watched Lauren cross the yard toward the stable. No doubt she was going to see her father.

"Sweetheart, why have you forgiven your father and not me?" he whispered to the empty room.

He shook his head. Lauren would probably forgive him long before he forgave himself.

Estaban stood over the fresh earth where Garret's father had been buried. He picked up a wilted flower and crushed it in his fist. He turned his attention in the direction of the big house. Grief hung over the place like a dark cloud.

Estaban had once again struck at Garret's heart. He would let him grieve for a short time; then he would strike again.

It had made him happy to see the *patrón* standing over his father's grave, weighted down with sorrow. Let Garret Lassiter suffer and weep as Estaban had suffered for his father—let Garret Lassiter live in the same kind of hell his family had created for Estaban's family. Let him cry out in pain, wondering what was happening to his safe, secure world.

Estaban had once considered killing Señora Lauren just so Garret would suffer the deepest kind of grief. But he did not consider himself a cruel man, and the señora was blameless for the sins her husband and his family had committed.

He would even be sorry to cause her pain, but her grief would not last long. She would be a wealthy widow, and she was beautiful, so she would have no trouble finding another husband. Estaban's eyes burned, and tears moistened them. He was almost finished with his task. Soon his family honor would be restored, he thought with grim resolution.

Now only Garret Lassiter stood between him and total revenge.

Chapter Twenty-five

Lauren had to take two steps to one of Jeb's long strides. He paused at the apple bucket, inspected an apple, then nodded with satisfaction before peeling it. He cut a slice, handing it to Lauren.

"So what do you think, Jeb?"

He took his time answering her, thinking over what he would say. "I don't rightly know who would want to kill Mr. Lassiter. I 'spect when a man has the Lassiters' kind of wealth, he's going to have enemies. But I agree with Chase—it was no Indian that killed him."

"Why do you say that?"

"In the first place, an Indian would never shoot a horse. They'd more likely shoot the man and take

355

the horse. And Comanche don't use bow and arrow anymore—they have guns."

She bit into the apple. "How about Apache?"

"Nope. An Apache would have a gun same as a Comanch, but they'd eat the horse since it was dead."

Lauren took another slice of apple and looked at Jeb speculatively. "I know we've been all over this before, but since you're the one who found the body, do you have any suspicions?"

"I'd be lookin' at someone who bore him a grudge. It was a planned killing. It wasn't robbery, 'cause he still had his belongin's when I found him."

"Garret will find no peace until he knows who killed his father. I wish . . . I wish . . ."

"You wish you could help him."

"Yes. Of course I do."

"Lauren, just stay by him. That's all you can do."

She could never tell Jeb that Garret did not want her beside him, that he did not want her anywhere near him. "What's left to do that we haven't yet done?"

Jeb tossed the apple core to one of the horses, who nibbled it right away. "Chase questioned everyone who might know somethin'. But to my way of thinkin', there might be someone at San Reanido who might talk to you when they wouldn't talk to a lawman. You could ask around and see if one of the hands heard or saw anythin'."

Lauren shook her head. "I know most of the hands, and they would have told either me or Garret if they knew anything."

"One of them might know somethin' he don't know he knows. It never hurts to ask."

She stood on tiptoe and kissed his ruddy cheek. "I'm going to see my father before riding home. How is he today?"

Jeb was looping a rope and hung it on a rusty nail. " 'Bout the same. Although I can see he's gettin' weaker."

"The whole world is sad," Lauren stated softly. "Is there no happiness anywhere?"

He searched her face carefully. "How is it between you and Garret?"

Lauren could be totally honest with Jeb. "About how you would expect it to be when the groom doesn't love the bride."

He grimaced. "Even sadness passes, Lauren."

"I want to believe that." She gave a wave and moved out of the barn on her way to the house.

It was much later when Lauren rode home in the gathering dusk. Her father had been too ill for her to stay long. She had managed to get through the visit without seeing Clare, and that was a blessing.

Over dinner that night, Garret was more talkative than he had been of late. He told Lauren about the five new Arabians that would be arriving next month, and he seemed to enjoy the duck in orange sauce that Mrs. Whit had prepared just to please him.

"How was your day?" Garret asked.

"I rode over to the Circle M. I talked to Jeb and saw my father."

Garret wiped his mouth with a napkin and laid it beside his plate. "Is your father the same?"

"About the same. He tires more easily now, and I need to keep my visits with him short." She decided against commenting on how tired Garret looked. There were lines under his eyes as if he had not slept well. She wished she had the courage to ask him if he would be sleeping in his study tonight, but she did not.

"How was Jeb?"

"Like the glue holding us all together."

"He's a good man. I wish he'd come and work for me."

Lauren shot to her feet, suddenly angry. She had been patient with Garret while he grieved for his father—she had endured his silence and his seeming lack of interest in her, but for him to suggest that Jeb might come and work for him made her suddenly angry.

"That will never happen, Garret. Just because my father bribed you to take me off his hands, that doesn't mean he'll let Jeb go, too."

He winced at the cruel words. "I don't consider that I was bribed, Lauren."

"Then what do you call it?"

Garret got to his feet. "I'll leave that for you to figure out. If you need me, I'll be in my study." He stopped near her, and a firm grip pulled her up and against a hard chest. "I'm sorry for what happened between us. If I could make it right for you, I would." He released her and walked away.

Lauren stood there long after the sounds of Garret's footsteps faded. What had he meant? That he would undo the marriage if he could?

She went to her room knowing she would spend another night alone. Tomorrow she intended to question Charley, Will, and some of the others about Garret's father's death.

Lauren came slowly awake when something soft touched her cheek. "Garret?"

He went down on his knees beside her and gathered her in his arms. "I tried to stay away, but I couldn't."

He brought his face level with hers. "I want you so damned bad. But if you don't feel the same way, I'll leave."

She took his hand and indicated that he should get in bed beside her, and when he did, she went immediately into his arms. Oh, the glory of being held against him, to have his mouth touch her cheek and hover above her lips—to hear his heavy breathing and know he wanted her passionately.

"I can't help myself," he said, his mouth grinding against hers.

Feeling feverish, Lauren wanted to rip her gown off so Garret could get to her. He must have sensed her desperation, because the gown was yanked away, and he moved on top of her, crushing her into the soft mattress.

When she looked into his dark, blazing eyes, a fleeting wish wound its way through her mind. She wanted his love, and she wanted to tell him about her love for him.

His kiss gentled, and he urged her mouth open with his tongue. Intense feelings lashed through her body as he swelled against her. Her thighs parted, and Lauren welcomed him inside her with a groan of pleasure.

"Sweetheart," he muttered, holding himself still inside her and resisting the urge to plunge deep and hard into her softness. "I have been unbearable, and I'm asking you to forgive me."

"Of course."

He cupped her chin and made her look at him. "I want you to understand that I had to work things out in my mind."

"I know that." She moved her hips the merest bit, and he stilled her.

"No, don't do that, or I'll never be able to tell you what's on my mind. I think I denied myself the pleasure of your body as a way of doing penance."

At the moment, all she could think about was his searing heat, and she moved her thighs upward, enticing him. Her hand moved up his muscled back and rested against his shoulder. "You didn't have to deny yourself. I have always been here for you."

"Lauren, I—"

She moved her hips sharply, and his eyes darkened. What he'd been about to say was never uttered. He jabbed deeper into her, his ragged breathing touching her cheek.

Lauren held Garret while his body shook and trembled with relief just as her body did the same.

Garret kissed and held her, his hands moving over her silken skin. He would never let her go. She was more important to him than his own life. He had been incomplete all those years he had waited for her. She was his as much as the air he took into his lungs.

And he would always be hers if she but knew it.

"I won't be spending any more nights in the study," he said forcefully, pulling back and looking into her serenely beautiful eyes. It had meant so much to him to have her beside him, grieving with him for his father. There had never been a woman like her.

"I'm glad," she said, trembling at his touch. His lips traveled over her breasts to her stomach. She groaned and lifted her hips, inviting him to take what he wanted from her.

And he did.

* * *

When Lauren awoke the next morning, Garret was getting dressed. "I'm sorry, sweetheart. I tried not to wake you." He shoved his foot into his boot and straightened. "Estaban sent word that he'd spotted several horses running free in Box Canyon. We're going to drive them to the east pasture." He bent over and kissed her lips. "I should be home before dark."

Lauren smiled, stretching like a kitten, remembering the things Garret had done to her during the night. He had been a tender lover and had left her flesh quivering with fulfillment.

He laughed and moved to the door. "Stay in bed if you're tired. You should be."

After her bath, Lauren went to the stable to speak to Charley. He was using the curry comb on one of Garret's prize Arabians, so she picked up a mane comb and ran it carefully through the thick white mane.

Lauren felt that she could talk freely to Charley; they had been easy in each other's company since the day she helped him deliver the foal.

"Charley," she said, using long strokes now that the tangles had been removed from the silken mane. "Has anyone had a theory about how Mr. Lassiter was killed?"

"Yeah. They all talk and state their opinions, but

no one really knows what happened. It's a pity . . . a real pity, ma'am."

"Can you think of anyone who wanted to kill him?"

Charley paused as if he were thinking. "Now that I think about it, there was something kinda peculiar. I didn't think much about it at the time, and I don't know that it means anything."

"What, Charley?" Lauren urged.

"You don't know Frank Nelson 'cause he'd gone before you came to San Reanido."

"What about him?"

"Well, sir, one day he just up and hightailed it outta here." Charley leaned against the stallion and scratched a day's growth of beard. "Frank kept saying the Spaniard was plumb loco. Said he talked like he wanted to kill the boss."

"Garret's father?"

"No, Garret."

"Who is this Spaniard?" Lauren asked, although she thought she knew who he was. It had to be Estaban Velasquez. She had always felt uncomfortable around him. "Is it Estaban?"

"Yeah. That Spaniard's a strange 'un, as strange as they come. He don't never like to mix with the rest of us. Keeps mostly to himself. The others don't like him any too well."

Lauren froze. "Could he be responsible for Mr. Lassiter's death, Charley?"

"I don't think so." He dropped the curry comb

in a wooden bucket and dusted his hands on his trousers as a troubled frown creased his brow. "I'm going to do some checking. The Spaniard's trunk is in the bunkhouse. I'll just see what he's got in it."

Lauren moved out of the stall and watched Charley latch the half-door behind them. "But if he wanted Garret dead . . ." Fear gnawed at her insides. "Go quickly and search."

While Charley was gone, Lauren paced back and forth. As if the horses could sense Lauren's unsettled mood, they whinnied and tossed their heads, nervously shifting their hooves.

Charley came back running and grasping his rifle. "I had to break the lock, but I found enough to prove to me that Estaban did it—a bow and arrows."

Lauren shook her head. "Dear God, no! Garret rode out with Estaban to Box Canyon! We have to get to him." She was frantic. "Let's go now!"

"The others are riding fence, and Will's in Sidewinder. I can't let you come with me. I'm going alone."

"No, you aren't. I'm coming, too!"

Lauren ran to Sultan's stall and yanked the door open. Charley was beside her, moving her out of the way. "I can do it faster than you," he said grimly, knowing there was no way in hell he could keep her from riding out with him.

It seemed to Lauren that it took Charley forever

to saddle her horse and his, but in truth it was accomplished in a matter of minutes.

They rode out of the stable in the direction of Box Canyon. As they galloped across a pasture, horses scattered, and some ran along beside them for a short distance.

All Lauren could think about was that Garret was in danger, and she had to get to him before it was too late.

The sun was hot and bearing down on them, and the horses were already lathered, but Lauren and Charley did not slow their pace.

Garret gazed at the white-hot sky, feeling the discomfort of the heat. He glanced over at his companion and slowed his horse. "I don't see any hoofprints, and Box Canyon's no more than a mile away. The horses would have come this way since it's the only entrance to the canyon."

Estaban stared straight ahead, a lie coming easily to his lips. "I saw them there just yesterday when I rode this way."

Garret squinted against the glare of the sun. Not only did he not see hoofprints, there was also no evidence that Estaban had ridden that way the day before.

"Let's ride on," Garret said, kicking his mount into a gallop.

When they reached the canyon, Garret dismounted, looking about him. "You were mistaken.

There hasn't been any stock in this canyon since the last rain." He bent down and examined some small hoofprints. "Only deer."

Estaban dismounted and rested his hand near his rifle. "I was not mistaken, *Patrón*. I lied to you."

Garret stood up and swiveled in the Spaniard's direction. "What in the hell is that supposed to mean?"

"It means I have a score to settle with you. You are the last of your family to pay for what the Lassiters did to me."

Garret nodded. "I have been expecting you to voice your objections to working on a ranch that was once owned by your family."

"You know who I am?" Estaban asked in surprise. "I used my real name, but you never said you knew me."

"Of course I know who you are. My father knew when he hired you that your family once owned San Reanido. He thought you needed the work and a place to stay. As far as I know, my father never regretted hiring you, because you're a good hand."

Estaban's eyes narrowed with hatred. "That was your father's first mistake. But it was also his last."

Garret moved closer to Estaban. "What are you talking about? Did you have something to do with my father's death?" His voice was low and held an ominous tone. "Did you?"

Estaban's hand inched toward his rifle, and he gripped the stock. "*Sí.* I did. And it felt good to watch Lassiter blood soak into the ground. Your family has robbed me of everything. It will be good to know I have killed you before I join you in death."

"You bastard!"

Estaban merely smiled. "I want you to know it was no accident that your mother was run down by the doctor's buggy. I untied the horses and sent them toward her. It worked better than I had hoped, and no one ever suspected me."

Garret's eyes flamed with sudden rage. "I will kill you for that!"

"I do not think so, *Patrón.* I have a gun, and yours is out of reach."

Estaban had not expected a man as tall as Garret to move so fast. Garret lunged at him, knocking the rifle out of his hand and sending him sprawling backward onto the hard-packed ground.

When Estaban got to his feet, Garret landed a hard punch to his midsection. Estaban's breath came out in a gust and his knees buckled, taking him to the ground once more.

But Garret had made one tactical mistake. Estaban had landed near his rifle. He rolled over, grabbing it and taking aim.

"Stop right there, *Patrón.* I do not want to kill you until you understand my reasons."

"I know your reasons," Garret said in a hard voice. "And I'm not afraid of you."

"You should be, Señor. You have a lot to answer for."

"Such as?"

"My mother died of sadness because she lost her home, her jewels—everything! My father killed himself because he could not live with the shame of losing our ranch. The woman I loved turned away from me and married someone else."

"I'm sorry about your mother, but as for your father, the way I heard it, he gambled away San Reanido brick by brick. I also heard that he gambled away the money my father paid for the ranch."

Estaban raised the rifle. "Do not say it! You are not to say such things about my father!" Tears were running down the Spaniard's face, and the gun trembled in his unsteady fingers. "It is time for you to die!"

Garret knew he could not reach his rifle and his only chance was to dive behind a big limestone boulder some ten feet away. With a swift lunge, he bound forward just as the shot rang out. Pain hit him, dropping him to the ground.

With the instincts of a survivor, Garret rolled until he was behind the boulder. But even that would not deter the Spaniard for long.

Chapter Twenty-six

When Lauren and Charley reached Box Canyon, they heard a shot.

Lauren's frantic gaze swept the area until she saw Estaban . . . but where was Garret? Then, in a split second, she realized that Garret was behind a big boulder, and Estaban was aiming his rifle at him.

Without pausing to consider her actions, Lauren slammed the heels of her boots into Sultan's flanks, and the animal sprang forward. Every instinct she had cried out for her to help Garret. She dropped low across the horse's neck, praying she would make it in time. She vaguely heard Charley call out for her to stop, but nothing would deter her, and Charley's horse would never catch Sultan.

Estaban turned toward Lauren, stunned as he saw the giant Arabian bearing down on him. He had been so intent on cornering Garret that he had not heard the two riders. Making a quick decision, he turned his rifle on her. He had not wanted to kill her, but now he must. Estaban cocked the hammer, raised the rifle against his cheek with his finger on the trigger.

Garret saw that Estaban had turned his attention to Lauren, and his heart froze as he cried out, "Lauren, no!" Unmindful of the searing pain in his thigh or the danger to himself, Garret rushed toward Estaban. "Lauren, go back," he cried. "Do as I say!"

Estaban swiveled back to Garret, undecided which one to shoot first. He could kill the señora and let her husband watch her die, or he could do what he had originally planned and kill Garret.

"I know what you're thinking," Garret said in a cold voice. "Estaban, the way I figure it, you only have time for one shot before Charley takes you down. It's me you want, not her—so do it!"

Estaban smiled, aiming at Garret. "*Sí*, it is you I want. I will see you dead this day, and then I can die in peace."

Estaban squeezed the trigger, but the shot went wild and ricocheted off the stone cliff.

Lauren had no gun, but she aimed Sultan at the Spaniard and kicked the horse hard. Sultan seemed to sense what she wanted from him. He slammed into Estaban, sending him tumbling against the cliff wall. Lauren urged Sultan forward and used the horse's huge body to wedge Estaban against the cliff.

She untangled her legs and slid from the animal, running toward Garret. She could see that his trousers were bloody—he had already been wounded.

By now, Charley had dismounted, and his rifle was aimed at Estaban, who was screaming in pain. Sultan would not move no matter how hard Estaban shoved him. The animal looked placid as he kept the man trapped between his flanks and the wall of the cliff.

Charley gathered Sultan's reins, trying to move the horse so he could get a better aim at the Spaniard. He pulled and he tugged and he cussed, but the stallion would not budge.

"Get this horse away from me," Estaban cried, pushing and shoving to no avail. "He's crushing me!"

"Garret, you're hurt," Lauren said, moving closer to her husband. "Is it bad?"

"Lauren," Garret said in an angry voice. "Don't ever do anything so foolish again! What were you thinking?"

"I was thinking," she said gently, "that a crazed man was going to shoot my husband. I was thinking I could stop him."

There was no sign of gratitude in Garret's demeanor. He gripped her shoulder and held her firmly against him. "Didn't you understand the danger you were in?"

"I didn't think about it." She shoved his hand away and bent down to examine his leg. "That'll need a tourniquet until we can get you back to the house. Can you ride?"

"It's nothing," he interjected angrily. "I was speaking of your recklessness, Lauren. I thought I was going to be forced to stand here and watch Estaban shoot you."

"Lauren," Charley called out. "I need you to get this damned horse to move. He won't budge for me."

"Go ahead," Garret said, limping forward. "We'll talk about this later." He slid his rifle out of the saddle and hobbled after Lauren.

She gathered Sultan's reins and gave a tug, and the stallion moved forward as submissively as a tame lamb.

"I'll be damned," Charley said, shaking his head and watching the Spaniard slump to the ground unconscious. "That just beats all I've ever seen."

Lauren rubbed Sultan behind the ear and laid her face against his. "It's extra oats for you tonight," she promised.

San Reanido was in upheaval.

Estaban Velasquez had been shackled and locked in the tack room while Will and George stood guard. Doc Pierce had been sent for to treat Garret's wound, and Chase had been sent for to take charge of the prisoner.

Lauren and Mrs. Shaughnessy had made Garret as comfortable as possible. He had refused to be put to bed, so he now reclined in his study, his leg bound and elevated on two pillows.

Lauren sat in silence staring out the window, waiting for the first sign of her brother or the doctor.

When she glanced back at Garret, his gaze seemed to slash into her, and she knew he was still angry.

"How are you feeling?" she asked, ignoring his dark mood and placing a cool hand on his forehead.

"Like hell."

"You don't seem to have a fever. That's good."

"Lauren, what you did today was foolish and could have cost you your life. Didn't you hear me telling you to go back? Estaban didn't want to hurt you—he only wanted me. But you forced him to make a choice, and he was going to shoot you— make no mistake about that."

Lauren had heard Garret goading Estaban, trying to draw his attention away from her. "But he didn't. If I hadn't distracted him, he would have shot you again. I wasn't going to let that happen."

Garret saw her smile, and it made him angrier. "I find nothing funny about what happened.

You've always been so damned audacious, and you take chances that could cause you harm."

"I know I do. I'm just that way."

She was still smiling, and that made him angrier still. She was not taking the situation seriously. "Being in danger amuses you?" he asked bitingly.

"Actually, I wasn't thinking of that." She laughed aloud. "I was thinking about Sultan. We can always use him in place of a gun and aim him at an enemy. Wasn't he amazing!"

Garret felt the anger drain out of him. Lauren was so adorable, he could never stay mad at her for very long. "He *was* amazing." He smiled now. "Charley couldn't get Sultan away from Estaban. But he followed you willingly, just like I do."

She pulled the footstool closer to him, and her green gown cascaded about her. "You're the horse breeder—do you think Sultan knew what he was doing today?"

"Not in the way you mean. People often give animals human traits when, in fact, you have to use a different yardstick to take their measure. Sultan didn't know that you were in danger. What he did know was how to respond to your commands. You were signaling him to keep Estaban pinned to the cliff, so that's what he did."

"It's still remarkable."

"Yes, it is. He responds to you and to you alone. That horse knows he belongs to you. Sometimes, although it's a rare occurrence, a horse will become a one-person animal. That's what happened with you and Sultan."

Lauren touched Garret's forehead again just to reassure herself that he still felt cool. "He was my wedding present from you."

"Yes."

She stood up and paced restlessly about the room. "I wish Doc would get here. What can be keeping him?"

"I want him here for a different reason than you do. Estaban admitted that he'd killed my father and my mother. Doc had always felt guilty because it was his buggy that ran my mother down. I want to assure him that it wasn't his fault."

"Garret, I'm so very sorry for all you've suffered."

"I still have you," he said, his eyes burning into hers. "I could have lost you today, Lauren."

Chase was the first to arrive. He burst into the room, and there was a look of relief on his face when he saw Lauren.

"You're all right?"

"Yes, I'm fine. But Garret took a bullet in his thigh."

Chase pulled up a chair beside his brother-in-law and looked him over carefully. "From what I've heard, you could be dead."

Garret nodded. "You heard right."

"Is the bullet still in you?"

"Yeah."

"Hurts like hell, doesn't it?"

Garret groaned. "My very words."

"I'll be taking the prisoner off your hands, but first, tell me everything that happened," Chase said, taking on the tone of authority.

"First," Garret said, glancing at Lauren, "would you talk to your sister? Maybe you can get somewhere with her. She won't listen to me."

Chase met Lauren's gaze. "No, I don't think I will. From what I know about her, all the talking in the world wouldn't do any good if she had her mind set on something."

"Don't I know it," Garret said, trying to shift his weight and being rewarded by a sharp pain. "She certainly has a mind of her own."

Chase winked at Lauren. "Stubbornness seems to run in the McBride family."

The house was quiet—everyone had gone to sleep but Lauren. Doc Pierce had taken the bullet out of Garret's leg, and luckily it had not hit a bone but lodged in a muscle. Garret had been carried upstairs, and Lauren had just sent the doctor on his way after feeding him cold chicken and a cup of coffee.

She lifted the oil lamp from the hall table and ascended the stairs, the flickering light making dancing patterns across the wall. She was bone-weary, and she could rest now that she knew Garret was going to be all right.

She turned the lamp off and set it on a hall table outside the bedroom, not wanting to disturb Garret's sleep. Doc had given him a sleeping draught, but Garret had fought against it until he finally drifted off.

Pale moonlight filtered through the open French doors, and a slight breeze fell upon Garret's cheek. Lauren stood for a long moment watching him sleep. What would she have done if she had lost him today?

She reached out and touched his face. He was in a deep sleep and did not know when she bent forward and touched her mouth to his.

She smiled to herself. He was asleep all right. He was so hot-blooded that he would certainly have responded to her kiss if he had been awake.

Lauren quietly undressed and climbed into bed beside him, taking care not to bump against his bandaged leg. She snuggled close to him, brushing a dark lock of hair from his forehead and kissing him again. For tonight, he was all hers.

"You put yourself in danger today because of me. You must love me a little if you were willing to give your life for me," Lauren whispered to her sleeping husband.

She touched her lips to his mouth, which was warm but unresponsive. "I love you," she whispered. "I love you so much."

Garret groaned in his sleep but did not awaken.

Lauren brushed her fingers against the hair on his chest, then pressed her cheek against him. He was warm, and his breath touched her cheek, making her weak inside.

"Who is the woman you love, Garret? Is she worthy of a man such as yourself?"

He continued to sleep.

"She can't love you half as much as I do."

Lauren closed her eyes, too tired even to think.

Probably she would never know the identity of the woman who had captured, and still held, Garret's heart.

Chapter Twenty-seven

Lauren walked hurriedly down the street, her arms full of packages. She rushed past a saloon as loud laughter drifted out to her. She was on her way to visit Chase.

Annabelle Chapin called out to her from across the street. "How's Garret doing?"

Lauren crossed the street and dumped her parcels on a wooden bench outside the stage office. "He's much better, thank you. He walks with a slight limp, but Doc says that will pass in time."

"From what I hear, he's lucky to be alive," Annabelle said. "Folks say the Spaniard is going to hang next week."

"Yes, he is. I can't pretend to be sorry after what he did to my husband's family."

"Ladies—" The drawling tone of William Hanes cut into their conversation. "What a pleasant surprise," he declared, doffing his hat and bowing gallantly. "Two lovely ladies at that."

Lauren smiled at her father's attorney. "You always know the right thing to say, Mr. Hanes. It's good to see you."

"Lauren, if you have the time, I'd like to speak to you in my office," he said in his stiff official tone.

"Go ahead," Annabelle said. "I'll look after your packages, and you can pick them up later."

Lauren was curious as she entered the lawyer's office and sat in the uncomfortable wooden chair he indicated.

"I'm glad you're in town today. I have some papers for you to sign."

"Papers for me to sign?"

"Yes. Garret had them drawn up some time ago, but he never got back to me about what to do with them. You have only to sign them and Cedar Creek reverts back to you."

"What are you talking about?" she asked, wondering just how much Bill Hanes knew about her situation. She had a hunch that very little went on in her family that he did not know about.

"As you know, Garret paid your pa ten thousand dollars for that land."

"No, I didn't know. I thought . . ." She fell silent.

"I assumed that Garret had told you all about your pa's little transaction."

"He didn't."

"Well, if you'll sign where I put the X, the property will be yours."

"I don't understand. Garret wanted that property."

Mr. Hanes looked pensive. "If he did, he doesn't want it now. He was very adamant that the land be in your name alone."

Lauren stared at the document with unseeing eyes. If Garret had not wanted the land, then why had he married her? Oh, what did it mean?

"Mr. Hanes, I have a feeling that my husband did not intend for me to see this document at this time."

He looked troubled. "Garret didn't make that clear to me. I hope I haven't done anything unethical."

Lauren stood. "I don't think I'll sign that title just now. And I would appreciate it if you didn't tell my husband about this meeting."

Bill Hanes appeared to be flustered. "I hope I haven't done anything wrong. I just assumed you knew."

Lauren shook her head. "I'm glad you told me about this."

The lawyer watched her rush out of his office and smiled. "You wily old fox, Thomas J. McBride. You're still in control of your children's lives. But you were probably right about Lauren and Garret—they just needed a little shove."

Lauren found Charley standing by the horses. "I left packages with Annabelle. Please take them home for me."

Charley looked at Lauren suspiciously. "Where're you going?"

"I'm riding to the Circle M. When you get home, tell my husband that I'll be there later this afternoon."

"The boss won't like it if I don't go with you," Charley warned.

"Tell him I had to see my father. He'll understand that."

Scratching his stubbly beard, Charley watched Lauren climb onto her saddle and ride out of town, hell-for-leather.

Lauren arrived at the Circle M just after the noon meal. She waved at several of the cowhands as they went about their daily tasks.

She strode into the house and climbed the stairs to her father's room. She wanted some answers, and she wanted them now!

Tiny heard Lauren's footsteps and opened the door for her. His eyes lit up as they always did when he saw her. He nodded toward the bed, indicating that her father wanted to see her.

Tom was sitting up in bed, and he actually had

a smile on his face. "I thought you'd be here some-time this week, Lauren."

"Now, did you?"

"Yeah. You saw Bill Hanes today, didn't you?"

"You know about that?"

"Of course I know." He leaned heavily into his pillow. "I suspect you have some questions to ask me."

"Damned right I do."

He arched a brow. "Your ma wouldn't have approved of you using such language."

"Mama would have understood because she had to deal with you every day of her married life."

"Now, gal, don't go getting in an uproar. You know I'm not supposed to be upset."

"Don't use that ploy with me, Papa, because it won't work this time. I want to know about your deal with Garret. Did he, or did he not, pay for Cedar Creek?"

"He did—and right handsomely, too. Garret paid much more than it's worth, but then so did I when I bought it."

Lauren sank into a chair. "I don't understand. If he bought the land, why would he be forced to marry me?" She shook her head. "Tell me, Papa. You owe me that much."

"He didn't have to marry you, Lauren. He *wanted* to marry you. But I told you that before."

Tears gathered in her eyes. "If he thought he had to marry me to get the creek, then it would have ruined his chances to be happy with that other woman. But he didn't have to marry me, so why didn't he go to her?"

"I know who the woman is," her father said. "I've known for a long time. Garret told me."

"Then why did you make me marry him?" Her voice was pleading. "Tell me who she is so I can know, too!"

"Hand me that box on the window ledge. The metal one that's locked."

Puzzled, she did as he asked. He took a key that was tied about his neck and unlocked the box. "I believe this is yours," he said, handing her a letter.

Lauren gasped when she saw that it was addressed to her; she recognized Garret's bold handwriting.

"You know what that is, don't you, gal?"

"It's the letter Garret wrote me before I left Texas."

"If you know that, then take it with you and read it when you're alone. Your visits always take so much out of a sick old man like me."

She automatically rose and kissed her father's cheek. Why was he being so mysterious? "How did you get this letter? I left it with Jeb."

"Let's just say that Tiny went on a little hunting trip and discovered lost treasure."

"Clare?"

He nodded. "Now leave me in peace."

Lauren left the room and stood in the hallway

for a long time, trying to decide what to do. If she read this letter, she would know all about the woman Garret loved. Did she really want to know? Could she stand the pain of knowing?

She went downstairs slowly and entered the parlor, dropping onto a straight-back chair. She glanced at the envelope, hesitant to read it, knowing that Clare had already read it . . . a thought that choked her with rage.

Her hands trembled as she slid the letter out of the envelope. She began to read the words she had been meant to read four years earlier:

My dearest Lauren,

I had not planned to say good-bye to you in a letter, but perhaps it is the best way. You will be in my thoughts every day, and I will be awaiting your return so I can tell you all that is in my heart. I would have told you long ago how much I love you, but you were too young—you are still too young to understand how deeply committed I am to you. I will patiently wait for you to grow up and come home, hopefully to me. I stand in fear that you will meet someone in Savannah and lose your heart to him. Keep your heart for me alone, my dearest love. When you come home, if you return my affections, no one will keep me from making you my wife. How long will be the days, weeks, years, before I look

*upon your face again. I would like to corre-
spond with you while you are in Savannah.
Of course, you will have to write me first so I
will have your address. I cannot see your father or Stone giving it to me. If I do not hear
from you, I will understand that your feelings
for me are not what I hoped they would be.
Dearest one, I will keep you in my heart,
please keep me in yours. I love you with each
breath I take.*

I remain faithfully yours
Garret

A deep, trembling sob tore from Lauren's throat
as she read the beautiful words penned by a man
who loved her deeply. She pressed the letter to her
heart.

Garret loved her!

She was the one he loved! The one he had told
her about that day when she thought he was speaking of someone else!

Tears made it hard to see the words when she
reread the letter. She raised her head and angrily
brushed the tears away. If only she had read this
letter when Jeb had tried to give it to her, it would
have saved so much trouble between her and Garret.

Garret loved her!

He had been steadfast and true, had loved her
in silence for all those years. She had to get to him

at once. She wanted to feel his arms around her—she wanted to tell him that she had always loved him, too.

Lauren ran out of the house and mounted her horse.

"Where are you going in such a hurry?" Jeb called out.

Lauren caught a movement on the front porch, and she saw Clare watching her. "I'm going home to the man who loves me," she said, brushing tears from her cheek.

Jeb looked confused, and Clare looked spiteful.

Clare glared at Lauren when she rode close to the porch and halted her horse.

"Clare, nothing you can do will ever hurt me again." She touched her pocket where she had put Garret's letter. "I have love, Clare. What have you got?"

Rage tore at Clare's mind as she turned away and entered the house. She had nothing! She was married to a sick old man who was dying. Tanner, the man she wanted with such passion, could not stand her. Lauren would have her Garret, and the bastard son, Chase, had been accepted by the others. All she had was the Circle M, and even that would be divided four ways . . . five, if Stone came home.

"Señora," Manuelo said, coming up behind her. "Is something wrong—are you upset?"

Clare's shoulders slumped. "I've lost everything."

"That is not so." He wanted to comfort her. "You will always have me."

Clare heard her husband's raspy voice calling for her, and she shuddered. Her worst punishment happened every time she stepped into that bedroom and pretended she loved that shriveled old man. If only Tanner had loved her as much as she loved him.

"I'm coming," she called out to her husband in despair.

Garret was rein-training a spirited little mare. The horse was on a long rein, and Garret was gradually drawing her in as she ran around in a circle. "This little filly is gentle enough for a child," he called out to Charley, who watched from his perch on the fence. "Lauren wanted a good horse for Luke. I think this one will do just fine."

Lauren dismounted and walked toward the paddock. Garret glanced up at her and frowned. "I was about to send someone to look for you."

She concentrated on Garret's eyes, the windows to his soul, that revealed his feelings. He had been worried about her, and his eyes showed relief that she was safely home.

"I need to talk to you as soon as possible, Garret."

"Now?"

"If you don't mind." She turned away and walked toward the house, soon hearing Garret's heavy steps just behind her. She could not wait to be in his arms, to tell him that she had read the letter, and that she loved him.

"Is something wrong?" he asked, catching up with her and slowing his pace to match hers. "Are you all right?"

She smiled to herself. "I have never been better."

He looked puzzled as they climbed the steps to the house. "What do you want to talk to me about?"

She continued across the foyer and up the stairs, knowing he would follow. When she reached their bedroom, she turned to him.

"Lauren, you're leaving me, aren't you?" He reached out to her and gripped her arm, then moved away from her. "That's what you want to tell me, isn't it?"

"No. That's not what I want to tell you." She took a step toward him, not knowing how to explain what she was feeling. "I just wanted you to know that I'm desperately in love."

She watched those glorious brown eyes widen with hope, and then doubt crept in. His voice sounded detached, but she could feel the tension in him; his eyes were incredibly sad.

"And who is the fortunate man?"

"Oh, my dearest love," she said as her eyes

shone with tears. "You are that man!"

He took a step toward her—his hand clamped her shoulder. "You love me!"

Tears rolled down her face, but she did not bother to brush them away. "Most desperately."

He clutched her to him, and she could feel his body tremble. "Lauren, don't say it if it isn't true. I don't think I could . . ." He tilted her face up to him. "Are you sure?"

"Garret, how could you not know I love you when I showed you in every way I could? I didn't say the words, but the feeling was there every time you made love to me."

Garret was still unconvinced. "Why have you decided to tell me now?"

Lauren reached into her pocket and withdrew the letter. "I read this today."

She touched his face, and he closed his eyes, trembling with the overpowering love he felt for her. "The words of a desperate man, Lauren, one who loved a young girl too deeply, I'm afraid. I had to do the honorable thing and wait for you to grow up, even knowing I could lose you."

"Oh, Garret, if only I had known! There was never a day I didn't love you. You allowed me to think you loved someone else. I thought you only married me to get Cedar Creek."

"That damned creek has caused me more trouble than it's worth."

"You signed it over to me."

He moved away from her, hoping his heartbeat would return to normal. "I was going to give you the deed when I gathered the courage to tell you how I felt about you."

She went to him and laid her head against his back, her arms sliding about his waist. "You were so much in my heart while I was in Savannah that I was never interested in any other man."

Garret turned to her, lifting her chin. "If you only knew the hell I've gone through. If I could just go back and do it all again."

Fresh tears were trailing down her cheek, and he gently brushed them away. "Why did you accept my father's offer?" Lauren asked.

He gathered her close to him, laying his face against the top of her head. "Because I was so damned afraid that your father would make the same offer to someone else. I couldn't take that chance. I did insist on paying him for Cedar Creek, though, so I wouldn't feel obliged to him."

"My father would not have made the offer to anyone else." She laid her cheek against his. "You see, he knew I loved you, and in his own way, he's been trying to gather his children about him and make up for the wrong he's done. He even brought Chase home." She looked into Garret's eyes. "And he gave me the only man I'll ever love."

He hugged her tightly to him. "Lauren, sweetheart."

She rubbed her cheek against his. "How could you not know how I felt about you?"

"I knew I could make you happy in bed." He shook his head. "I knew that you were infatuated with me when you were fifteen, and I had hoped that your infatuation would turn to love as you matured. I was full of hope the day you arrived in Sidewinder. But you scared the hell out of me when you acted so indifferent to me when we met. It dashed my hope, but not my determination to have you at any price—even my pride."

"Garret, I wasn't indifferent to you that day. I realized when I saw you that I loved you even more than ever. And I was scared, too."

He let out a long breath. "If only we'd been honest with each other that day."

She smiled. "We could even have told each other how we felt the day you shot Raja."

He touched his lips to her brow. "I couldn't do that because you were so young then. I had to keep a tight hold on my feelings for you at that time. But when I learned that you would be leaving, I had to write you the letter."

She touched her lips to his, and his arms tightened about her.

"Just the thought of you makes me crazy," Garret whispered. "I can be doing some menial job, and you'll come into my mind, and I want to make love to you."

"Sir," she said in mock horror, "you're so passionate in nature."

He watched her eyes soften. "Damned right. I'm married to this fiery little redhead, and it takes a lot to keep her satisfied."

"This fiery little redhead wants you to take her to bed right now and make her satisfied."

Garret laughed with the assurance of a man who knew what he wanted and was about to take it. His head dipped, and he kissed her gently as his fingers deftly unbuttoned her blouse. He was still kissing her as he unfastened her skirt and shoved it downward. He lifted her into his arms and placed her on the edge of the bed so he could remove her boots.

"Now you," Lauren said, reaching up to unbutton his shirt.

They tumbled onto the bed, and Garret seemed to touch every part of her—her shoulders, her breasts, between her legs.

Lauren was aching and frantic for him. She pulled at him, opened her legs, and he laughed as he lowered himself and slid into her. Then the laughter stopped as his eyes became whirling storm centers.

"When I'm inside you, it's the most powerful feeling, a little like dying, I should think." He moved slowly forward and then back. "Then I do this, and the agony is more intense, but, oh, so sweet."

"I know," she murmured, sliding her mouth along his strong jaw line.

"I can never get enough of you. If I stayed in you as much as I wanted to, you wouldn't be able to walk."

She smiled against his lips.

Garret's forceful mouth angled against hers, and Lauren clasped him to her. The lovemaking was not so frantic this time. It was gentle, lingering, the union of two people who knew that love was what melded them together and also knew there would be many other days and nights when they would find pleasure and fulfillment.

Garret's thrusts became more powerful, and Lauren gasped, straining to receive him. As their bodies were joined, so were their hearts. Then, so sweetly, her body found satisfaction, and so did his.

The sun was just going down as Lauren laid her head against Garret's arm, gazing into his beautiful eyes. "Love is painful, isn't it?"

"It was for me for many years." His gaze settled on her breasts, and his hand followed. "But not now. I have everything I want."

"Me, too." She raised herself up and touched her lips to his. "Well, not everything."

"Name what you want and it's yours."

"Promise?"

"I promise."

Lauren laughed. "Then give me a baby."

There was joy in his laughter as he eased Lauren onto her back and covered her with his body. "Boy? Girl?"

Lauren looked bemused. "At the same time?"

"We could try."

Her fingers slid into his dark hair, and she kissed his mouth. "I like this part."

"Sweet little redhead, I got my money's worth when I bargained for you. You put me through hell, but you were so worth the winning. You see before you a happy man."

She touched her lips to his. "I'm glad."

With gentleness he parted her legs and slid inside her quivering flesh.

"Then excuse me," he whispered, completely caught in her power. "I have a promise to fulfill."

And he did.

TYKOTA'S WOMAN
CONSTANCE O'BANYON

Tykota Silverhorn has lived among the white man long enough. It is time to return to his people. Time to fulfill his destiny as the legendary tribal chieftain he was born to become. So what need has he for the pretty white woman riding beside him in the stagecoach, trembling beneath his dark gaze? Yet when Apaches attack the travelers, when one of his own betrays him, Tykota has to rescue soft, innocent Makinna Hillyard, teach her to survive the savage wilderness . . . and his own savage heart. For, shorn of the veneer of civilization, raw emotions rock Tykota. And suddenly, against his will, blue-eyed Makinna is his woman to protect, to command . . . to possess.

___4715-2 $5.99 US/$6.99 CAN

Dorchester Publishing Co., Inc.
P.O. Box 6640
Wayne, PA 19087-8640

Please add $1.75 for shipping and handling for the first book and $.50 for each book thereafter. NY, NYC, and PA residents, please add appropriate sales tax. No cash, stamps, or C.O.D.s. All orders shipped within 6 weeks via postal service book rate. Canadian orders require $2.00 extra postage and must be paid in U.S. dollars through a U.S. banking facility.

Name_____
Address_____
City_____State_____Zip_____
I have enclosed $_____ in payment for the checked book(s).
Payment <u>must</u> accompany all orders. ❏ Please send a free catalog.

San Antonio Rose

Constance O'Banyon

Sam Houston knows he needs all the help he can get to defeat Santa Anna's seasoned fighting men. But who is the mysterious San Antonio Rose, who emerges from the mist like a ghostly figure to offer her aid? Fluent in Spanish, Ian McCain is the one man who can ferret out the truth about the flamboyant dancer. Working under Santa Anna's very nose, he observes how the dark-haired beauty inflames her audience, how she captivates El Presidente himself. But as she disappears with a single yellow rose, he knows that despite the tangled web of loyalties that ensnare them, he will taste those tempting lips, know every secret of that alluring body. And before she proves just how effective she can be, he will pluck for himself the San Antonio Rose.

___4563-X $5.99 US/$6.99 CAN

TEXAS PROUD

CONSTANCE O'BANYON

Rachel Rutledge has her gun trained on Noble Vincente. With
one shot, she will have her revenge on the man who killed her
father. So what is stopping her from pulling the trigger?
Perhaps it is the memory of Noble's teasing voice, his soft
smile, or the way one glance from his dark Spanish eyes once
stirred her foolish heart to longing. Yes, she loved him then . .
. as much as she hates him now. One way or another, she will
wound him to the heart—if not with bullets, then with her
own feminine wiles. But as Rachel discovers, sometimes the
line between love and hate is too thinly drawn.

___4492-7 $5.99 US/$6.99 CAN

ATTENTION ROMANCE CUSTOMERS!

SPECIAL TOLL-FREE NUMBER
1-800-481-9191

Call Monday through Friday
10 a.m. to 9 p.m.
Eastern Time
Get a free catalogue,
join the Romance Book Club,
and order books using your
Visa, MasterCard,
or Discover®.

Leisure
Books